SPECIAL MESSAGE

THE ULVERSCROFT F
(registered UK charity n
was established in 1972 to p ___ for
research, diagnosis and treatment of eye diseases.
Examples of major projects funded by the
Ulverscroft Foundation are:

- The Children's Eye Unit at Moorfields Eye Hospital, London
- The Ulverscroft Children's Eye Unit at Great Ormond Street Hospital for Sick Children
- Funding research into eye diseases and treatment at the Department of Ophthalmology, University of Leicester
- The Ulverscroft Vision Research Group, Institute of Child Health
- Twin operating theatres at the Western Ophthalmic Hospital, London
- The Chair of Ophthalmology at the Royal Australian College of Ophthalmologists

You can help further the work of the Foundation by making a donation or leaving a legacy. Every contribution is gratefully received. If you would like to help support the Foundation or require further information, please contact:

THE ULVERSCROFT FOUNDATION
The Green, Bradgate Road, Anstey
Leicester LE7 7FU, England
Tel: (0116) 236 4325

website: www.ulverscroft-foundation.org.uk

DEATH HOLDS THE KEY

Western Australia, 1928. Out on the Tolhurst farmstead, Detective Constable Hartley is working on his very first assignment, looking into reports of a mysterious prowler. Suddenly he is startled by three gunshots ringing out. Investigating the noise, he discovers the corpse of family patriarch Fred O'Donnell, shot in the chest — alone in a room that has been locked from the inside.

The dead man was almost universally despised, which doesn't help Hartley narrow down his pool of potential suspects. But fortunately for him, chasing a tenuous clue leads him to meet one very useful man — a nameless mendicant friar with prior experience of solving crimes . . .

ALEXANDER THORPE

◆

DEATH HOLDS THE KEY

Complete and Unabridged

ULVERSCROFT
EST. 1964

First published in 2024 by
Fremantle Press

First Ulverscroft Edition
published 2024
by arrangement with
Fremantle Press

*A catalogue record for this book is available
from the British Library.*

ANZ: ISBN 978–1–39914–056–0

UK: ISBN 978–1–39916–889–2

Published by
Ulverscroft Limited
Anstey, Leicestershire

Printed and bound in Great Britain by
TJ Books Ltd., Padstow, Cornwall

This book is printed on acid-free paper

This story takes place on the lands of the Ganeang, Wilman and Whadjuk Noongar peoples. Sovereignty of these lands has never been ceded.

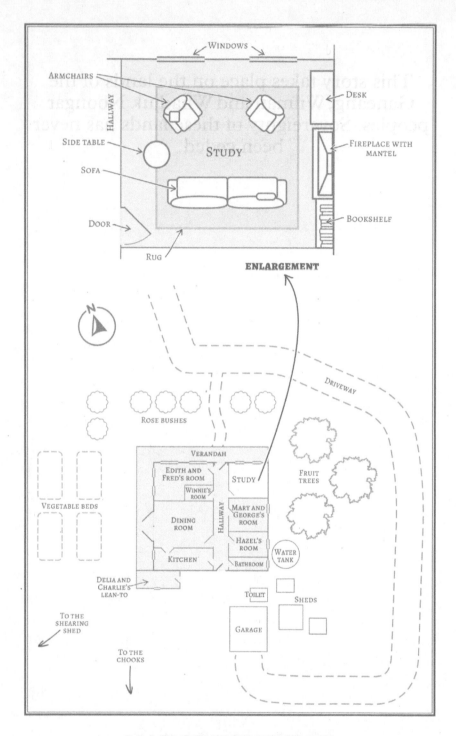

MAP OF TOLHURST

Prologue

The exact nature of the north-east room at Tolhurst had always been the subject of some dispute.

Fred O'Donnell claimed it as his study, though he seldom bothered the few books kept within.

Edith called it 'the good room', though there was nothing in either function or furnishing to justify the name.

Winnie, under the influence of the *Ladies' Home Journal* and other equally indecent imported literature, referred to it as 'the living room', and was undoubtedly the furthest from the mark. Fred's uncompanionable air meant that very little living took place in the room at the best of times, but the events of the tenth of September, 1928, would forever render the epithet wholly, hideously inaccurate.

1

Detective Constable Hartley slowed his motor car to a shivering idle.

The town of Kojonup rolled down the gentle slope before him as if unfurled from inside a carpet, little buildings of stone and red brick chasing the main road through a green-gold patchwork of paddocks. The whole scene would have been altogether idyllic had his bones not been shaken numb by a full day's drive from Perth on largely unsealed roads.

Squinting through the windscreen — by this point a grimy slab of dust and dead insects hiding a pane of glass somewhere inside it — he located the squat, thick-walled cottage that served as the headquarters of the local constabulary. A figure stationed outside the building hailed his vehicle with a wave: not a police officer, Hartley noted on approach, but a well-dressed young woman wielding a parasol. He pulled into the gravel driveway, turned the engine off and sat, listening to it cool. Feigning interest in one of the instruments beside the steering wheel, he forced himself to take a few slow, deliberate breaths.

It was Hartley's first assignment since becoming a detective, and he was determined to make a good impression. There was every chance, he well knew, that the whole business would turn out to be a hoax — his superior had made little effort to hide a sardonic smile when allocating him the case — but whatever the outcome, nothing would prevent him from acquitting himself with all the professionalism expected of an officer in the Western Australian Police Force. He caught his reflection in a dial upon the dash and found himself wishing, not for the first time, that his face would make some sort of effort to embody the gravity of his profession. The freckled cheeks and boyish brows framed eyes as widely guileless as ever, while his new hat sat upon a shock of ginger hair dishevelled beyond all attempts at re-shevelling. Hartley sighed and took a moment to fasten the top button of his coat before stepping down from the vehicle, at which point he slipped on the gravel and fell headfirst to the ground.

The woman with the parasol scrambled to help him up.

'Are you all right?' she asked. The genuine concern in her eyes was enough to weaken the detective's already unstable composure, and he began to laugh as he climbed to his feet.

'I think I shall survive, thank you.' From somewhere beneath the dust, his mind drew forth the particulars of the case. 'Ah — Mrs O'Donnell, is it?'

'Hazel,' she nodded. 'And you must be Detective Hartley.'

'Call me Jamie,' he said, taking again the hand that had helped him up. 'I hope you haven't been waiting too long.' He glanced around. The front door of the police station was closed, no signs of life visible through the barred windows.

'Oh, only half an hour or so. The local lawmen had some pressing business to attend to, it seems, but kindly allowed me to loiter out here.'

Hartley followed the young woman's pointed gaze across the street to a building that quite plainly housed a pub, feeling himself inflate slightly with indignation. Not content with having him dragged out to the middle of nowhere for what would almost certainly prove to be a dull jape or simple misunderstanding, the Kojonup police now appeared determined to tarnish with their provincial work ethic the reputation of all those who wore the uniform.

'Now, really!' he spluttered. Then, finding further words and the desire to take any tangible action equally elusive, he added: 'Really, now!'

This might have gone on for some time had Hazel not taken it upon herself to interject.

'Shall I show you out to Tolhurst?' she offered, to the detective's great relief. 'Only if you have room in your auto, of course. I imagine you'll be wanting to take a look around before it gets dark.'

'Not a bad idea,' said Hartley. He turned back towards the car, shifting his weight so as to discreetly stretch still-aching calves. 'How far is it, would you say?'

'Just a few miles. Not much more than twenty minutes, certainly.'

Though he didn't know it, 'not much more than twenty minutes' was also the amount of time that remained to Hartley before his nascent career would sustain its first fatality.

* * *

A white milk-can letterbox marked the beginning of the driveway, which curved through wheatfields and past windmills for more than half a mile before reaching the house and its attendant buildings. From behind the rusting gate, only one corner of the main dwelling could be seen, peeking out around a row of pines. Leaving the engine running, Hartley went to help his guide with the gate.

'This is usually locked in the evenings, is it?' he asked, eyeing the sturdy padlock and chain.

'Every night,' said Hazel, 'and the one on the side road, too.'

'I see.' The detective struggled to keep his voice steady against the weight of the iron frame as he pulled it wide. 'And were both gates closed on each occasion that . . . well, each time . . .'

'The spectre paid us a visit?' There was a hint of challenge in the young woman's voice, as though she were daring the newcomer to doubt her.

'I suppose so, yes. The encounters, as it were.'

Hartley let the gate fall wide of the driveway, tossing his head a little in what might have been a bid to shake off scepticism or an attempt to suppress a shudder — the detective himself would have been hard-pressed to say which. He was sure of one thing, though: the bucolic scene before him was almost impossible to reconcile with the dark business that had called him so far from the city. The wheat was nearly ready for harvest, green and shifting slightly in the breeze. Rows of towering lemon-scented gums bordered the road while smaller conifers helped to demarcate the paddocks, several of which played host to grazing flocks of sheep. The very image of antipodean Arcadia, especially with the golden light of the spring afternoon ripening towards evening. The idea of cloaked figures creeping through the darkness in a place like this seemed absurd.

'You were the first to see it, weren't you?'

'The first, but not the last,' said Hazel. She spoke

6

in an automatic, offhand way, gazing out towards the house. A distant form in the garden raised a tiny hand in acknowledgement, and Hazel responded in kind, though her face remained hard. 'It was three weeks ago,' she went on. 'Plenty of others have seen it since then. The local police laughed it off at first, but after the third or fourth testimonial, they were forced to take note.'

Hartley had read the statements. Though they came from various members of the O'Donnell family and sundry associates, they never differed in the key details. The figure came at night, swathed in a black cloak and hidden beneath a heavy hat. The witnesses described it as more of an impression than a person — a mere shape, a suggestion of something dark and unwholesome.

'I'm not a child,' Hazel said. 'I don't believe in fairy stories or haunted houses. No, he's a man — he must be — but he's a man who knows how not to be seen. No-one has ever gotten close to him.'

'No-one other than Fred,' the detective pointed out.

Fred O'Donnell, the family patriarch, overlord of Tolhurst's two-thousand-odd acres, was undeniably the one in whom the phantom was interested. If the witness statements were to be trusted, the visitor never appeared save when Fred was present, and it usually contrived to have him alone, fleeing into the darkness the instant an onlooker made themselves known.

Hazel huffed at the mention of her father-in-law's name.

'That's him over there, in the garden.' She indicated the faraway figure, which was now heading back towards the house. She glared after it for a moment or two, waiting until the man had disappeared from

7

view before continuing. 'The problem is that he won't admit to anything. Fred O'Donnell is far and away the most stubborn old man I've ever encountered. He claims that there's nothing to be seen, and never has been. Imagine it!' She laid a hand on the letterbox as if for balance, grasping it with enough force to whiten her knuckles. 'Imagine having the unrestrained gall to tell grown men and women — your own family, no less — that what they've just witnessed with their very own eyes never took place.'

'The dossier did leave me with the distinct impression that Fred O'Donnell can be a difficult man,' said Hartley, choosing his words with care.

'Difficult? I'll tell you what's difficult! It's difficult to understate just how much of a bloody tyrant —' The young woman pulled herself up short, looking back at her interlocutor with a tight smile. 'You must forgive me, Detective. The last few weeks have not been easy. The cloaked man has come to us time and again, and we've all been worried senseless. He seems to appear and disappear at will. We've never heard a horse or a car. He doesn't even leave footprints. If he wanted to do anything to us, or to the children, I doubt we'd be able to stop him.' She sighed. 'He does want *something*, though, I'm sure of it. And whatever it is, Fred knows.'

Hartley studied the woman. Her honey-coloured hair was pulled back into a loose bun from which a few ringlets bobbed loose, brushing against cheeks reddened from sun, or pique, or both. Her face was long and pleasant, despite the strain it wore, and she spoke with a slight cockney accent, dampened by the long years which must have separated her from London. Hartley found himself sympathising with her.

'If his statement is anything to go by,' he said softly, 'it would seem that Fred doesn't believe the cloaked man exists at all.'

'I'm well aware of Fred's beliefs,' Hazel sniffed. 'He never shies away from inflicting them on us. He accuses us of imagining things, or daydreaming, or inventing outright nonsense. Last week, Edith pulled him aside — Edith, that's his wife — and told him she'd seen the cloaked man creeping past the window. She was afraid, quite naturally. Terrified! And do you know what he did? He told her to 'stop bloody wool-gathering' and get back to the dishes.'

'I'd have thought wool-gathering was in demand around here, especially during the shearing season.'

Hartley froze as the words left his mouth. The quip had sprung unbidden to his mind, and he hadn't been fast enough (travel-addled as he was) to prevent its escape. He cursed himself. Less than an hour into his first case and he was already belittling the witnesses.

'I'm terribly sorry,' he stammered. 'I didn't mean to make light of —'

He broke off. Hazel was laughing.

'Quite the wit, Detective. I only hope it functions as well in the investigative sphere as in the comedic.'

Hartley felt himself redden. 'I'll certainly give it my all. I can't make promises, of course, but I am convinced that there must be a rational explanation for all of this. And if an explanation exists, it can be found.'

To the detective's surprise, Hazel responded by turning away. 'To be honest,' she said, 'I can't say I hold much hope of that.' Then, seeming to catch hold of herself, she faced him once more. 'Really, I'm just glad that you're here. The local police did nothing but shrug at us for weeks. It was only when we heard the

9

shots —'

So thoroughly unlikely was the prospect of a gun-shot ringing out at that precise moment that Detective Hartley found himself doubting the evidence of his own ears. If it hadn't been for the flock of sul-phur-crested cockatoos which took flight from the direction of the homestead, jabbering indignantly, he would have dismissed the sound as the work of his imagination. In fact, he was still half inclined to do so. As if sensing his uncertainty, a second shot rang out, followed by a third.

'Come along!' he called, rushing back towards the vehicle. Hazel stood as if frozen. Every trace of col-our had fled her face. It was only when the engine clunked into gear that she seemed to regain the power of movement and ran to join the detective.

The car tore along the driveway, an incongru-ous beast of noise and dust amidst the peace of the paddocks. As they rounded the final stand of pines, the house came into full view, a large single-storey brick-and-limestone construction with an iron roof, bounded on two sides by a wide verandah. Hazel ges-tured for the detective to stop the vehicle beside a small gap in the front hedge. She leapt out and ran down the path to the front door, Hartley in tow. Fly-ing up the stone steps, she crossed the verandah and was reaching for the handle when the detective caught her arm. He drew her aside to the nearest of the two large windows which looked into the room on the left.

It was not a particularly sizeable room, boasting little of note besides a desk, a couple of overturned chairs, a long chesterfield sofa, and a fireplace. It did, however, contain the body of a man lying face-up on the floor, his head and torso just visible over the back of the sofa. A couple of holes in the far wall, ringed with cracked plaster, spoke to the fate of the first two gunshots, while the third appeared to have found its mark in the man's chest. The room was dimly lit, the curtains having been drawn across the far window, but Hartley could see well enough to know that no breath passed those half-parted lips.

Stepping around the ashen-faced Hazel, he tore through the front door and into the hallway.

'Police!' he called. 'Is there anyone here?'

No reply.

The door to the front room was the first on the left. Hartley rattled the brass handle and stooped to peer through the keyhole. It was locked from the inside.

'Mrs O'Donnell,' he said, 'I need you to find me another key to this room, please, as quick as can be.'

The young woman shook herself out of her stupor. She was on the verge of vanishing into the dark heart of the house when a sudden thought seemed to strike her. Turning back, she dropped to her knees before the door.

'The children like to make a game of locking themselves in the woodshed,' she muttered, reaching up to retrieve a hairpin from beneath her hat. 'As a result, I've had to become something of a housebreaker.' She prodded around in the keyhole, then gave voice to a string of syllables that would not make it into the detective's official report as the hairpin snapped. The key could be heard clattering to the floor on the other side of the still-locked door.

'Never mind!' said Hartley, already starting back towards the front of the house. 'You keep looking for a spare while I try the windows. And be careful!'

The window through which he had first glimpsed

the dead man was bolted from the inside, affording a maddeningly inaccessible view of the scene within. Hartley considered breaking the glass but was loath to risk disturbing anything inside the room. There could be fingerprints on the casements, he reasoned, or boot marks in the dust on the sill. The second window, about four feet further along the northern wall, proved to be locked just as securely, but Hartley felt something move as he tried to lift the sash. He ran his fingers around the edge of the frame and came away with a tightly folded piece of notepaper about half the size of his palm, darkened at the corner with what could only have been blood. Something slipped from within as he opened it. Animated by instinct, he was quick enough to catch the first object as it fell, but several others dropped to the floor, clinking and ringing. He knelt to scoop them up, casting cautious glances about the verandah, then spread his collection upon the windowsill. The item Hartley had managed to catch proved to be the brass casing of a shotgun cartridge, flattened into a crude circle by the application of some significant force. Beside it lay a ridged steel ring about an inch in diameter, a small coin of tarnished copper and the notepaper itself, across which had been scrawled, in an ostentatious hand: *With this, a little of what was wrong is now put right.*

All items being, at present, equally unilluminating, he pocketed the lot and returned his attention to the far more pressing matter of the dead man on the other side of the window. As far as he could discern, the still-locked door was the only other way in or out of the room. How, then, could the shooter have escaped? Notwithstanding the disarray of the chamber itself — and, notably, the bullet holes — nothing

12

in the immediate vicinity indicated the recent presence of another person. The detective stood still, watching the body and thinking, until his attention was arrested by a series of muted sounds from within the house: the sort of dull creaks and thuds which could be caused by anything from possums in the ceiling to settling walls or bare feet on floorboards.

'Mrs O'Donnell!' he called, taking a cautious step into the dim hallway. 'Hazel?'

There didn't seem to be a light on anywhere in the building. The obscurity ahead was broken only by the vague outline of the distant back door, which looked as though it was standing slightly ajar. He was just about to go and verify this when Hazel materialised from the darkness, key in shaking hand. The detective breathed a sigh of relief. Taking the key, he turned back to the door of the frontmost room. The lock opened without a sound, and he was able to kneel beside the victim at last.

The unfortunate man was on the older side of middle age, rather tall and strongly built. He was clean-shaven, clad in solid boots and a cotton shirt tucked into heavy trousers. It was the work of a few seconds to confirm that he was no longer living, though the warmth had yet to leave his cheeks. A cigar, near whole, smouldered on the floor beside him, while another glowed in an upturned ashtray nearby.

'Is it him?' asked Hartley, knowing full well that the lifeless hand he now held had waved at him from the garden only minutes ago.

Hazel nodded. She still stood in the hallway, apparently unwilling to cross the threshold into death's dominion. Her fingers were clasped tight, blanched and bloodless.

'That's Fred,' she said, quietly. 'That's my father-in-law.'

The detective's shoulders fell.

'I must confess to having doubted the danger facing you and your family,' he said. 'I see now that I was wrong. I'm sorry.'

Hazel shook her head but said nothing.

'You should summon the rest of the O'Donnells, I'll take care of things here and send for the local police. They'll need to make a record of everything while I look for whoever did this.'

'It's the cloaked man,' Hazel said, in a curiously dull voice. 'It has to be.'

The young woman disappeared back into the darkness of the hallway, leaving Detective Constable Hartley alone with the body of the person he had been called down from Perth to protect. Maybe there was something to this phantom after all. What about the rest of the statements supplied by the family, then? Did the man he was looking for really appear and disappear at will? Did he really leave no footprints? He looked again around the room. He couldn't doubt the evidence of his own eyes: each door and window was locked from the inside. What kind of killer could walk through walls?

2

The Cuballing Hotel was crowded on Thursday evening. People clustered around tables and clamoured at the bar, cradling their pints of Castlemaine. Shearing season was in full swing, and the town's meagre population was swollen with roustabouts, shearers, wool classers and truck drivers from all corners of the state. The talk revolved for the most part around the horse races over at the Narrogin racetrack — slurred excitement from the lucky punters, bitter mutterings from the less fortunate — but, as in any crowd, there were still the inevitable few who insisted on talking shop.

Hartley sat alone at a corner table, attempting to appear inconspicuous and failing quite remarkably. Straight-backed and silent, he stared at the door over an untouched glass of stout. It had been three days since the shooting at Tolhurst, and he had made not a jot of tangible progress. Three days of mourning relatives, expectant looks and fruitless footprint searches. Three days of pacing the same impossible room. Three days of questions without answers. All his interviews with the farm's residents had turned up nothing, and asking around Kojonup had only served to provide him with a greater pool of suspects.

Hartley had started with what he thought to be a fairly logical first line of enquiry. Who, he wondered, would want to kill Fred O'Donnell? Unfortunately, the victim himself had sabotaged this investigative angle by way of being almost universally despised, and the detective was still coming across people who raised a glass to Fred's death in hotels and pubs several hours distant from the old man's property.

Changing tack, Hartley had then spent the better part of a day chasing reports of cloaked men, a search which led him to the creaking corner table where he now sat. Though barely more than a rumour, it was the first hint of any headway he'd had in the whole case. A truck driver passing through Cuballing a day or two prior had stopped in at the pub for a drink and had seen a man wearing something like a robe or a hooded cloak lurking about the back door. It was, admittedly, a tenuous link to the Tolhurst business, and Hartley had driven the eighty-odd miles more to comfort himself with the illusion of action than out of any real hope for progress.

The detective drained his glass over the course of half an hour, weighing the need to soothe frayed nerves against the desire to maintain some measure of mental clarity. A similar balancing act was visible in the frequency with which he got up to walk out to the lavatories: often enough to give him a chance at sighting his cloaked quarry behind the building, but not quite so frequently that any of the bar staff should feel the need to pull him aside and recommend a physician.

Another hour passed without incident.

Starting in on his third pint of stout, Hartley felt his mind begin to wander. He sought something to distract himself from the abject failure which his first case showed every sign of becoming and found the conversation at the next table to be of great utility. A gentleman seated nearby was putting forth the extraordinary claim that he had been able to shear three hundred and twenty sheep in a day, laying Dan Cooper's world record to well-deserved rest. One of the boastful shearer's companions gave him to understand — through statements sprinkled liberally with invective — that his assertion was not widely believed, citing (amongst other weighty evidence) the claimant's inability to state with any real confidence the number that came after twelve. Over roars of laughter from fellow drinkers, the shearer blamed his arithmetical shortcomings on the quantity of Swan lager he had imbibed, following this up with the logically tortured argument that the only reason for such prodigious consumption would be the celebration of some great achievement, surely serving to give further proof of his record-breaking feat.

Hartley found himself enjoying this battle of wits and had very nearly managed to put aside his fears for his professional future when he was brought back to reality by the sight of a cloaked man at the bar. He froze, glass halfway to his lips. The man wasn't drinking. Though his face was inscrutable, turned away from the light, his posture gave every indication of waiting for something. Soon, one of the kitchen staff emerged and handed him a brown paper parcel. With a deep nod, the cloaked figure turned and vanished into the hazy crowd.

Hartley leapt to his feet, knocking his chair backwards into the *soi-disant* world champion, and pushed into the throng, muttering apologies as he turned this way and that. There was no sign of the cloaked man anywhere. He elbowed his way over to the service area and, raising his voice to be heard over the bar-room din, asked the publican if he had seen the mysterious

17

figure make his escape. In response, the publican placed another glass of stout in front of him.

'No,' the detective yelled, 'the man in the hooded cloak! Which way?'

The barman nodded his understanding and plonked a bottle of ale down beside the glass.

'No, I need —' Hartley broke off, catching a dark movement towards the back of the room. 'Never mind,' he cried. Throwing a few coins on the polished jarrah, he ran down the corridor and out to the open back verandah, past the lavatories.

The verandah backed right on to bush, and Hartley arrived just in time to see a slip of dark fabric vanish between the trees. Coming to the beer-dampened realisation that the sun had set while he'd been moping inside, the detective hesitated for only a moment before setting off into the darkness in pursuit. He stumbled through the sheoak scrub for a minute or two, pausing here and there to catch the sound of his quarry's progress or disentangle himself from the grasp of a prickly dryandra bush. Finally, the foliage gave way to a small, moonlit clearing, into the midst of which Hartley would've stepped had he not been suddenly captured by a net strung between two trees.

'What on Earth?' he cried, struggling.

The man in the centre of the clearing looked up from the pile of firewood he was arranging. His round face was outlined in dark curls and short, greying whiskers.

'Good evening,' he said, implacably.

Hartley, for his part, was unbalanced — to the extent that such a thing is possible for someone whose feet are no longer on the ground — by the quotidian greeting.

18

'What's going on?' he yelped, with slightly less authority than he had hoped to project. Then, remembering his station, he tried again. 'Release me at once!'

'Not to worry,' said the man, approaching him with hands extended. 'It's just a hammock. Here, allow me to assist you.' With deft fingers, he disentangled the detective and guided him to the ground.

'What the devil have you got a hammock strung up there for?' complained Hartley, stuffing his shirt tails back into his waistband.

'For sleeping, mostly,' the man said. 'If I'd known I had company coming, I would've arranged for a *chaise longue*. Can I offer you some tea? I was just about to put the billy on.'

Hartley's ability to maintain his outrage was further hampered by the undeniable fact that a cup of tea sounded thoroughly delightful. He sighed, rubbing his face with both hands. 'Go on, then,' he said, and sank heavily onto a nearby log.

At such close quarters, any remaining hope that this stranger might be connected with the murder of Fred O'Donnell had finally evaporated. The Tolhurst murderer was tall and swathed in black, while this man was of diminutive stature, his garment brown. It couldn't even really be called a cloak, if Hartley was being honest with himself. It was a single piece of coarse fabric, something like calico or hessian, which covered the little man from his neck to below his knees. If anything, it looked more like a monk's robe.

With an abrupt cry, Hartley sprang to his feet again.

'I know who you are!' he said. 'You're that wandering chap.' He clicked his fingers furiously, trying to call half-buried facts to mind. 'You helped the Geraldton fellows with that body in the bush and

19

unearthed the stolen cash from the Wyalkatchem bank business. What is it they call you? A mendacious something — some sort of medicine man?'

'A mendicant friar,' said the man in the brown robe. 'It means, broadly, that I keep no possessions and rely on the generosity of others to keep myself fed.' As if by way of demonstration, he unwrapped the parcel from the Cuballing Hotel kitchen, revealing a fresh loaf of bread, a slab of cheese and a bundle of leafy greens. 'I aim to repay the public in whatever small ways my modest abilities allow. Some spiritual counsel here and there, a kind ear to those in need — and yes, occasionally, the application of the logical faculty towards the solution of such issues as may require it. I must say, though,' his smile widened, 'this is the first time the news of my work has preceded me. It's quite an unusual feeling. Rather difficult to describe.'

Hartley thought that the word 'pride' would have encapsulated the phenomenon neatly but had no desire to offend the friar's self-denying sensibilities. He settled back on to his fallen log, accepting a tin mug of tea and a slice of bread with cheese. He chewed slowly and thoughtfully, and by the time he was through with his supper, he had come to a decision.

'I need your help,' he said. 'Please. This is my first case, and I can't go back to Perth empty-handed.' He told the friar everything he could about the murder at Tolhurst. The words came haltingly at first, then began to escape in a jumbled rush as Hartley realised what a gift it was to be able to share his burden with another. The mendicant listened without comment, his face warm in the flickering firelight. When the tale reached the locked room, his eyebrows rose.

His interest was palpable.

'If you'll allow me the night to tie up my affairs here,' the mendicant said, 'I shall certainly accompany you and render whatever assistance I am able. I'm afraid I can't promise results, though,' he grinned. '*You get what you pay for*, as the saying goes, and I don't accept much in the way of remuneration.'

It was all the relieved detective constable could do to stop himself from embracing the little man.

'Thank you,' he said, earnestly. 'I was at a loose end. You've no idea how grateful I am . . .' He stopped short, remembering that not one of the rumours of the peripatetic holy man had contained a name. 'What shall I call you?'

The mendicant shrugged.

'You may call me whatever you wish. I've given up my name along with everything else.'

'Given it up?' Hartley laughed. 'You can't be serious.'

'I am more than capable of being serious,' said the mendicant, 'though I find it tiresome to do so too often. Now,' he said, stooping to clear some gnarled branches from beside the fire, 'have you managed to find a room at the inn, so to speak, or shall I have my valet make up the guest chamber?'

21

3

Hartley and his newfound partner stood at the threshold of St Mary's Anglican Church in Kojonup and peered inside. Save for the two frontmost pews, the building was deserted.

'Perhaps we have the wrong time?' suggested the friar.

'I don't think so,' said Hartley, digging a notebook out of his jacket pocket. 'No, here we are — ten o'clock, Friday the fourteenth.' He stepped back and cast an eye over the wooden entryway. 'Could be the wrong church, I suppose.'

'Very few of my Roman brethren would refer to it as the right one, certainly,' the friar muttered, 'but this is hardly the occasion to succumb to sectarian debate.'

It was the occasion, ostensibly, for mourning. The two investigators had arisen early and driven for several hours to get to Kojonup in time for the funeral, but there wasn't much before them in the near empty nave to suggest that a ceremony was imminent.

'They may be running behind time.' Hartley tapped his wristwatch. As if summoned by the gesture, a granite-faced man emerged from the shadows.

'Fred O'Donnell?' intoned the man, whose black, weighty attire marked him as a minister.

'No, Hartley. Detective Constable Hartley,' the policeman replied automatically. He was on the verge of extending his hand when the meaning of the minister's query dawned on him. 'Oh, I see. Sorry.'

He fought the ill-timed urge to laugh off his own error. 'Yes, we're here to farewell Mr O'Donnell. Are we in the right place?'

The man in black inclined his head in the direction of the rear pews and melted back into the darkness. Hartley took a seat, sliding along the hard, cold wood to make room for the friar. Now that his eyes had adjusted to what little light the narrow windows admitted, Hartley was able to identify the mourners in the front row, with only one or two exceptions.

'That's Fred's widow over there,' he whispered, indicating the woman closest to the aisle on the front-left seat. 'Edith. Quite an impressive woman.'

The validity of this assertion was palpable, even across the dim distance of the church. The matriarch sat straight and unmoving, head held high. Her unveiled profile was strong in silhouette as she stared out across the aisle. At forty-seven, Edith O'Donnell was thirteen years younger than the man who had predeceased her, a fact that Hartley had been surprised to uncover, as her vigour and bearing gave the impression of a woman still some way shy of middle age.

'Who is it that has managed such a monopoly on the good widow's attention?' the friar enquired. Hartley followed the line of Edith's gaze.

'That's the youngest O'Donnell daughter, Winnie. She and her mother do not often see eye to eye. I imagine that today's quarrel is a sartorial one.'

'I doubt you're far from the mark there,' said the friar, taking in Winnie's knee-length cream dress, short sleeves and dark, bobbed locks. 'And beside her?'

The detective craned his neck.

23

'I don't recognise the couple immediately beside her,' he said, 'but the fellow on the outside is Les Thompson. Though he's a hired hand, strictly speaking, he functions more as a member of the family. Increasingly so since Fred's death, if I'm not mistaken.'

The friar glanced up in interest. 'Who gave you to understand that?'

'No-one in particular,' said Hartley. 'It's more an impression than anything else. Just a few remarks here and there.'

'From whom?' pressed the mendicant.

Hartley's high brow crinkled with the effort of recollection. 'I can't be completely sure. Several people have mentioned changes. He takes dinner at the house more often than he used to. Gives his opinion in areas he never would've ventured to do so before. That sort of thing.'

'Ah.' The friar sat back. 'He does have a certain enterprising air.'

The man under discussion was exactly what one might expect to eventuate if a political cartoonist were commissioned by a patriotic newspaper to represent the noble Australian frontiersman. The seams of his sombre suit were rendered almost indecent by the sheer volume of muscle rippling behind them, while the line of his jaw posed a danger to the eyes of all those nearby. Although he was bareheaded, being inside a house of worship, there was something in his posture and steely squint which effectively conveyed the idea that a broad-brimmed leather hat should be pictured upon his blond curls — tilted, if possible, at a rakish angle.

'It is certainly hard to imagine that an increased

presence from Les Thompson would go unremarked upon,' said the mendicant. 'And on the other side of the aisle, next to Edith . . . is that another daughter?'

'Yes, that's Mary. The elder O'Donnell daughter, though she's now properly Mrs Bamonte.'

Shorter and rounder of face, Mary seemed somehow to be the inversion of her mother, projecting a solid maturity beyond her twenty-seven years. Her unadorned grey gown sat taut over a protruding midsection. She gripped Edith's slim shoulder with her right hand and held her husband close with the left.

'Gino Bamonte,' said Hartley, nodding towards Mary's spouse. 'They tend to call him George. Married into the family nearly a decade ago and seems to have taken to the farming life quite well. I believe he was once a soldier.'

George's black hair fell forward in a soft curtain as he bent to the two children beside him. While his words could not be heard across the church, Hartley gathered that he was attempting to settle a dispute about who held page-turning rights to the shared hymnal. This particular Gordian knot was untangled through the simple act of stretching over the back of the pew to obtain a second volume.

'Do both children belong to Mary and George?' enquired the mendicant. Hartley had made attempts to brief him on the family as they drove down from Cuballing, but a good deal of the information had been lost to engine noise and the wind, and he was working hard to make use of this opportunity to fill in the gaps. The children were of similar ages, one dark-crowned and the other lost in a cloud of strawberry-blonde ringlets.

'The lad is theirs. Charlie. He's around eight or

25

nine years old, I believe. They have another on the way. Due in February, if I recall correctly.'

'I see. And the girl?'

'That's Delia. Quite a sad story, really.' The detective sketched a family tree in the air as he spoke. 'Her father was Jack O'Donnell: Fred and Edith's eldest, and their only son. I doubt she remembers him, though. It sounds as though he died not long after Delia was born. Made it through the Great War only to come home and catch the Spanish Flu. Got through it, but his lungs were never the same, and he died from pneumonia a year or so later. Fred'll be laid to rest beside him in the churchyard.'

The friar made a sympathetic noise deep in his throat. 'Delia may also lay claim, one assumes, to a mother? Not that I have any wish to publicly denounce the idea of immaculate conception, you understand — it's just that the whole thing would be rendered altogether less maculate if the sole parent were male.'

Hartley was beginning to wonder if soliciting aid from such an eccentric quarter had been a wise move.

'Delia's mother,' he said, 'is quite human, to the best of my knowledge. Her name is Hazel. She's the one who was with me when —' he faltered. 'Well, when it all happened. The murder, I mean. I can't imagine why she isn't here now, though.'

The detective's imagination was relieved of its burden by the sudden ringing out of a few robust chords from a piano in the corner of the hall. At the keys sat Hazel O'Donnell, focussed and austere in funereal black. Hartley pointed her out to the mendicant and then, with the full cast assembled, whispered a swift rendition of the alibi given by each on the day

26

of the shooting: George and Les were out shearing, Edith had driven Mary into town for a check-up with the doctor and Winnie had taken the children shopping for new school shoes. Kojonup being a relatively small settlement, the family was known to all, and there had been no shortage of witnesses to shore up each of these statements. The friar merely nodded, his thoughtful gaze roaming about the pews.

The few mourners took to their feet as the minister appeared, and Hartley noticed for the first time that Fred's coffin was already in position beside the pulpit. Though not a vain or proud man by nature, the detective found himself hoping that when he reached the end of his days, he would still have friends enough to provide a full complement of pallbearers. He made a mental note to reply to some of the personal letters that had been accumulating on his desk back in Perth.

In response to a murmured imperative from the minister, all those in the church resumed their seats. The next half hour dragged on in dour ceremony, Hartley's thoughts almost immediately lost to the drone of psalms and biblical admonitions. It was only when the meagre congregation rose for the final time that a nudge and a quiet nod from the friar directed his attention back towards the door. Hartley turned to see a wiry man in a grey suit standing in the entryway. He was half hidden in the shadows and had neglected to remove his hat, so that almost nothing of his face could be discerned. One thing, though, was plain — the man was staring straight at Hartley. The detective glanced back once or twice more during the final blessing, but by the time the service had officially drawn to a close and the mourners reached for their coats, the man in grey had disappeared.

27

4

Hartley was not looking forward to the wake. A wake is, in general, not the sort of thing one anticipates with any real relish, but the knowledge that the O'Donnells would be expecting an update on the investigation further hobbled his enthusiasm.

The gravel chattered beneath the tyres of the Australian Six as they passed through the front gate at Tolhurst. Hartley slowed the vehicle to a crawl, as much to delay the inevitable as to give his passenger the chance to become acquainted with the property.

'This is where you heard the shot?' enquired the friar.

'Shots,' Hartley nodded. 'Three in all.'

'Did you drive directly to the house?'

'Of course. That was where the gunfire came from, after all.'

'As it transpired, yes, but how did you know that at the time?'

Hartley considered this, looking out over the waving wheat. 'Well,' he said, 'it just sort of felt right, really. There weren't too many other options. Who gets shot in a shed?'

'I suppose it would lack a certain gravitas,' said the mendicant. He pointed at the ramshackle outbuildings, growing steadily closer. 'What do the sheds contain, then, if not murderers?'

'Oh, everything under the sun.' Hartley searched his memory, considering each of them in turn. 'That

28

one's a woodshed, I think. That's a sort of garage, with a stable on the other side of it. The smallest one is an outhouse lavatory. And that one over there is — well, as far as I understand, it's just a place to put things that don't really belong in any of the other sheds.'

'I see. There are also stockyards and silos some-where, one presumes?'

The detective nodded. 'And a shearing shed. They're all away beyond the home paddock, hidden behind that low hill with the row of salmon gums. The driveway curves around in a sort of arc, you see, connecting the main road to a loading track that runs along the side of the property. Apparently, the person that laid this place out was very keen that the appear-ance of a genteel estate be preserved when viewed from the main road, while all the grubby business of actually running a farm could carry on in the wings.'

As the car drew level with the front of the house, the grubby business of running a farm leapt out to greet them in the form of three wildly enthusiastic dogs. One was a kelpie, and a fine example of the genre, while the other two were less identifiable as any specific breed, merely exuding a general sense of the canine. In a matter of seconds, the animals had come round the vehicle and were doing an admirable job of herding it towards the garage, barking all the while.

'Don't worry,' said Hartley. 'They're always like this. I'm told it's only visitors who are subject to this treatment — stay here for a few nights and not one of the beasts will so much as bat an eye when you approach the house.'

'I see.' There was a definite trace of nervousness in the friar's voice as the car shuddered to a halt. He eyed the dogs warily through the dust-marred window.

'Are they friendly?'

Hartley paused, shamefully savouring the novel sensation of not being the one to lose his composure. 'Absolutely,' he said, when he felt the friar to have suffered enough. 'Having said that,' he hastened to add, 'friendliness can be shown in many ways.'

'What do you mean by that?'

'Well, I mean to say that while I feel thoroughly well disposed towards you, for example, I wouldn't necessarily express it by knocking you to the ground and coating your face in spittle.'

'An act of restraint for which I extend my deepest gratitude,' said the friar, his face still not entirely free of fear. Outside, the dogs sniffed about the car like sharks circling a vessel in distress. Another taut silence passed, the mendicant apparently unwilling to open his door and expose himself to the wildly quivering jowls, the detective unwilling to open his door and reveal that the animals were, in fact, thoroughly harmless. This tension was shattered by the arrival of Winnie O'Donnell, who flew around the side of the garage from the direction of the main house. Though still in the beaded knee-length dress she had worn to the funeral, she was barefoot, dancing lightly over the gravel.

'I say, you beasts!' she said, cocking an elbow against her hip in studied insouciance. 'You're causing an awful stir. Be a pack of darlings and lower the volume, won't you?'

Hartley gave a tentative wave, hoping that the admonition was directed at the dogs. Winnie took no notice of him, and the dogs took no notice of her, the friar's unfamiliar scent seeming to make another round of frenzied barking a necessity. With a huff,

Winnie shook the bobbed fringe from her eyes and strode forward.

'Oi!' She grabbed the nearest animal by the scruff of the neck and yanked it bodily away from the car. 'I said get out of it, ya mongrel!' The other dogs backed off immediately, appearing to understand from experience that the youngest O'Donnell daughter was not to be provoked. Hartley saw the friar's eyes widen; though he'd experienced it several times before, the detective remained equally awed by Winnie's ability to transform in the space of a moment. She stood before them now as a farmer with a fistful of fur, where a second or two earlier, she could easily have passed for a misplaced member of the Bloomsbury Set. By the time the investigators had descended from the vehicle — the friar doing so with considerable caution, still eyeing the hounds — Winnie was once again in Mayfair mode.

'My dear Detective Constable,' she cooed, planting a kiss on Hartley's startled cheek. 'How delightful of you to return to our humble family seat. I do hope the service wasn't too dreary for you. And you've brought us some sort of Jesuit-type creature,' she added, eyes running up and down the dusty robe. 'The next best thing to a bottle of Chablis, I suppose. How do you do?' She extended a hand which Hartley knew to be roughened with work, belying the silver bracelets clinking at her slender wrist.

'A pleasure to make your acquaintance,' the friar bowed. 'I only wish I were doing so under more agreeable circumstances.'

The young woman gave him a quizzical look. 'How d'you mean?'

'I believe he was referring to your late father,'

31

offered Hartley.

'Oh, *him*.' She gave a dismissive wave. 'Awful old bore. I will admit though, he's been a trifle less tiresome these last few days. Come along, won't you?' With a giddy laugh at the shock on her guests' faces, she spun and skipped off along the path towards the back door of the house.

'Is that indicative of the general sentiment towards the late patriarch?' enquired the mendicant.

'It's not far wide of the mark.' Hartley rubbed his temples. 'You'll see soon enough.'

★ ★ ★

The back door of the house was the main point of entry and egress at Tolhurst, being closest to the stable and garage. The front door — the one that Hartley had rushed through on the day of the murder — appeared to be largely ornamental, opening as it did onto the carefully manicured rose garden. The detective found himself wondering what sort of occasion might be grand enough to merit the use of that stately portal. A visit from the Prince of Wales, maybe? For whatever reason, Fred O'Donnell's wake appeared not to have made the cut, and the guests were forced to pick their way over a pile of muddy boots and unidentifiable farm ephemera as they passed through the tiled rear alcove and into the kitchen.

Mary Bamonte stood before the oven, a faded apron tied over her dress. She loaded a large silver tray with pastries and passed it across the counter to her mother, who scrutinised the arrangement with a critical eye. After making a few all-but-undetectable changes, she nodded for Hartley and the friar to follow her into the dining room, where the rest of the family was already seated. Only the dead man's immediate relatives had regrouped for the wake, the muted formality of their clothing and the conspicuous space at the head of the table serving as the sole indicators of solemnity.

'Our pet policeman has returned,' announced Edith. 'He brings, I presume, news of the killer's conviction.' She kept her hands close upon the tray of pastries as she laid it down, as if to indicate that only good boys who solved homicides were rewarded with sweets.

'Well, not as yet, no.' Hartley felt his face grow hot, his collar tight. 'We've made a good deal of progress, though, especially in ruling out certain suspects that —'

Edith waved his words away in irritation. 'What's this you've dragged along with you, then?' She looked down her patrician nose at the friar.

'He's a darling sort of hermit,' Winnie put in, skipping forward to rest a possessive hand on the cassock-clad shoulder. 'Very chic. Very Catholic. I want to take him down to the Andersons' place tomorrow and show him off before everyone gets one.'

Aside from George rolling his eyes in the corner of the room, this statement met with no response. The family was obviously well accustomed to Winnie's flights of fancy.

'Never mind her nonsense. Do you have any information about who killed my father?'

This question came from Mary, who had shed the apron and joined her husband on the other side of the table, one hand resting atop her belly. The room became preternaturally silent, all eyes fixed on the holy man. Hartley was just about to interject when the friar spoke.

'Funnily enough,' he said, 'I rather think that I do.'

Edith tapped her long, lacquered fingernails against the table in order to quiet the resulting clamour.

'Tell us,' she commanded.

'I can't tell you, I'm afraid,' said the friar, 'but I can show you. I'll have the murderer here, in this room, one week from today. I shall also, if there are no objections, try one of these delightful-looking cakes.' He reached for the tray as the room erupted in clamour and chaos.

★ ★ ★

'Well?' Hartley hissed. They stood on the verandah, some minutes later, having finally managed to slip free of their interrogators.

'Yes?' The friar looked up, munching innocently on one of the cucumber sandwiches he had pilfered from the dining room.

'What the hell was all that about?' Hartley forced himself to whisper for fear of being overheard. 'Why didn't you tell me you knew who the murderer was?'

'Ah. Because I don't.'

The detective groaned. 'Are you telling me you were lying in there?'

'Absolutely not. I was merely showing faith in your capabilities.' The mendicant took another bite.

'What on earth do you think will happen in a week, when I've nothing to show them?'

The friar shook his head. 'That's no way to approach it. You've got to have confidence! I've secured us a seven-day allotment in which to work. Think of it as my creating the conditions for the resolution to present itself.'

'I think of it as you creating the conditions for the end of my career.'

'Nonsense. I've already seen several promising leads rear their heads. The most important result of my declaration, though,' the friar continued, seemingly deaf to Hartley's pleas for more detail, 'is that I have won the trust of the new head of the family. Edith has asked me to stay here for the week.'

'Really?' This brought the detective up short. He had taken a room at the Royal Hotel in Kojonup, and while the distance afforded him some welcome respite from the O'Donnell clan, he was quick to recognise the potential benefits of having someone at Tolhurst both night and day. It was an idea made all the more pleasing by the fact that the person in question was not him. 'Well, I suppose that's nothing to scoff at.'

The friar stood, brushing crumbs from his cassock, and went to investigate the sturdy support posts of the verandah. 'I think I shall string my hammock out here,' he said. 'If we reconvene tomorrow morning, I have no doubt we'll find ourselves much closer to a solution.'

5

The following day was a Saturday.

All traces of the previous afternoon's ceremonials had been erased and life at Tolhurst had returned to something approaching normality. By the time that Hartley drove over after breakfast, most of the family were engaged in various agricultural errands: George had gone to ferry supplies down to the shearing shed, Winnie was checking the water levels in the property's three dams and Edith had taken the truck into town for repairs of some sort. Hazel was holed up at the piano, practising a waltz for the wedding of a local couple that evening, while Mary worked the domestic sorcery that kept the entire household fed and clothed, the children roaming in her wake.

Only one dog came to herd Hartley into the garage this time — the other two were working down at the sheep yards. This animal was the eldest, the fur beginning to grey about her neck and along her spine. Age and absent comrades did little to dampen her enthusiasm, however, and she barked loud enough to shake the corrugated-iron walls of the garage as she chased the vehicle to a halt. The friar followed upon her stiffly furred heels.

'I see you've managed to overcome your phobia,' said the detective, stepping down from the car.

'We found some common ground.' The friar gave the dog an affectionate scratch about the haunches. 'This is Kaiser. She sleeps on the verandah, too.'

'Kaiser?' Hartley had, for whatever reason, not yet been introduced to the non-human residents of the property.

'That's right. The other two are Queenie and Shah. Quite the regal bunch, though no-one has been able to satisfy me on the provenance of the names. It would seem that honorific titles are not so strictly tied to gender in canines as they are in humans.'

'Well, that's progress of a sort, though not exactly what I was hoping for. Did you manage to encounter any murderers out under the awning, or will we have to cast the net wider?'

They began to make their way along the gravel path to the house, the dog running large, lazy circles around them.

'I thought we might start by having each of the O'Donnells describe their encounters with this mysterious cloaked entity.'

Hartley frowned as the friar led him around the corner to his encampment on the verandah. 'But I've done that. I held an interview *en masse* in the dining room. Didn't you read the notes I left you?' He nodded towards the pile of notebooks which now sat on the weathered boards beside the hammock.

'I did indeed,' said the friar. 'They were marvellously detailed and most illuminating. I would appreciate the opportunity, however, to speak with each member of the family individually. There are certain questions I would like to have answered.' He gathered up the books and thrust them into an ancient-looking satchel. 'Despite my appreciation for antiques and heirlooms, I have found that some things are best acquired firsthand. Testimony falls into this category, as do undergarments.'

37

Hartley regarded his grinning partner with some curiosity. 'At some point,' he said, 'you're going to have to describe the series of events that led to your spiritual awakening. For whatever reason, I have no end of trouble picturing you in the seminary.'

* * *

They found Mary in the kitchen. She had just finished clearing away the breakfast things and was busy putting the scraps into a tin for chicken feed.

'I've already told you what happened,' she said, wearily. 'While we're prattling on, the man who killed my dad is getting farther and farther away. He's probably halfway to Melbourne by now.'

'You do think it was a man, then?' asked the friar.

'Too tall for a woman. Big boot prints, too.'

'You didn't get a clear look at him, though?'

Mary jabbed her wooden spoon at a clump of burnt porridge caked along the bottom of a pot. When it finally slid free, she scooped it into the scrap tin. 'No, I didn't. And now that you mention it, I haven't been able to get a clear look at much else, either, not since I lost my spectacles. If you really want to make yourself useful,' she said, waving the spoon in agitation, 'go and find my eyeglasses so I can read the mail without giving myself a headache.'

Hartley ignored this affront to his professional dignity, hoping that the friar would do the same. He was immediately disappointed.

'When did you lose them?' the little man asked, with what sounded like genuine concern.

'I haven't seen them since last Sunday.'

'The day before your father was shot.'

'Well, they say bad luck comes in threes.'

The investigators shared a puzzled look.

'I'm not sure I'm aware of a third piece of misfortune,' the detective hazarded.

Mary gave a thin smile. 'Keep wasting my time and you will be.' She thrust the tin of scraps into his arms. 'Take this out to the chooks. Get one of the kids to show you the way, or better yet, have Hazel take you. She can show you where she had her encounter with the bloke in the cloak. It'll keep you out of my hair for a few minutes, at any rate.'

6

Following his initial interviews with the O'Donnells, Hartley had managed to identify three separate occasions on which the cloaked man could indisputably be placed at Tolhurst.

There were plenty of unverified accounts from lone family members — often correlating remarkably with Sunday afternoon brandy consumption or return trips from the pub — but only those three in which the cloaked figure's presence could be attested to by more than one witness.

The first such sighting was on the twentieth of August, several weeks prior to Fred's death, when Les and George had spotted the cloaked man near the shearing shed at knock-off. A fortnight later, the figure had been observed for the final time, lurking outside the kitchen window up at the house. The remaining encounter, almost exactly midway between the other two, had as its backdrop the incongruous environs of the henhouse.

Scraps were taken to the Tolhurst chickens immediately following each meal, a strict schedule attributable not so much to concern for their nutrition as to Mary's desire to keep the kitchen free of ants. The job of feeding the poultry belonged to Charlie and Delia, it being one of the very few tasks they could be trusted to perform independently, if not entirely without supervision. Prior attempts to discharge this duty unaccompanied had resulted in a sprained ankle (Delia's reward for courageously driving a fox away from the coop) and Charlie somehow managing to lock himself inside one of the laying boxes while retrieving eggs (a feat which had never been satisfactorily re-enacted or explained). Playing chaperone to the children was rarely viewed as a chore because the distance to the henhouse was ideal for a post-prandial stroll. Mary's dinners, though widely appreciated, were famously dense, benefitting from any available aid to digestion.

'There were four of us that evening,' said Hazel, as she led the investigators past the garage. 'Cordelia, Charles, Winifred and myself.' The two children were again present, but had run a dozen yards ahead, immersed in some imaginary mission.

'You are referring to the twenty-seventh of August, correct?' the friar asked.

'That's right.' Hazel stretched her arms out over her head with a contented sort of sigh. Hartley imagined that she must be savouring her temporary freedom from the saccharine wedding waltz. 'It was about an hour after dinner. Mary and I had finished up the dishes, Edith and George were debating the purchase of a new stud ram and Fred had disappeared into his study as usual. We decided to leave old Kaiser back at the house. She takes a bit too much pleasure in terrifying the chickens.'

'Was it a clear night?'

'Not particularly, no. There were a few clouds about. I don't recall seeing the moon.'

Night was a hard thing to bring to mind. As they spoke, the sun was climbing ever higher in the sky. The daylight didn't have the fierce heat it would acquire in the coming months, but Hartley could already feel a distinct warning tingle on the freckled skin of his forearms.

'The children had pestered Winnie into reading to them from one of her American periodicals,' Hazel went on. 'When it came time to take the chicken scraps out, they refused to go unless she accompanied them. I joined out of solidarity. The poor thing spent the entire evening being interrogated on everything from the exhibitions at the World's Fair to the current Manhattan social hierarchy.'

Hartley could hear the chickens before their enclosure came into view, sheltered behind a wall of lilly pilly. They scratched at the ground and pressed against the rusted wire fence, clamouring in anticipation.

'We were about here,' said Hazel, 'when I first became aware of the voices.'

'Even over the sound of the poultry?' asked the friar.

The young woman stifled a laugh. 'I'm sorry!' she said. 'I keep forgetting that neither of you actually met Fred. There were marching bands incapable of drowning him out.'

'Could you actually hear what he was saying, though?' pressed Hartley. 'Anything that might help us identify the cloaked man?'

'He said, 'I'm gunna kill you!'.'

This interpolation came from somewhere in the vicinity of the detective's knees. Looking down, Hartley realised that they had finally managed to catch up with Charlie and Delia, the latter of whom was now engaged in a rather menacing impression of her grandfather.

'He did *not*, Delia! Stop making stuff up!' Charlie protested.

'Yes he did. You just couldn't hear him because

your ears are always full of rocks.' She bent to pick up a pebble. 'Look, this just fell out of your ear.'

'Did not!'

'Did too! Everyone saw it.'

'Auntie Hazel,' came the boy's plaintive appeal, 'that rock didn't come out of my ear, did it?'

Hazel sighed. 'Of course not, darling. Cordelia, take this to the chooks and stop tormenting your cousin.' She handed the scrap tin to her daughter. After scrabbling over it for a moment, the pair ran off to unhook the gate to the chicken coop. 'I think she's right, though,' Hazel went on, once the children were out of earshot. 'Fred was in a foul mood.'

'He was threatening to kill the cloaked man?' asked Hartley. 'Not the other way around?'

'That's the way it sounded. To tell you the truth, though,' she added, after a minute's reflection, 'I couldn't hear much of what the other man was saying. He was much quieter than Fred.'

'Could you get a clear look at him?'

Hazel shook her head. 'Only an impression — an outline, through the fence. They were over behind that corner of the enclosure.'

The chicken coop consisted of a covered wooden structure about six feet high which gave out on either side to an area completely enclosed by wire fencing. On the western side — the side closer to the garage and the homestead — the fenced area was much larger, containing about a dozen hens. Patches of torn and mended wire bore testament to a history of incursions from foxes, feral cats and chuditch. The further portion, about half the size of the hen-house, was home to a couple of roosters who strutted back and forth along the line of the fence like major

43

generals. It was to this section of the structure that Hazel was pointing.

'Did you hear Fred say anything else?' pressed Hartley.

'They were arguing about money, I think. The only words I heard distinctly were 'not one penny'..'

'You think it might've been blackmail, then?'

'In all honesty, I don't know what to think.' Hazel's voice trembled:.the cumulative frustration, Hartley guessed, of several uncertain months. 'It's all so hard — all the secrecy. Fred must've heard us approaching, because he hissed something to the cloaked man and they both disappeared around the back of the enclosure. When we got back to the house, his study door was locked, and he refused to let anyone in.'

'Did you ask him about the cloaked man?'

Hazel nodded. 'The next morning.'

'And what did he say?'

'The same thing he always said.'

' 'It's all in your thick bloody head!' ' The children had returned, and this time it was Charlie in the role of their late grandfather. Evidently, his impersonation wasn't far wrong, as Hazel had to stifle a smile before rebuking him for his language.

'But that's what he used to say!' Charlie protested.

'Your grandfather used to say a great many things I wouldn't care to hear repeated. Now let's get this tin back to Auntie Mary.'

The two children raced off towards the house, having mutually arrived at the understanding that the last one to the kitchen would be cast out of the family in shame. The friar turned his head to watch them go.

'They seem to entertain each other well enough,'

44

the little man said with a smile.

'Thank God,' said Hazel. 'I don't know how I'd manage with Delia if Charlie weren't there to keep her busy.'

'It must be difficult raising a child without the aid of your husband.' Though phrased as a statement, there was a note of enquiry in his voice.

Hazel was silent, watching the red dust settle in the children's wake. 'It can be,' she said, carefully, 'but I'm very lucky to have the O'Donnells. I think it's important for children to grow up amongst family.'

Something in the way she spoke made it clear that Hazel had not experienced this herself.

'Were you an only child?' asked Hartley, who had often longed for the companionship of a younger sibling.

'At times.' Hazel's gaze was still fixed firmly on the path ahead. 'I was raised in an orphanage in Lambeth. Children came and went. There was one they said was my brother, but he wasn't there for long. Polio.'

'I'm sorry,' the detective murmured. He cast around for some way to move the conversation on to brighter things. 'Lambeth, you say? I thought I heard something of London in your accent.'

'There's little enough left now. I sailed out to Australia at quite a tender age. They found a distant aunt of mine in New South Wales and sent me off as soon as she wrote back. She was quite nice, in her own way. Married to the owner of a theatre down by The Rocks.'

'How on earth did you get from Sydney Harbour to Kojonup, of all places?'

'I met Jack O'Donnell.' Hazel smiled. 'But that came later. I lived in the theatre for years, learning the ropes.

45

Everything from cosmetics and costumes to marking up the scripts and running lines with the understudies. My aunt hoped to see me become her assistant stage manager, but it was the music that called to me. Whenever I wasn't working, I'd be watching from the orchestra pit. They didn't mind, so long as I stayed out of sight. When I got older, I began to beg lessons from the pianist, and it soon became clear that I had a knack for it. Within a year or two I was travelling up and down the east coast with a touring company. That's where I first ran into Jack — during a run of shows in Melbourne. We were so young, then. He was only seventeen when he fled the farm, dreaming of the stage.'

'Much to Fred's delight, I'm sure,' said the friar.

Hazel shuddered. 'I can only imagine what it was like to be at Tolhurst then. Jack slipped away in the middle of the night.' She shook her head. 'Fred kept a gift for him by the front door, just in case he ever came home.'

'What was it?'

'His shotgun. Always loaded.'

Hartley grimaced. 'He must have calmed down eventually, though.'

'I thought so, too, but that gun was the first thing I saw when we arrived at Tolhurst, six years later. Fred stood on the verandah over there and pointed it at us while we climbed down from the truck. I believe he really would've fired it, too.'

'What stopped him?'

'It must have been my enormous belly,' Hazel laughed. 'I was nearly nine months pregnant. Then again,' she added, sobering, 'I could be giving the old man too much credit. He may simply have been unwilling to waste ammunition. It was pretty clear by that point that Jack was not long for this world.'

Silence descended on the party as they drew to a halt by the back door.

'It was pneumonia that took him, wasn't it?' said the friar, quietly. 'Not a pleasant way to make one's exit.'

'No. In many ways, a bullet may have been kinder. Still, he survived the war and lived long enough to meet his daughter. I'm grateful for that, as I am for so many things.' Hazel steadied herself against the wall as she kicked the dust from her boots. 'Shall we leave all this talk of death outside and go in for a cup of tea?'

'Tea,' said the friar, 'is something for which we can all be truly grateful.'

7

Morning tea was served at the kitchen table by the window, so that those partaking were able to look out over the verandah to the well-kept vegetable garden and rolling paddocks beyond. Mary fussed about, arranging dishes and trays on the table with a fastidious eye. Only when everything was fully to her liking and the children had been sent away with a scone each did she take her seat alongside the investigators and her sister-in-law.

'Winnie shouldn't be far off,' she said, reaching for the enormous porcelain teapot, 'and the boys will be back from the shearing shed in a minute. By the time that lot've had at it, there'll be nothing left, so grab what you can now.'

Hartley did not require any further encouragement. While he had breakfasted passably well at the hotel, the anxiety generated by this seemingly interminable investigation left him famished at all hours. He let his eyes roam hungrily over the freshly baked bread, warm scones, homemade cheese and sliced red apples, unsure of where to begin.

As promised, the diners were still stirring sugar into their tea when they caught sight of George's hat above the wind-rippled wheat. Within a minute or two, he was padding through the kitchen in his socks, having left his sheep-soiled boots at the door. He bent to kiss Mary on the cheek, nodded to the others and took a seat with his back to the window.

'Is Les not joining us this morning?' Hartley enquired.

'No, I'll wrap some tucker up and take it back down for him,' said George, sawing a thick slice of bread from the loaf. 'He reckons he doesn't need a break. That'll change the moment he smells this, I wager.'

'How are things down at the shed?'

'Ah, nothing out of the ordinary,' George shrugged. 'Just the usual, you know.'

Hartley didn't know but nodded regardless. Hailing from Nedlands, in Perth's western suburbs, the detective had spent very little time on the land. Though he believed himself to be concealing this inexperience well, he was strikingly mistaken, and nearly every member of the O'Donnell family had found great enjoyment in discreetly mocking the city dweller. Moved, perhaps, by mercy, the friar intervened to change the subject.

'Tell me, Mr Bamonte,' he said, 'is it true that you were the first to actually see our cloaked mystery man?'

'Seems that way. Well, Les and me, anyway.'

'Would you mind telling me your impressions?'

George chewed thoughtfully. 'There's not a lot to tell, really. It was just around dusk, and they were on the west side of the sheep yards — I'll show you the exact spot if you come down — which meant that they were both sort of silhouetted against the sunset.' With the light from the window behind him, George wasn't much more than a shadowy outline himself at present. The friar watched him with an expression of intense focus.

'When you say *they*, to whom are you referring?'

'Oh, sorry — Fred was there, talking to the cloaked

49

man.'

'Could you hear what they were saying?'

'Not really, no. The sheep make quite a bit of noise.'

'The ovine element aside, could you hear anything else?'

George lifted an eyebrow. 'What sort of thing?'

'Engines, bird calls, shots.' The little man shrugged. 'Anything that might tell us more about what was happening at the time.'

'Nothing out of the ordinary,' said the shearer, after some consideration. 'There would've been cockatoos around, I suppose — they usually come out around that time — but I don't remember anything specific.'

The friar broke into a wide smile, to the bemusement of everyone else present. 'Brilliant. Now then, tell me about the cloaked gentleman. You must've been able to make out enough to distinguish him from your father-in-law.'

'Well, he was about Fred's height. Maybe an inch taller.' George frowned with the effort of recollection. 'He had a cloak on, obviously, or a coat. Whatever you want to call it.'

'How long would you say it was?'

'Fairly long. Almost down to the top of his boots. And he had a hat on, too: a huge, big thing. The brim was about as wide as his shoulders.'

'Black?'

'It looked that way, but again, it was hard to tell.'

'Was he holding anything?

'I don't think so. In fact, come to think of it, I'm pretty sure he had his hands in his pockets. I wish I'd gotten closer, now, but at the time it was all I could do to stay out of Fred's way.'

'You weren't to know,' the mendicant said, gently.

'How long did their conversation last?'

George rubbed his chin, the two-day smattering of stubble rasping audibly. 'Couldn't have been longer than a minute or two. As soon as they noticed us watching, they wrapped it up right quick.'

'Were you able to find anything left behind?'

'I didn't really look. Would've been nice if there was a watch chain or something left behind, wouldn't it? Like in the police stories. Special type of silver chain that was only ever made in a certain factory at a certain time. Leads you right to your killer.' He chuckled. 'I suppose that sort of thing doesn't really happen in real life, does it?'

'I'm afraid not,' put in Hartley, eager to reinstate his authority after the friar's extensive interrogation. 'In modern detective work, we don't really hold out much hope for fingerprints or distinctive piles of cigarette ash. It's a mental science now. All about understanding how criminals think.' He tapped his temple, savouring the three or four seconds which passed before this assertion was ruthlessly undercut.

'I say, a trail of bloody footprints! Frightfully thrilling, don't you think?'

Everyone looked up. Winnie stood in the doorway, dressed incongruously in tattered overalls and a silk *lavallière*. Before her, leading from the back door to the kitchen table, was a faint but undeniable trail of blood. A brief commotion ensued, at the end of which George — or more specifically, George's right foot — was identified as the culprit.

'It's nothing,' he said, squirming free of Winnie's attempted ministrations. 'There was a rock or something in my boot, but I could barely feel it. If I'd realised it was bleeding, I wouldn't've tracked it

51

across the tiles.' This last statement appeared to be a valiant, if ultimately hopeless, attempt to appease his wife, who had already risen for the mop with a great show of martyred sighing. George struggled once more against his assailant. 'Get off it, would you, Winnie?'

But Winifred displayed not the slightest intention of getting off it. She had finally managed to catch hold of the injured foot and proceeded to wrench it skywards.

'Things of this sort simply must be elevated,' she declared, tugging at her brother-in-law's sock. The others hastened to push back their chairs, corralling plates and cutlery to keep them clear of the errant extremity. When the sock came free, Hartley's ever-deepening appreciation of pastoral life was further enriched by the scent of freshly unbooted feet.

'For God's sake, don't put it on the table!' cried Mary, but it was too late. The sock was off, and George's bare foot lay against the butter dish, revealing an untidy smear of blood along the instep and a slightly underwhelming nick in the pale flesh.

'Hold still, will you?' demanded Winnie. 'I think I see it.'

With exaggerated care, she worked at the wound. Then came a triumphant cry and a barely audible clatter, and piece of clear glass half the size of the woman's little fingernail was deposited in the bowl of a nearby teaspoon.

'Really!' Hazel swept in to take the spoon and remove it from the ruins of the meal, her face as white as the bone china. 'Was that entirely necessary, Winnie?'

'I'm sure I've no idea what you mean, dear.' Winnie

flashed a grin. 'I may well have saved a life here today. Georgie, darling, you'd better start thinking of ways to repay me. I'm partial to *éclairs*, you know.'

'You're partially mad, that's what you are,' he said, as he stomped off to the bathroom to wash up.

'That's it!' said Mary, waving the mop. 'Everyone clear out. Morning tea's done. Off with the lot of you!'

'I say, the service in this place is just too barbarous,' drawled Winnie, darting in to grab a scone before the tray was whisked away. 'Come on, chums. We shall regroup on the verandah.'

8

Being evicted from the kitchen filled Hartley with a transgressive, boyish thrill which helped sustain him as he waited for the day's final interview. He and the friar spent the afternoon shoring up the statements they had taken before lunch. Winnie offered ready support for Hazel's version of events at the henhouse, Les was only too happy to back up George's account of the *tête-à-tête* by the shearing shed, and the two youngest members of the family contributed a helpful pantomime recreation of each and every occasion on which the cloaked man had visited the property, including the time he had ridden in on a flying horse and distributed poisoned magic toffees — an event that had managed to slip the minds of all those over the age of ten.

Delia and Charlie had also been present for the cloaked man's third and final confirmed visit, but the investigators could glean little in the way of reliable information from them. The only indisputable piece of intelligence was that Charlie had been sent to bed early after dinner that night for locking Kaiser in the woodshed. This was a crime he still denied, though Delia supplied compelling evidence that the poor old dog had played the role of hostage to Charlie's masked bushranger in a particularly engrossing game which had occupied most of the afternoon. In the interests of reconciliation, the detective pointed out that locking Kaiser in the woodshed had likely kept her clear of the all too real gunfire which was to come later in the evening, and was therefore a net positive action. After some discussion, both cousins were able to agree on the wisdom of this point and went off together in companionable silence.

According to Hartley's notes, the other two witnesses to the final visitation had been Mary, who still stalked the kitchen in furious silence, and Edith, whose business in town appeared to have grown to consume a significant portion of the day. Soon enough, the sun began to set, and the detective found himself growing restless. The prospect loomed of another night spent in the smoking-room at the Royal Hotel, fretting over a case which showed no sign of nearing its solution. He was relieved, then, to finally hear an engine outside, and happier still when Edith entered, bearing both the box which contained her purchases from Kojonup and an invitation to dinner.

★ ★ ★

After the meal — another hearty triumph of assorted starches — Edith led the investigators to the vegetable garden on the western side of the house.

'This is where I saw him,' she said.

'I was under the impression that you were in the kitchen,' said the friar. He reached for one of the notebooks that Hartley had lent him, but Edith forestalled him with a gesture.

'You are quite correct,' she said. She nodded at the bright expanse of the window, through which they could see Mary clearing the dishes. 'I was at the table with the children. Fred was out here with the cloaked man.' The kitchen window was tall and wide, running most of the room's length. A wooden bench had been crafted to fit snugly beneath the outer windowsill, looking out upon the greenery. The friar's hammock hung nearby. Though the sun had set, the western sky still burned a deep orange, and the white pebbled path fairly glowed between the garden beds.

'What were the men doing?' Hartley asked.

'I couldn't tell,' said Edith. 'Not for a minute or two, at any rate. They seemed simply to be talking, though I couldn't hear them at such a distance, of course, especially with the window closed.'

'Did your husband seem agitated?'

'My husband spent his life in a near constant state of agitation. He was forever in and out of the house at all hours, taking abrupt trips into town or driving the auto round the paddocks to clear his head. He'd recently taken to sleeping in the study, presumably so I wouldn't turn him out of bed for smelling of cigar smoke. All of this is to simply say that it would probably have been more remarkable, on the night in question, had he managed to appear in command of his emotions.'

'You weren't concerned by the interaction, then?' This question came from the friar.

Edith turned calmly to face him. 'My dear, when one has been running a farm for as long as I have, raising children and whipping stockhands into shape, one becomes far more accustomed to inflicting concern upon others than retaining it oneself.' She gave a tight smile. 'You must remember, too, that young Hazel had been going on about this mystery man for the better part of a fortnight, so his appearance did not come as any great surprise.'

'Surely the gunshot gave you pause, though.'

Edith was silent, as if choosing her next words with care. 'Knowing how Fred was killed,' she said, 'it may be easy now to see the import of that particular shot. Still, you must remind yourself of where you are. Shots ring out across the paddocks every day. We use the rifles to scare off foxes, to keep our fruit trees free of birds, to hunt for rabbits and kangaroos.'

'The younger members of the family were not quite as phlegmatic, were they?' The friar spoke almost serenely, bending to take in the scent of a nearby flower.

It was the shot under discussion — fired on the third of September, a week prior to Fred's demise — which had finally forced the Kojonup police to act. Winnie and Hazel had been needling them to despatch a detective ever since the first sighting of the cloaked man. A local constable rode out to take a look after the first call to the station, more from boredom than anything else, but quickly came to the conclusion that there was no credible threat and nothing to be done. Subsequent requests were either politely refused or ignored outright. It was only after the shot in the garden that the local officers had finally agreed to send to Perth for a detective — partly because they knew that if a murder did eventuate and they were found to have done nothing to prevent it, there would be serious repercussions but largely, Hartley thought, out of a desire to pass responsibility on to someone else.

'The round was fired from Fred's shotgun,' Edith said, shortly. 'It was the police themselves who established that. The local lads. It was his usual ammunition, a Remington 12 bore. Nothing like the bullet that ended his life.'

'Were you confident of that fact at the time?' pushed Hartley, with a discreet look at the friar. The pressed brass cartridge base enclosed in the note at the crime scene had been a Remington.

'All I will say,' said Edith, turning back towards the house, 'is that it certainly wasn't the first time my husband fired at a visitor, and I had no way of knowing it would be the last. Now, if you'll excuse me, I really must help Mary with the dishes.'

With that, she strode for the door.

★ ★ ★

'Well, there's another day gone,' sighed Hartley, when he and the friar were alone once more. 'You know, I can't see how those interviews helped. Not one of our witnesses told us anything we didn't already know.'

'I find myself compelled to disagree,' said the mendicant.

'You may as well make that your personal motto.'

The little man laughed and said, in a disorienting change of conversational pace: 'I don't suppose you know anyone who wears a toupée?'

Hartley blinked. 'Not really, no. I'm fairly sure there's a fellow downstairs from me at headquarters who uses one, but I wouldn't say I know him well.'

'Yet you are sufficiently acquainted to see his coiffure for the absurd fiction it is.' The friar lifted a hand to his own greying curls as he spoke. 'Being young — and in possession of an enviable auburn mane — you probably have no interest in what happens above your eyebrows. When you get to my age, though, I daresay you'll pay it more heed.' He sighed. 'The thinning usually starts at the temples, sometimes the crown. No-one else will notice, at first. Not unless you make the mistake of trying to conceal it. There is nothing that approximates a natural head of hair less believably than a toupée. The colour is uniform, either flat and lustreless or shining like a polished stone. There are no whorls, no variation in thickness or direction; the thing lies over your own sparse locks like a discarded pelt.'

There was silence as Hartley processed this image. 'Very evocative,' he said, 'but I'm not quite sure I see the connection to matters at hand.'

'This murder,' the friar assumed an earnest expression that served only to heighten the absurdity of his assertion, 'is wearing a toupée. Someone has tried to pull together a covering, but it is bulky and obtrusive. The stitches can still be seen.'

'Through the holes in the witness testimonies, you mean?' hazarded Hartley, struggling with the extended metaphor.

'Or lack thereof. The narrative woven by all these accounts is, much like a poorly made wig, curiously watertight. Though only three visitations have been definitively attested, the cloaked intruder has managed to be seen by every member of the household. In fact, with the exception of the children, who encountered the figure twice — and Fred, whose testimony will regrettably go forever unheard — every person at Tolhurst has seen the murderer precisely once. Not only that, but each of these sightings can be corroborated by at least one other person.'

'You're right. The sightings must have been planned somehow.' The detective cursed. 'It should have been obvious from the start.'

'Don't be too hard on yourself. There are others in this case far more deserving of your vitriol, and our task now is to find them. Luckily, we may be aided by a witness constitutionally incapable of deception.' He reached out to run his fingers through the silver-flecked fur of old Kaiser, who had followed them from the garden. 'The person responsible for fabricating the cloaked sightings made two particularly telling choices. Firstly, they did not choose to appear when the entire household was assembled. It would have been fairly simple to stage a sighting at dinner, when everyone was in attendance — including, on certain nights, Les Thompson.'

'That would certainly have saved some time,' agreed Hartley. 'What was the second choice, then?'

'Each of the three sightings occurred in situations where the canine element was absent or otherwise engaged. At the sheep yards, the working dogs would have been too focussed on their duties to notice a distant stranger in a field. You and I have felt firsthand the strength of their herding instinct. The other two sightings took place in territory traditionally under the control of Kaiser.'

'. . . except for the fact that the family has begun to keep her away from the chooks,' said the detective, nodding slowly. 'That's why the figure appeared by the coop. And the final sighting took place when she was locked in the woodshed.'

'Precisely. I think we shall find that young Charlie's protestations of innocence in that matter were quite genuine. The unjust detention of Kaiser was carried out by another.'

'The cloaked man — or an accomplice — wanted to avoid being mobbed by the dogs when speaking to Fred.' Hartley suddenly clicked his fingers. 'No! He had to make sure the dogs weren't given the opportunity to make a fuss, because they wouldn't have done so. They knew him! It's like that old story, the one where the bloke is identified as the one who broke into his own stables because no-one heard his dog barking in the night.'

The friar exerted absolutely no effort in trying to conceal his grin. 'I think you'll find that old story is 'The Adventure of Silver Blaze', by inveterate fantasist Sir Arthur Conan Doyle. Which is surprising, really, because I could have sworn to having heard you in the kitchen, scant hours ago, expounding most volubly on how modern police work has nothing in common with the childish imaginings compiled in volumes of detective fiction.'

Hartley struggled with irritation before allowing himself a chuckle. 'Yes, all right. Go on, then. I'll take all the ridicule in the world if it gets me through this God-awful case.' He rubbed his hands together. 'At least we'll be looking in the right direction now. The man in the cloak was known to the dogs and couldn't appear when the whole household was gathered together.'

'Quite right,' said the friar, sobering. 'We are forced to face the very real possibility, then, that the man in the cloak was no stranger, no outsider, no figure from Fred's dark past. He was well known at Tolhurst. A friend, perhaps a family member. When we sat down to dinner this evening, we may well have been sharing the table with a murderer.'

61

9

It was about half an hour later, once darkness had crept in and the Southern Cross had staked its claim to the horizon, that Detective Hartley found himself cast as an inadvertent eavesdropper. He was reclining on the verandah, relishing the cool evening air and scribbling in his notebook by the light from the dining-room window, when he heard the latch above him click. He ducked aside as the sash creaked open, the muted murmur of conversation from within resolving into something suddenly intelligible. Though his view of the interior was obscured by the bulk of gathered curtains, Hartley had no difficulty recognising the voices of those who spoke.

'That's better,' breathed Winnie, her artificially accented tones unmistakeable. 'The atmosphere in here has been altogether oppressive of late.'

'What do you expect, with all these police traipsing all over the place?' Mary's voice, though emanating from somewhere deeper within the room, was still quite audible. 'It's enough to put you thoroughly on edge.'

The younger sister gave a derisive laugh. 'More so than the dire pall of death?'

'It stands to reason you wouldn't bat an eye at having a bunch of strangers rifling through your things. You're as private as you are modest. That's without mentioning your feelings regarding gentlemen in uniform, which you take great pains to broadcast to all and sundry.'

Winnie laughed again. 'If that's an allusion to the young detective, I can tell you with perfect candour that the uniform doesn't enter into it. In fact, the opportunity to see him sans uniform — or other vestments, for that matter — is something at which I would not turn up my nose.'

Hartley heard nothing further over the thundering of his own pulse. Flushing all over, he wriggled away from the sill, crouched and crablike, aiming to put as much distance as possible between himself and the window. In this he was impeded by the friar, who materialised out of the darkness grin-first, a Cheshire cat in reverse.

'Overheard something distasteful?'

Hartley held a frantic finger to his lips. 'The whole situation is distasteful,' he whispered, scuttling further along the verandah. They were now clear enough of the dining room's light that his scarlet cheeks would not be visible, but he worried that the friar might be able to feel the heat of his embarrassment through the few scant inches of evening air that separated them. 'I'm never one to intrude on private conversations, I can assure you. Not if it can be avoided.'

The little man cocked his head at this. 'It would greatly interest me to hear, when we are able to speak at liberty, what precisely you imagine the duties of a detective to be. I can't help but feel that our understandings of the role differ wildly.'

'What are you implying?' whispered Hartley.

'Merely that being privy to an unguarded moment between the inmates of this house — each of whom, as we've recently ascertained, should now be considered a murder suspect — is a rare opportunity, and not one to be dismissed out of hand.'

'Even so, you can't —' Hartley began to protest, but the friar ploughed onwards.

'I would make the further case that your duties in the service of the Crown might outweigh any personal discomfort incurred by the odd spot of eavesdropping. Not that I feel any particularly compelling loyalty to His Majesty, you understand,' the friar flashed a grin, 'but I am terrifically nosy, and not too proud to exploit your sense of professional responsibility in order to learn what's being discussed in the living room.'

'Fine,' huffed the detective. 'But you'll come with me and help yourself to half the shame.'

'I think I shall manage to shoulder the burden somehow.'

Silently, the pair crept back to crouch beneath the windowsill, the weathered wood hard against hands and knees. Hartley sighed in covert relief to hear that he was no longer the topic of conversation, which had now taken on the cadence of a well-trodden sibling dispute, its points worn dull through time and repetition.

'. . . utterly unbecoming,' Mary was complaining. 'Not to mention the way you behave around the children. God knows where you get the nonsense you fill their heads with. Sometimes I think dear Jack was right. He always said you were left here as an infant by a troupe of travelling circus folk.'

'And you wonder at the font of my nonsense?' Winnie snorted. 'Who else but our brother could've had you picturing a passable band of entertainers within a hundred miles of this tedious backwater?'

'Well, I'm certainly not forcing you to stay. Off you go, out into the world. Go out and try to make your own way — see how long you last!'

'And leave the children to wither in your grey clutches? Not likely! I have the vital duties of an eccentric aunt to carry out.'

'Of course you do. Where on Earth would they be without mad Winnie convincing them to leave food out for the fairies at the bottom of the garden?' The sounds of Mary's sarcasm drifted about the room, punctuated by exaggerated footfalls and clinking china. 'We'd have fewer ants about the place, for a start. No, it's fine. I'll clear away the tea things. Don't get up and make yourself useful, whatever you do. Wouldn't want to throw the universe into complete disarray.'

'You know perfectly well that you'd be lost without me, darling,' drawled Winnie. 'You all would. After all, 'it's in stories that we store our souls' — do you know who said that?'

'Haven't the slightest.'

'I did, just now.' The younger woman tittered, chuffed at her own wit. 'Honestly, it's as though you don't pay attention to a word I say.'

'Why should I? You either make it all up as you go along or regurgitate nonsense from the pages of some foreign newspaper. At least Jack's tales had some substance to them. Remember Tim Mittens the Tailor?' Mary sighed. 'Oh, Jack spun a story around him to rival Dickens. I'll remember that one as long as I live. Or what about Benjamin the Bunyip? The way he'd lurk around the creek, bellowing —'

'Wait!'

So abrupt was Winnie's interjection, her tone so transformed, that Hartley was certain he'd been discovered. He flattened himself immediately to the

65

floor, awaiting the inevitable accusations, but none were forthcoming.

'What are you playing at?' demanded Mary, setting down the tea tray with an audible rattle. 'Half startled me out of my skin.'

'Benjamin the Bunyip!' Winnie cried. 'I'd forgotten all about him. Don't you remember where he came from?'

'Well, I s'pose he came from a billabong, in Jack's imagining. I don't see what that has to do with anything, though.'

'No, I mean the story itself, the inspiration. It came from Dad.'

'Dad? Telling fairy stories?' Mary scoffed. 'Not bloody likely.'

'But it wasn't a fairy story. Not to begin with. Don't you remember?' Urgency stripped Winnie of her affectations, roughening her vowels and rendering her a farmer's daughter once more. 'Dad sat the three of us down one night after supper. It was after school, I think. I was still too young to go, but you and Jack were in your uniforms. Dad was pacing up and down. I've never seen him so unsettled, before or since.'

'It really doesn't ring a bell . . .'

'Just try to remember!' Winnie insisted. 'We all thought we were getting in trouble for something, maybe climbing on the plough again, but Dad just told us that we had to be on the lookout for a stranger. There was a man, he said, who might try to grab us from outside school or follow us back to the farm.'

Hartley heard a sharp intake of breath, followed by a dull slap that he guessed to indicate a hand striking a thigh, or possibly the side of an armchair.

'You're right!' said Mary. 'That mad, scared look in

66

his eye. I remember!'

'It was the only time I ever saw him like that. And all he'd tell us was that this strange man was called Ben, and that he was dangerous. If we noticed anyone unusual or heard anything about Ben, we were to report to Dad immediately.'

'I don't think I ever heard anything more about it. Did you?'

'Not from Dad, no. He never mentioned it again. He settled down after a week or two, then went on as though nothing had happened. Jack seemed to find the whole episode hugely amusing, for his part. He claimed to have seen Ben one day after school, then began using him as a sort of bogeyman. You must remember, surely! Whenever something went missing, he'd tell us that Ben had gobbled it up, and that we had to be careful near the windows at night, or we'd be eaten, too. I suppose things began to grow in the telling, and that's how we ended up with Benjamin the Bunyip haunting all corners of the farm.'

'Poor Jack,' Mary's voice was tender now, thoughtful. 'It wasn't easy for him, but he did his best to keep things bearable. Wait — you're not trying to suggest some sort of link between Ben and the cloaked man who shot Dad? That was fifteen years ago. No, longer! Surely there can't be any connection?'

'It seems almost impossible,' allowed Winnie, 'but so does everything else that's happened to us these last few weeks. Look at the way Dad was killed. Look at that strange, nameless little man that the detective managed to dig up from the middle of nowhere. Every semblance of normality seems to have gone out the win —' She pulled herself up short. 'The window! Mary, look — there's someone outside the window!'

This time, Hartley didn't so much as flinch. Both body and moral compass had been contorted for so long as to make him glad of the discovery. Sighing with relief, he clambered to stand from aching knees, an apology already half formed on his lips.

The words made it no further.

Both of the women in the dining room were staring, wide-eyed — not at the detective, but past him. He spun around just in time to glimpse a heavily dressed man ducking away into the darkness of the rose garden. There was a moment of shocked silence before the night came alive. Hartley leapt from the verandah to give pursuit, Winnie's cry of alarm ringing in his ears. Other sounds reached him as he ran: Kaiser barking, distant, but growing closer; queries and exhortations from other quarters of the house; the ragged breath of his quarry from somewhere in the darkness ahead.

Thorns caught at his clothes as he pushed through the rose garden. The dark shape in front of him maintained its distance, reaching the fenceline before him and vaulting over into the home paddock. Hartley leapt after it, landing awkwardly on an unstable ankle and losing a few precious seconds in the recovery.

They were well clear of the house now, with nothing but the stars above to light the scene. The friar must have given up the chase or — more likely, to the detective's mind — had decided to sit it out from the beginning. Hartley trotted forward at a more cautious pace now, moving carefully across the uneven ground. Kaiser whined behind him. Foiled by the fence, the old dog paced up and down the length of the paddock, pawing at the ground. The other two must still have been out at the shearing shed. Hartley registered their howls at the edge of hearing as he strained to catch any indication of movement from the intruder. He crouched low, reasoning that the man's silhouette would be easier to see when outlined against the starry sky. His quarry must have had the same idea; Hartley spied a huddled form by the fence about ten yards ahead, shifting slowly in an apparent attempt to hide behind a low, rocky rise.

The detective crept onward, almost on hands and knees. In darkness, he put his trust in stealth over speed, not wanting to give himself away until the last possible moment. Finally, with only a few feet separating him from his target, Hartley pounced. He charged forward with arms flung wide, an indistinct cry rumbling up from somewhere in his shuddering chest.

What happened next would never appear in the pages of any official police report. It would never reach the ears of the chief, nor would it be whispered with a knowing wink at the pub by the station, where officers could often be found confiding a casual bit of excess brutality or the partial personal reappropriation of recovered goods. In fact, Hartley would go the rest of his law enforcement career without speaking of it to another living soul.

He hit the low figure at full force, momentum carrying him forward and over his target. Off balance and afraid of losing his advantage, the detective scrabbled for purchase on the most immediately available surface, sinking his fingers deep into the man's hair. Very deep. Too deep, thought the detective, dazedly, as both hands disappeared almost to the wrist in his opponent's thick, heavy curls. By the time he realised his mistake, it was too late — he had already hit the hard soil of the paddock, pulling the creature along with him. He watched the dark shape of his adversary topple towards him, blotting out the stars as it rolled. Then the wind was knocked out of him by a hundred and fifty-odd pounds of sheep.

The ewe recovered long before he did, bleating indignantly as she regained her legs. Through a fog, Hartley realised that several of the things he had taken to be rocks were, in fact, lambs. As he watched, they began to sleepily unfold themselves and trot away after their mother. Left dazed in the dirt, the detective lay still, attempting to ascertain the extent of the damage he had suffered. The pain was concentrated largely in two points: the lower back and the ego. A series of exploratory movements led him to believe that the former would probably recover in time, while the latter had better be taken behind the shed with a shotgun for the sake of mercy. Groaning, he sat up and began to take stock of the situation.

Above the furious percussion of Kaiser's bark — apparently, she had still not managed to breach the fence — Hartley could hear movement from the direction of the house. Footsteps in the garden, though indistinct, gave him the impetus he needed to finally right himself and brush the dust from his uniform. No sooner had he done so than a series of muted explosions rang out on the other side of the paddock: not gunshots, but an automobile engine rattling into life. The vehicle swung out onto the gravel driveway and rumbled towards the main road, headlamps guttering in and out of view amongst the pines. Hartley stood, helpless, watching the lights grow small and gradually disappear in the distance, until a hand at his elbow broke the trance.

Edith O'Donnell stood beside him, peering into the darkness.

'What on Earth was all that about?'

The detective sighed. 'A man in a dark suit, or something similar, lurking about the shadows. I only saw him for half a second before he took off. Gave me the slip without too much difficulty, I'm afraid. I doubt I'll be able to catch him up now, even in the auto.' Then, brightening suddenly, he added: 'There's a chance, though, that he may already have given himself away.'

He filled Edith in on the friar's latest theory as they turned back towards the house.

'You believe a member of my family was responsible for what happened to Fred?' There was something dangerous in the matriarch's tone.

'It's a possibility. Based upon a logical deduction,' Hartley hastened to explain, 'not a reflection of my personal feelings.'

'That wouldn't be a deduction but an inference,' corrected Edith, 'and not a particularly sound one. Besides, look at how worked up poor Kaiser is now — there's no question she caught the scent of a stranger.'

Upon hearing her name, the dog stopped pacing and sat, waiting for orders. Hartley gave her a desultory scratch.

'She may simply have been excited by all the action,' he ventured, but his conviction was shaken. It suffered another blow as, nearing the verandah, he caught sight of George and Les approaching from the direction of the shearing shed. Winnie and Mary were still visible through the dining-room window, too, the latter fussing over the friar with a tea set. As if on cue,

71

Hazel wandered into the garden to complete the cast.

'All present and accounted for,' Edith observed, taking her daughter-in-law's arm. 'Unless you intend on routing out and arresting my grandchildren, I think that this particular theory can safely be put to bed. Good night, Detective.'

'Now, wait a minute,' said Hartley, as the women made to enter the house. 'Aren't you at all concerned about the fellow returning? That could've been *him* — the murderer, I mean.'

'Rubbish. It was just some local lad having us on. You forget, perhaps, that my late husband's irascibility made Tolhurst the preferred target of every bored and malicious youth for miles around. That was one of the reasons dear Winnie had such trouble getting the local police to lend her credence in the first place. Even in the unlikely event that the perpetrator were to return tonight,' she added, forestalling Hartley's protestations, 'Les and George are here now. I'll have them prepare the rifles, if that'll put your mind at ease.'

Hartley's mind was neither at, near nor anywhere remotely approaching ease, but he found himself exhausted and ill-inclined to pursue the point any further. Under the pretence of attempting to pick up the trespasser's trail, he bid a good evening to all and drove off into the night.

10

As the following day was a Sunday, Hartley decided to take the opportunity to examine the house unsupervised while its inhabitants were at church. He nursed a cup of coffee at a table by the hotel window, looking out over the main street, and only when he saw the O'Donnells arrive — pulling up outside the church in a miniature convoy comprising an old Chevrolet Tourer and a flatbed truck — did he descend to his own vehicle and strike out for Tolhurst.

'No worship for you this morning?' the friar asked, greeting him on the verandah.

Hartley began to fidget. This was always a topic to approach with care. 'No,' he said. 'I have never been aligned with any particular religion. My father is . . . well, the family was Jewish originally, based in Prussia. Dad didn't take to it, though. He actually became rather prominent amongst the local socialists and got himself into a bit of hot water. He ended up having to flee to Australia — the most remote place he could think of — where he married a thoroughly conventional Anglo-Saxon girl and took her surname, the better to blend in. A good bit of foresight on his part, and one I've since had cause to thank him for. Being a skinny red-headed heathen made school trouble enough for me, but navigating those halls come nineteen fourteen would have been unimaginably harder as a Schmitz than a Hartley.'

The friar chuckled, his face a picture of jovial

73

sympathy. 'Nothing wrong with red, in one's hair follicles or one's politics. The teachings of Jesus align with those of Marx more often than the followers of either would care to admit.'

'It doesn't bother you, then?'

'Not in the least. I'm of the belief that every creed has something to offer. If we limit ourselves to a single set of teachings, what chance do we have to grow?'

Hartley was taken aback. 'I must say, it's surprising to hear this sort of talk from a member of the Catholic Church. I've always thought of it as quite a dogmatic faith.'

'Oh, I'm not a member of the Catholic Church,' said the friar, lightly. 'Now, shall we take a look around the house?'

'Hold on,' the detective scrambled to follow him through the door. 'What are you talking about? You're a priest, aren't you?'

'I *was* a priest,' the friar said, heading for the front of the house, 'though I found the office to be . . . well, how best to explain it? Let's just say that it was incompatible with certain aspects of my personal philosophy.'

'Wait a minute, now. Wait a minute!' Hartley protested. 'What about the robe? What about your name? I thought you'd taken some sort of monastic vow when you gave it up.'

'Oh, I did that too.' The friar sighed, placing a gentle hand on his companion's shoulder. 'Let me put it this way: having a role to play makes everything a little easier, especially when you're wandering from place to place. The exact nature of that role is not particularly important, in my experience, nor is the degree to which it provides an accurate representation of one's thoughts or beliefs. When I arrive in a new town, people don't see me, they just see a sort of frame upon which to hang the familiar robes of a holy man. Instead of asking where I come from, what I'm planning, what my motivations are, they just think *here's a zealot of some sort. Harmless enough, but best to give him some food and leave him be.*'

'You're a fraud, then,' said the young detective, a touch more bluntly than he had intended.

'In a sense,' the friar smiled, 'though not necessarily the sense you're imagining. I may not fully embody the ideals I profess to follow, but as I said, playing a role does have its benefits. When seeking truth — whether in a moral quandary or a murder investigation — I begin by thinking the way I was taught to think, in the manner of Boethius, of Aquinas, of Saint Teresa. The only real difference,' he gave a vague wave, 'is that I then allow myself the liberty of departing from said doctrines, should it better suit my present purposes.'

'But surely that's some sort of blasphemy, isn't it?'

'Possibly. I can only hope that in attempting to bring a murderer to justice, I may work towards balancing the scales. I'm sure that God, should such a being prove to exist, will grant me His forgiveness. Or Hers,' he added, visibly relishing the shock on Hartley's face. 'Now, let's not waste any more time. Where shall we begin?'

★ ★ ★

The house was large and low, a corrugated-iron roof settling over whitewashed brick and dark wood. The front door faced north; seen from this angle, the broad verandah was the first thing to catch the eye, extending across the front of the house and down the

75

length of the western side, presenting a respectable face to the main road. A long hallway ran through the centre of the building, an arterial thoroughfare giving way on either side to the rooms in which the O'Donnells slept, ate, argued, and — in Fred's case — died. The study, already well known to Hartley as the scene of the inscrutable crime, was the first room on the left as one entered the hallway. Beyond this was the bedroom belonging to Mary and George, followed by Hazel's chamber and the bathroom.

On the opposite side of the hall, Fred and Edith's bedroom was frontmost, its wide windows opening onto both the northern and western portions of the balcony. The linen closet behind this enviably situated suite had been converted into a cave-like dwelling which Winnie filled with magazines, nylon stockings and shelves of fiction and poetry. Next was the dining room, the largest space in the house, communicating with the western balcony via a large French window and with the kitchen via a small, open-ended passageway. On the southern side of the kitchen — found on the right as one exited through the back door — was a lean-to which Fred had apparently built with the idea of keeping his grandchildren at an inaudible distance. Shabby looking but solid, this structure extended beyond the western wall to close off the end of the verandah, forming the sheltered corner in which the dogs piled themselves each night. It was also in this area, free of biting breezes, that the friar had strung his hammock.

The house was almost entirely enclosed by gardens: roses welcomed visitors at the front of the building, vegetables were hidden away to the west and several fruit trees helped to shelter the windows on the eastern side from the morning sun. A large, free-standing water tank also worked to keep the light at bay, hulking outside Hazel's bedroom window with its pipes pushed through the bathroom wall and into the ceiling cavity.

Hartley and the friar began their investigations in the study, the door swinging open soundlessly on well-oiled hinges. The local officers had removed Fred's body and cleaned away all but the most stubborn bloodstains, but the room had otherwise remained largely untouched since the killing. One of the more notable changes was the extraction of the bullets from the wall; the dark pits left by their absence were ringed in shattered plaster, cracks spiderwebbing off into the paint. The furniture lay where it had tumbled or been pushed aside in whatever struggle had filled Fred's final moments. Both windows remained obstinately, infuriatingly locked.

'For the life of me, I still can't fathom how it was done,' complained Hartley. 'I don't suppose your flexible belief system stretches far enough to include malevolent spirits? No ghosts, ghouls, daemons or the like?'

The friar knelt to examine the worn floorboards. 'I've not encountered anything in the way of incontrovertible proof of life after death, ill-intentioned or otherwise,' he said. 'Mind you, nothing I've seen conclusively rules it out, either. I can't imagine that a spirit would require something so mundane as a rifle, though, to take a man's life.'

'It was a pistol, actually.'

The friar looked up. 'What's that, now?'

'The bullets we retrieved from the wall were fired from a revolver, not a rifle,' said Hartley. 'We still haven't been able to locate the weapon, but the rounds themselves are quite unmistakable.'

'Are any revolvers kept at Tolhurst?'

'Not that we've been able to determine, no. Just a couple of rifles and Fred's old shotgun. As Edith told us yesterday, there is no shortage of rural applications for a firearm, but I can't see any advantage to having a pistol around.' The detective cocked his head to the side. 'Does that change your understanding of the crime?'

'Not appreciably,' said the friar, though his manner appeared to intimate the opposite. He bent to collect a fallen mantel clock from beside the fireplace, running a finger across the splintered crystal face. 'Why don't we do a spot of tidying? I often find that by putting a room in order, I encourage my thoughts to follow suit. With any luck, it may help us to form a clearer picture of what happened here.'

Hartley deliberated, weighing the possibility of unearthing new evidence against the risk of demolishing some previously undetected point. It had been nearly a week since the shooting, and he'd been over the room so many times that he now saw the floral pattern of its pressed-tin ceilings in his sleep. Deciding that the odds of anything truly significant eluding him for so long were slim, he consented to spend a few minutes in the careful examination of trajectories and reconstruction of movements. This process saw side tables righted, chairs replaced and even fragments of masonry slotted into the places from which they had been knocked loose.

While there was a certain calming aspect to the room's reconstitution, no single sequence of events arose to undeniably account for the state of the place.

The position of the holes in the wall did allow them to make a rough estimate of the gunman's location when the shots were fired — approximately in the centre of the room, between the sofa and the victim — but a threadbare rug hampered any hope of footprints. Before long, the detective found himself growing annoyed.

'We can come back later, if need be,' he said, replacing a fallen fire poker on its hook. 'None of the O'Donnells will set foot in here, so there's nothing to stop us spending all night staring round these confounded walls. Let's take a look through the rest of the house while we have the chance.'

After the chaos of the study, Mary and George's chamber appeared all the more unremarkable. A heavy double bed dominated the room, its head against the wall. There were no side tables and only a single chest of drawers facing the foot of the bed, with a plain vase and a few other banalities displayed upon its lacquered surface. The window, large and low, afforded views of fruit trees and the edge of the water tank, while a dark rug of rather magnificent pile fairly swallowed the feet of the investigators as they crept over to the wardrobe in the corner. Nothing of note having made itself known amongst the trousers and frocks, they were forced to beat an unenlightened retreat.

The next room, being the province of a young widow, presented a more mysterious prospect. Hartley felt untethered and indecent as he tiptoed through Hazel's little world, peering at pots of cream and scented bottles with unfathomable contents. A small dressing table displayed several devices whose proximity to hairpins and combs hinted at a cosmetic function, though their wicked curves bore a closer resemblance to certain implements of torture the detective had once glimpsed in a treatise on the Spanish Inquisition. The rest of the room was less alarming: a chair in the corner was piled high with piano scores, while the inhabitant's modest closet appeared to contain nothing untoward.

'Really, though, I can't claim to know precisely what it is we're looking for.' Hartley found himself whispering, even once they were safely back in the hall of a house he knew to be empty. 'It's not as if one of the O'Donnells would leave a pistol in plain view, is it? And even if they did, what would it prove? Every one of them has an alibi. I was there when the shots were fired, for heaven's sake. I just can't see how a member of the family could have managed it.'

'Nor can I, at present,' admitted the friar. 'But they must have done so, or at least facilitated the process in some way. Of that much, I am convinced. As to your first point, I can only say that when the object of our search presents itself, we shall surely recognise it.'

To Hartley's ears, this sounded more like an admission of ignorance than anything to inspire courage, but he could see no better course of action than to continue the search. After a cursory look through the already well-trodden kitchen and dining room, the pair found themselves before the door to Winnie's bolthole. Hartley turned the handle and opened the door halfway. It would go no further. The tiny room would have been cramped enough when clean, but the stacks of magazines, newspapers and sundry pieces of clothing which covered it from corner to corner made ingress nigh impossible. Nor was the clutter confined to the floor; sketches, sewing patterns and newspaper clippings had been pinned over every inch of available wall space, while the low bookshelf was crammed to overflowing with dog-eared volumes of verse, cheap versions of canon classics and even — Hartley declined to meet the friar's eyes — detective novels.

'It looks as though you may have found a comrade,' the little man said, nodding at the nearest cluster of press cuttings. Hartley craned his neck around a precarious tower of periodicals to take in the headlines. Though the larger and more prominent pieces drew mostly from the fashion and society pages of the Perth broadsheets, the detective quickly recognised the *Westralian Worker's* familiar masthead peeking out from amongst the photographs of film stars. A smattering of updates from the world news section made it clear that Winnie had been tracking the progress of suffragette movements around the globe and revealed a concern with the ongoing Soviet wheat shortage. A polemic on the rights of native workers had been tacked nearby, too, half hidden by a triumphant photograph of Kingsford Smith on arrival in Brisbane.

'Miss O'Donnell appears to be a woman of no mean character,' marvelled Hartley, 'though she does a fair job of concealing it beneath that absurd Sloane Square veneer. Makes you wonder what else she's hiding.'

'I'm more inclined to wonder how the young lady is able to locate anything,' the friar said, with an almost audible shudder. 'I'll admit to occasional misgivings about the mendicant way of life, but the material element does not factor greatly amongst them. When one possesses a single pair of sandals, one is unlikely to misplace them.'

'True enough. If there's a pistol hidden in this

room, it'll stay hidden. There could be a cannon under those papers, and you wouldn't know it.' The detective checked his wristwatch. 'It'd take us hours to comb through this mess. We'd better move on.'

The lean-to at the rear of the house was next. The room was not exactly clean — no area housing two children under the age of ten can ever be said to be truly clean — but the clutter was spaced widely enough to be navigable. There was only a single small window cut into the southern wall, as if Fred had finished putting the structure together and then remembered, at the last minute, that living things need light and air, not unlike a boy who catches a mouse in an old tin and must be reminded to knock a few holes in the lid to keep his new pet alive. At either side of the room was a narrow bed with a wooden trunk for clothing and other essentials. The rest of the chamber was littered with playthings, though not all of the objects appeared to have been originally manufactured with that purpose in mind. There was a stuffed bear and a doll or two, but Hartley was also able to identify a couple of the steel ear-tags used for marking sheep, a rusted disc that must once have functioned as part of an engine and a roll of old wire that one of the children had fashioned into an inaccurate but still identifiable effigy of a horse. Had Hartley not spent a certain amount of time with the two youngest O'Donnells, he might have entertained concerns about the children's welfare, but he had seen them presented with the option of sleeping in the comfort of their parents' rooms. The choice to remain in this shed-like enclosure with its assortment of repurposed agricultural implements was a reflection of the cousins' shared sense of adventure rather than an atmosphere

82

of familial neglect. Happily, the crow-like collection of tools and trinkets did not appear to include anything resembling a firearm, and the investigators returned to the front of the house.

The final room to be searched was the one belonging to Edith and, until recently, to Fred. This chamber, overlooking the verandah and the rose garden beyond, was the only one in the house which seemed touched at all by luxury. Hartley found it hard to reconcile his impression of Fred O'Donnell, painted by all surviving relatives and associates as a cold, hard man, with the cream-coloured window seats and the finely stitched cushions populating the room's soft surfaces. In lieu of the drab, nondescript drapery which hung from window-rails around the rest of the house, the curtains in this room were cut from heavy velvet with climbing vines picked out in shimmering thread, and the lamps were all clean and freshly polished. The bed was large and impeccably turned down, with a small dressing table and cushioned chair on either side. The only intimation of anything at all out of order or unconsidered was the pair of suitcases which lay open on the floor by the foot of the bed, piled high with trousers, shirts and underclothes. The friar stepped over them to open the wardrobe, which hung half empty. Only Edith's share of the vestments remained, having migrated on their wooden hangers to invade the space once claimed by Fred.

'It doesn't seem as though her husband's death has left Mrs O'Donnell particularly distraught, does it?' remarked Hartley.

'Edith is a proud woman,' said the friar, kneeling to examine the cases. 'A social stalwart, someone who has spent decades learning to tame and trammel her emotions. Even if she were to exhibit the sort of wailing and hair-tearing that passes for bereavement in cheap paperbacks, I doubt anyone would be truly taken in by it.'

'You suspect her, then?'

'I wouldn't be surprised, let's say that much. One could easily make the case that she's profited by Fred's death. It looks as though she's taken the family helm unopposed, for one thing, but simply being free of him may have given her sufficient motive for murder. If the attitudes of those who remain are anything to go by, he was something of a tyrant.'

'That's putting it lightly. Plenty of the people in town are glad he's gone, though most are canny enough to hide their smiles. As for the O'Donnells — well, they're upset, certainly, but they appear to feel more as if they've been robbed of a possession than lost a loved one.'

'Love comes in many forms, you know,' the friar said. There was something in his voice — a slight rise in tone, or the prolonged drawing in of breath — that seemed to herald a profound meditation on the nature of human affection. Hartley was, then, more relieved than alarmed to have their conversation interrupted by the rumble of an approaching automobile engine.

11

The investigators retreated together to the study. Never an adept keeper of secrets, Hartley knew that the best way to prevent himself from inadvertently revealing his intimate and newly acquired knowledge of the O'Donnell family's living situation was to simply avoid speaking to any of them. To this end, he made a great show of being engrossed in recreating the crime, scarcely looking up to acknowledge the returning residents. In an exaggerated whisper, the friar gave Edith and her brood to understand that any interruption would greatly impede the progress of the case, and they quickly dispersed. From that point on, the detective and his itinerant advisor were acknowledged to have annexed the front room and, with the exception of the occasional tray of tea things deposited outside the door by Mary, were left largely to their own devices.

Inside the room, Hartley and the friar swapped theories and made cases for and against each suspect in turn, their voices kept carefully controlled for fear of being overheard. They knelt to look beneath the door and between the cracks in the floorboards, concocting ever more improbable methods by which the murderer may have made his escape. The locks on the windows and the doors were examined and re-examined, screws and bolts checked and the edges of the window sashes tested on the off-chance that the killer may have dislodged a pane of glass, slipped out through the resulting hole and managed to paint and reseal the window before the detective's arrival on the scene. While this was finally ruled to be roaringly unlikely, the hypothesis was equalled in absurdity by a dozen others put to the test that Sunday afternoon.

'Do you still have the note with you?' asked the friar, during a brief respite from re-enactment. The distant notes of a sonata drifted through the old house; Hazel must have been at the piano.

The detective sighed. 'Always,' he said, withdrawing the dreaded piece of correspondence from his breast pocket and spreading it out upon the writing desk. Since its discovery in the moments following Fred's murder, the thing had been unfolded and refolded so many times that it no longer lay flat, having a texture closer to ineptly ironed linen than notepaper. Riddled with creases and dark ridges, the message upon it was in danger of becoming illegible, but both men had long since begun to see it etched across the insides of their eyelids every time they blinked.

'*With this, a little of what was wrong is now put right,*' murmured the friar. Hartley shuddered to hear the familiar, inscrutable words afresh.

'I don't suppose you've had any additional flashes of insight?'

'There are shades of Paul's Second Epistle to the Corinthians. 'Behold, all things are made new',' he clarified, in response to the detective's blank look. 'Or even the anchoress Julian of Norwich, whose *Revelations of Divine Love* comforts us with the promise that *all manner of thing shall be well*. If it is a direct quotation, however, it does not come from a text with which I am familiar.'

'Let's assume, then, that it isn't a quotation,' said

86

Hartley. 'Why would a killer take the time to write out a message like this and leave it at the scene of the crime? It's undeniably a risk. Any additional evidence raises the chance of being found out, no matter how slightly.'

'Guilt?' The friar counted off the possibilities on his fingers. 'Pride? A plea for understanding, or a message to the surviving family members?'

'I've asked them all to look over the note. None seemed to glean anything more from it than you or I.'

'The phrase 'put right' would seem to suggest redress or restitution for some past wrong.' The friar sighed. 'But that line of enquiry is frustrated, as always, by Fred's almost unnatural ability to cause outrage. We could work for months and still fall short of a complete list of feuds and vendettas.'

Hartley reached into his coat pocket, withdrew the shotgun cartridge which had originally been enclosed within the killer's missive and laid it on the writing desk.

'At first glance, this would serve to narrow things down a bit. It's a match for Fred's preferred make — the twelve-gauge Remington Arrow black powder cartridge — and nothing similar has been located at any of the surrounding properties. If this were the only memento left with the note, I'd say we'd be entirely justified in treating this as a revenge killing or something of the sort. Unfortunately,' he sighed, taking out the steel ring and the copper coin, 'these do absolutely nothing to shed light on the situation. They could, in fact, point to something else entirely, if only I knew what to make of them.'

The artefacts glinted dully against the worn leather of the desktop. Like the shotgun cartridge — and, indeed, the letter which had enclosed all three — they had become fruitlessly familiar to the investigators, who now glared at them as though hoping to extract some sort of confession through sheer force of ire. Hartley reached first for the ring. Though more or less the perfect fit for his index finger, it was plainly part of some larger tool or device, its ridged teeth flecked with traces of machine oil. Comprehensive work on the part of his local auxiliaries had established that it had no place in any of the weaponry or agricultural implements in common use on the property, and whatever significance the letter writer had intended to impart with by way of its inclusion remained obscure.

The coin was equally enigmatic. What Hartley had taken, in the initial clamour and whirl of the shooting, to be a dirty penny soon proved to be something altogether less commonplace. When polished, the image of a wreath of bay leaves had surfaced from beneath the patina and with it, a set of foreign letters. As his schooling had brought him into only limited contact with languages other than the King's, identifying the alphabet as Greek was the more or less the extent of Hartley's contribution. Further information only came with the involvement of the friar, whose scholarship in this field had evidently progressed further.

'Five lepta, you said?' The detective squinted anew at the tarnished characters — lambda's sharp peak and the pi so drearily familiar from years of geometry lessons. 'How much would it be worth?'

'Not a great deal. There are a hundred lepta to the drachma, comparable to the cents in the American dollar. This coin is the smallest Greek denomination currently available, if memory serves. It is known colloquially as an 'obolos', after the manner of the ancient obol.'

The friar's tone made it plain that he expected some sort of reaction to this final word. Hartley thought hard. 'I seem to recall something, but —' He shook his head. 'The classics were never my strong point.'

'You are reminded, perhaps, of Charon's Obol,' prompted the little man. 'The funerary offering allotted to the dead, enabling them to buy passage across the river Acheron — or in some traditions, the Styx — and into Hades.'

'Of course! That's it. The fare for the ferryman.' Hartley turned the coin over and over in his hands, seeing each dint and ridge in a new and murky light. 'You don't think that the killer left it for that reason, do you? That he went to all the trouble of seeking out a specific Greek coin in order to allude to some ancient burial custom? It seems — I don't know. Excessive. Far-fetched, even for a case as unorthodox as this.'

'It would certainly complicate our understanding of the killer's feelings towards Fred,' said the mendicant. 'The act of ensuring entrance to the afterlife would seem to carry with it a degree of affection, or at least some sympathy. The payment for the psychopomp — the spirit guide — was an element common to many cultures, though it varied considerably by region and era. Coins were usually placed in the mouth of the deceased, or sometimes a pair upon the eyelids. Either way, the gesture is an undeniably intimate one.'

'How on earth do you know all this?' asked Hartley, quite overwhelmed by the flood of data. 'More to the point, *why* do you know all this? It can't be within the regular purview of a beggar-monk, surely.'

'You are quite correct. The pursuit of such knowledge is personal, not vocational.'

Though the friar seemed content to leave it at that, Hartley's curiosity was unquenched. He had long wondered at the fellow's breadth of experience, even as his investigation benefited from it. Thankfully, the last few days had taught him that inducing the friar to hold forth on any given topic was essentially as simple as not preventing him from doing so. If the detective were to merely sit back and let silence take the room, his friend would soon fill it. After a lull of less than a minute, the dialogue did indeed pick up again, albeit not along the anticipated trajectory.

'Have you ever sailed at night?' said the friar.

'What?' Hartley was taken aback. 'Ah — no. Not that I recall.'

'A certain evening is never far from my mind. When I was a young man — a period of time roughly contemporaneous with the invention of the wheel — I found myself on a boat. We were sailing from the docks of Canton down to Victoria Harbour, on the northern side of the island of Hong Kong. It was a warm night, and the Pearl River was languid, almost still. One of my fellow passengers, encouraged equally, I imagine, by the sparkling eyes of the young lady on his arm and a bottle of baijiu which was making its way around the deck, slipped the skipper a banknote and had him take a detour down to the mouth of the delta. As we rounded Cape Collinson, the South China Sea spread itself out before us, vast and dark. The city lights dropped away behind the headland and the steward put out all the gas lamps, leaving nothing to set us apart from the sky and the sea. I leant over the gunwale and gazed down into the fathomless deep. The vast sidereal swirl above me was reflected below, and I no longer knew whether I floated upon the water or amongst the lights of the heavens themselves. Of course,' he acknowledged, with a deprecating shrug, 'the aforementioned bottle may have had a part to play in shaping my experience. For the most part, though, it was the enormity of it all that held me captive. That vast expanse, filled at every point with an impossible number of stars. How could I stand before something so enormous, so ineffable? Worlds upon worlds, distances impossible to comprehend. I felt insignificant, microscopic. This feeling was intolerable at first, but I soon saw it differently. If, set against the sheer majesty of the ever-expanding universe, my every achievement dwindled away to nothing, then so too did each and every one of my transgressions.' His eyebrows hiked conspiratorially skyward. 'The consideration of sin, you see, had held me in thrall for a good deal of my life up to that point. It was more or less my bread and butter, being the currency in which the church trades. But in that instant, together with any number of similar concerns, the sum of every trespass I had ever committed — or even considered! — was reduced to a trifle. Via a simple shift in perspective, I had managed to attain a state to which nothing else, not even prayer, had brought me close. I had found peace.' Here, the little man paused, drawing a deep breath. Then, his voice suddenly lighter, he said: 'I suspect you're wondering how this rambling tale is in any way connected to your question.'

Hartley, whose thoughts had run precisely thus for several minutes now, found himself immediately launching into a vociferous denial. The friar cut him off, laughing.

'As I am no longer in the habit of hanging, half drunk, from boats of an evening, I have had to content myself

91

with more mundane methods of achieving equilibrium. In lieu of the manifold stars sprawled across the firmament, I gaze out at the many equally mystifying works of mankind. Instead of liquor, I drink deeply from the pages of almanacs, periodicals, journals. Lacking constant access to the magnificence of the open ocean, I let the currents of knowledge and culture rock me to some semblance of tranquillity. Each piece of information I glean, no matter how trivial, affords me a glimpse at the inconceivable totality of human experience. Language, geometry, history: these are constellations as humbling as Ursa Major or the Pleiades. I flatter myself that my memory is stronger than that of most men, but I could live for centuries and still not understand even one iota of the knowledge lost with the burning of that fabled library at Alexandria, or the collapse of the cities of the Zapotec. Even if one were to —' He drew himself up short. 'I don't suppose you have somewhere pressing to be, Detective?'

Hartley sat bolt upright, cheeks flaming like a scolded schoolboy. He had been caught stealing a glance at his wristwatch, despite exercising all the stealth at his disposal.

'No, no,' he said, hastily. 'Nowhere to be. Just keeping an eye on the time, you know. Just keeping my wits about me.' His protestations trailed off as he saw the mirth in the mendicant's eyes.

'A stern and vital thing, time,' the little man chuckled. He looked on the point of braiding the idea of time itself (a worryingly broad topic, thought the detective) into his musings, but something must have stopped him. He stood silent, and when he spoke again, it was with an urgency that had been absent

92

from the earlier oration.

'What time was Fred killed?' he demanded.

'At some point in the late afternoon,' said Hartley, hastening to take out his notebook. 'Here we go: twenty past four precisely. Why?'

The friar gave no immediate answer. Instead, he hurried across to stand before the fireplace.

'This clock,' he said, indicating the fissure-faced timepiece he himself had retrieved from the floor an hour or so earlier, 'has stopped at quarter past.'

12

The clock was unremarkable, a dozen Roman numerals chasing each other round an eight-inch block of polished oak. There was nothing to set it aside from countless other timepieces in catalogues and shopcases the world over. Nothing, that is, other than an apparent ability to anticipate death.

'It could be a coincidence,' said Hartley. 'Five minutes off is a forgivable margin, I'd have thought, especially out here in the country. I doubt the sheep are prone to complaining about missed appointments. Then, too,' he added, 'the minute hand may have been knocked about by the fall. Fairly delicate instruments, these things.'

As if to illustrate this assertion, a number of loose components tumbled out as the friar pried open the back of the device. He knelt to retrieve and examine them, turning his head this way and that and muttering quietly. Then, with a cry of satisfaction, he dashed back to the writing desk and picked up the mysterious ring.

'Look at this.' He brandished it in such an extravagant manner that Hartley had to grab his wrist in order to actually get a clear look at the thing. 'Notice the uneven points.'

'Well, yes. It's obviously a cog or a wheel of some kind. It has teeth.'

The friar shook his head. 'Not on the outside. On the inside.' He pointed to the near undetectable imperfections on the inner curve of the ring, then opened his hand to reveal a couple of tiny, twisted pieces of metal. 'The spokes snapped clean off as it was removed.'

'Removed from where?' asked the detective, more because it felt like the right thing to say than out of any real uncertainty; the friar had already turned back towards the clock. Hartley watched with dull unease as the friar indicated the ring's rightful place amongst the innards of the machine.

'It's a balance wheel,' he said. 'See how it fits in between the spring and the escapement, here. Without it, the clock is wholly unable to operate.'

The implications of this intelligence, Hartley felt, were enormous, if not immediately obvious. He thought for a few seconds, trying to reconcile the removal of the balance wheel with the established facts of the case.

'The killer must have removed it after Fred's death,' he said, slowly. 'They were wrestling in the moments prior. But why? And how did he manage to get it out, escape the room, slip it into the note and flee the scene before I arrived? It can't have taken me more than a minute or two to drive down from the front gate. Why waste precious time in meddling with a clock?'

'We certainly haven't done anything to reduce the number of questions facing us,' sighed the friar. 'If I might complicate matters by positing another scenario: could the killer have removed the clock component prior to his disagreement with Fred? It might even have been the precipitating factor.'

'It's possible, I suppose. There would have to be some hidden meaning attached to the whole business. I certainly wouldn't be thrilled if some bloke broke into my study and started pulling bits out of my clock, but I don't think it'd be enough to start a deadly brawl over. Unless —' The detective snapped his fingers. 'It was a signal! If, as we've assumed, the killer either lives at Tolhurst or has an accomplice who does so, the clock could have been stopped ahead of time — hours, maybe, or days — to let Fred know when to expect a visit. It would fit with the apparent pattern of the cloaked man confronting him at something of a remove from the rest of the family.'

The friar hummed pensively. 'It's certainly possible,' he conceded. 'It would also explain why the killer went to the trouble of actually rendering the clock wholly inactive: he'd want to ensure that his message was not obliterated by some well-meaning inmate of the house winding or resetting the thing.'

Delighted at having an ally in his theory, Hartley resolved to maintain the momentum. 'If the time of the rendezvous was shown on the mantel clock,' he reasoned, 'there may be further information hidden in plain sight. The killer could have indicated the date somehow, or even left a clue as to his motivation for the meeting.'

This line of thinking sparked a renewed scrutiny of the room's contents, particular attention being paid to the mantel and its surrounds. With all the fallen or displaced articles restored to their rightful positions — albeit, in several cases, somewhat the worse for wear — the area above the fireplace regained its air of stately domesticity. Besides the broken clock, there was an ashtray, a cigar box, a photograph of a rather dour-looking Mr and Mrs O'Donnell on what must have been their wedding day, an artless ceramic lamb, an imitation Wedgwood platter decorated with a likeness of the Crystal Palace, and a small, framed portrait of a girl.

'It's a wonder this survived,' mused Hartley, lifting the latter. It was about five inches high and, despite being knocked to the floor during the fatal scuffle, appeared to have sustained no major damage. The detective tapped the glass, snug in its gilt enclosure. 'Tough little thing.'

'Are you referring to the frame or to Cordelia?' asked the mendicant, for the subject of the portrait could be no-one else. It was a simple charcoal sketch, scarcely more than a few strong lines and a touch of shading, but the proud set of Delia's jaw beneath the mop of curls was unmistakable. 'Either way, I'd have to agree with you.'

Hartley replaced the picture. 'Odd that it's only one of the grandchildren,' he noted. 'Not a trace of Charlie to be seen.'

'Ah, but that's how things work in the world of a man like Fred O'Donnell,' the friar said. 'Believe me, I've known enough of his ilk. To Fred, girls are to be pampered and sketched and paraded around, and boys are to be beaten and pruned and shaped into men. Anything that didn't prepare Charlie to take over the farm would be seen as a waste of time.'

'Suppose the boy has no interest in running the farm?

'Suppose the girl does? Both ideas are equally abhorrent to the staunch and the staid.'

The friar's tone left Hartley with no doubt that he spoke from some measure of personal experience. He was on the verge of probing further, but something in the little man's furrowed brow stopped him. Making a show of returning to pore over the mantelpiece once more, the detective let silence retake the room. Soon, judging the shelf to have suffered enough, he knelt to examine the fireplace. It had been scoured inside and out over the course of the interminable search, but imagination had long since deserted the detective and inertia alone now dictated his steps.

With one knee on the hearth, he stuck his head into the sooty darkness. A vague hint of sunlight hovered at the end of the obscure tunnel, dim enough to leave no doubt that the top of the flue was at least partially covered. Unable to gauge the chimney's width in the dark, Hartley removed one of his boots and pushed it as far as he could up into the gloom. At the highest point of his reach, the passage was only slightly wider than the rugged length of the sole.

'That'd make it about a foot square, and still narrowing,' the detective said, his voice reverberating around the bricks. 'No chance of someone being able to fit through there. Even a possum would have trouble getting in.'

There was no response. The detective lowered his arm carefully, managing to knock only a few showers of soot loose in the process, and emerged from the fireplace, groaning.

'Yes, yes,' he said, working the boot back on. 'The local officers have already checked this off this list, but it was worth a look, wasn't it?'

When this, too, failed to elicit an answer from the friar, Hartley was surprised to find himself experiencing a flash of concern. He stood up and peered over the back of the chesterfield to see the ersatz holy man curled up on his side, snoring quietly.

'I suppose it has been a long day,' Hartley conceded. Reasoning that tired minds perform poorly, he decided to allow himself a short repose, too. Hanging his coal-smudged jacket on the poker hook, he settled into the armchair opposite the friar. Rest would do him good, he thought. Just a minute or two.

★ ★ ★

When he awoke, the room was almost completely dark. Only a faint glow from beyond the curtains allowed the detective to orient himself. Groggily, he moved to get up, but a gentle hand on the shoulder stopped him.

'Keep still,' whispered the friar, from somewhere in the shadows, 'and be very, very quiet.'

'What's going on?' He looked around the room. Not a glimpse of light shone through the gap below the hall door. The house beyond lay still and silent.

'There's someone outside,' the friar said. 'Listen.'

Hartley did so. For a long time, there was nothing. The only sound was the friar's low, steady breath in the darkness. Hartley was on the verge of speaking when he finally heard it: a careful footfall on the verandah, then another. It was a cyclical sound, almost machine-like. The muted tap of a heel on the hardwood, the slow groan of the verandah as it took the walker's weight, then the almost imperceptible sigh as the aged boards returned to their original positions.

'Does no-one sleep in this house?' Hartley breathed. Supporting his weight on the threadbare arms of the old chair, he slid forward until he was able to sink to the floor. On hands and knees, he crept across the rug and onto the jarrah, conscious of the friar creeping along behind him. He reached the wall and lowered himself until he heard the faint clink of his shirt buttons against the floorboards.

The two windows took up the majority of the northern wall. They stretched from roughly a foot above the floor to just below the ceiling. Each window was adorned with two sets of curtains: a coarse, dark fabric — gathered in thick rolls on either side of the pane, presumably waiting to be deployed against the full summer sun — and a flimsy floral affair, thin enough to twitch with the detective's breath as he craned his neck to see out. It was only two nights after the new moon, but the sky was free of clouds, the stars unfettered by gas lamps or arc lights. The verandah and rose garden were clearly visible, wheatfields stretching out beyond in silvery splendour. Outlined against this backdrop was the dark figure of a man, much closer than the previous night's specimen. His face could not be seen, pressed as it was against the windows of Edith O'Donnell's bedroom, but there was no mistaking the muscled forearms or the cavalier set of his broad shoulders.

'Les Thompson.' Hartley felt rather than heard the friar's words in his ear. The watchers held their collective breath, afraid to make any movement lest they alert the shearer to their presence. There was a distant creak, loud and sudden against the silence, and Hartley was able to see the faint glimmer of starlight on glass as Edith's window swung open. Les disappeared into the bedroom up to his shoulders, only to emerge again a moment or two later. Hartley froze to see the shadowed face turn slowly towards him.

The taut silence stretched on and on. Then, in an instant, the tableau was shattered. Thompson turned and slipped away into the garden, displaying astonishing agility for one so large. The window of Edith's bedroom was shut tight. No indication of any nocturnal activity remained. The world was colourless and still.

13

Edith O'Donnell drew the knife towards her, every movement rich with refinement and purpose. The detective watched over the rim of his coffee cup, waiting for his turn at the butter.

'Do try the marmalade.' She passed a jar across the table. 'Mary made it. It's quite good.'

Hartley accepted the preserve with a grudging nod of thanks, stifling a groan at the pain in his neck as he did so. His whole body ached after a night in the armchair, the majority of it spent turning the same few thoughts over and over. Exerting considerable nocturnal effort, he'd managed to come up with a few scenarios in which the midnight visit of a strapping young gentleman was innocuous and wholly removed from the recent death of an elderly, widely despised husband, but they didn't seem quite as convincing in daylight as they had on the edge of sleep.

He gulped again at his coffee and forced himself towards introspection. After a week of dead ends, why was he so unwilling to act on the evidence that had finally begun to present itself? Perhaps it was the fear of actually coming face to face with a killer. He'd seen fatal accidents as a uniformed constable, dealing with vicious assaults outside Hay Street pubs and

a brutal beating or two on the Fremantle waterfront, but they'd all been acts of mindless aggression, unplanned escalations or crimes of passion. Even the case that had seen him elevated to detective —

independent of his father's union connections, never mind the jealous grumblings of the rank and file — had been nothing more violent than a smuggling bust, brought to a close without casualties. The O'Donnell case was the first in which he'd been faced with the possibility of a planned killing, a murder fully mapped out beforehand. It was the idea of the *administration* involved that unnerved him so, the hours spent working towards the death of another human being.

'This is quite an achievement.' The friar's voice broke in upon his reverie. Hartley looked up to see him eating marmalade straight from the spoon. 'Do I discern a hint of quince?'

'I shouldn't doubt it. Mary has been known to add mandarin and bergamot, too. What do you think, Detective?'

Edith was regarding him closely, an inscrutable expression upon her proud features. 'Oh,' he said, flustered. 'Yes. Yes, it's very nice.'

'If I'd known you were spending the night, I would have saved you some bacon,' Edith said, without shifting her gaze. Hartley and the friar had only emerged from the study after eight o'clock in the morning, when the rest of the household had long since eaten and left to go about their business. Hoping to slip out unnoticed, the investigators were instead intercepted by the elder Mrs O'Donnell, who seemed to have been lying in wait for them.

'Yes, I must apologise again for taking advantage of your hospitality,' said Hartley. 'We were pursuing several avenues of investigation and simply lost track of time.'

'There's nothing to apologise for, Detective. I keenly await your conclusions,' the matriarch said with a controlled smile. 'In fact, I have discovered something that may even help them along.'

She pushed her chair back and rose with her usual careful grace, disappearing into the hallway. Hartley and the friar exchanged glances.

'I came upon this yesterday, in the process of packing away my late husband's effects.' Edith returned holding a sheaf of papers bundled together with rough twine. 'He had hidden them in a place which he believed to be unknown to me. He was, of course, quite mistaken. A man has very few secrets from the one who washes his undergarments.'

Hartley reached for the papers, but Mrs O'Donnell drew back suddenly, hugging them to her chest. It was the first hint of fear that Hartley had seen the woman betray, though she recovered quickly and resumed her seat.

'Before I give this up to you, I wish it to be a matter of record that I did so voluntarily,' she said, spreading long-fingered hands over the package. 'I have cooperated with the police at every stage, even to the extent of making an inventory of Fred's possessions and reporting one of his silk ties as missing on the off-chance that it would prove relevant. In good faith, I have glanced over the contents of this package and, fully understanding the implications, delivered it willingly into your hands, trusting that it will help in some way to identify the culprit. I would like that to be taken into account as the investigation moves forward.'

'Absolutely.' Eager curiosity made the blood beat in Hartley's ears. Edith slid the bundle across the table and he took it, working quickly to loosen the knot.

'It appears to be an insurance policy,' said the friar.

'The farm is insured through the bank,' Edith put in. 'I saw to that myself years ago. I realise that things will be different without Fred, but I fully intend to keep this place a going concern. I've already made an appointment to speak with the branch manager in Katanning next week.'

'But this is about more than just the property,' said Hartley, as he thumbed through the first few pages. 'It's from Great Southern Mutual Assurance. A personal policy, and quite a sizable one.'

He read on. Though the typewritten paragraphs were clotted with the usual inscrutable jargon — the terms possibly a little more exacting than expected — there were certain points that fairly leapt from the page. The date of submission was of interest: the tenth of August, 1928, exactly a month before Fred's murder. Then there was the sum to be paid out upon the claimant's accidental death, which amounted to nearly five times Hartley's annual salary. Of most immediate note, however, was the name at the bottom of the second page. Hartley pointed it out as he passed the document to the friar.

'The sole beneficiary of this policy,' the friar read aloud, 'is to be Mrs Edith O'Donnell.'

The woman in question was impassive.

'It is surely not uncommon for a man to ensure his wife is looked after in the event of his unforeseen death,' she submitted.

'Not uncommon at all,' said Hartley. 'Of course, the very existence of this document would seem to suggest that your husband's demise was indeed foreseen, at least by Fred himself.' He turned back to the friar, who was still thumbing through the papers. 'Can you find anything regarding the insurance agent who processed the application? If we can identify him, he may be able to enlighten us as to Fred's state of mind when he took out the policy.'

'The same thought occurred to me,' Edith put in. 'If you care to look at the particulars on the final page, you'll see that the application was submitted via post.'

The friar did as instructed. 'She's quite right,' he said. 'Fred O'Donnell — if, indeed, he was the person responsible for taking out this policy — sent away for a form, filled it out and mailed it in. The whole thing could've been done without his ever being seen.'

Hartley considered this. 'Submitting a life assurance policy in this manner is unorthodox, to say the least, especially when such a hefty sum is involved.'

'But not unheard of,' said Edith, pointedly.

'Not unheard of, no,' he conceded. 'And it would be your assertion, I suppose, that you knew nothing of this prior to finding the policy today?'

'That is correct.'

A few seconds of tense silence overtook the table.

'There's a signature here,' said the friar, at last, 'and a few orthographic amendments throughout. It shouldn't be too much trouble to verify it against a sample of Mr O'Donnell's handwriting.'

'Right you are,' said Hartley. He excused himself and left for the study, returning with a selection of letters and memoranda in Fred's stolid lettering. Extensive samples of written matter had been taken from each of the O'Donnells some days ago, to be compared with the enigmatic note found at the scene of the shooting.

'I'd have to ask one of the specialists up in Perth in order to be absolutely certain,' he said, squinting, 'but it does look to me as though this form was filled out by Fred O'Donnell in his own hand.' The documents were passed around the table for consensus, finally arriving in front of Edith.

'It's definitely Fred's writing, for all the weight my word holds,' she said. 'Except in the section declaring him to be of sound mind and body.' She indicated a page towards the end of the document.

'That form needs to be filled out by a physician, by the looks of it.' The friar began rifling through the papers once more. 'If you'll give me just a moment, I shall find the doctor's full name and the address of his rooms.'

'There's no need,' said Edith. 'The signature is quite well known to me. I believe you'll be wanting to speak to Dr Stephen Parry, whose offices are on Spring Street, Kojonup.' She paused, her gaze resting defiantly on the detective.

'This man is familiar to you, then?'

'In the truest sense of the word. He is my brother.'

14

Despite having been built fifteen years ago, the unassuming red-brick building in the middle of Kojonup's main street was known as the New Post Office. This was, of course, to distinguish it from the Old Post Office around the corner, which now played host to the headmaster of the local school, and the Post and Telegraph House further down the street, which had been robbed of its former functions and was now merely a House.

'I don't understand why they don't simply call this place the Post Office,' complained the detective, as he climbed the building's stone steps, 'and call the other place the Headmaster's House. It'd make things a lot simpler.'

'You've never lived in a small town, have you?' the friar chuckled.

Hartley laughed along, his knitted brow softening a little. It'd been a long morning, and there was no denying he'd let frustration get the better of him.

Upon arrival at the Spring Street medical practice, Hartley and the friar had been informed that Dr Parry was out on house calls for the morning and would not be back in his rooms until after lunch. Deciding to take this opportunity to catch up on correspondence, the pair managed to tour both previous iterations of the post office before eventually locating the premises in present operation.

The sense of relief Hartley felt on making it through

the door was premature, however, as the sole clerk within was engaged in a heated exchange with an irate elderly couple whose chief complaint seemed to be the price of postage to Norfolk Island. The investigators took their seats on a wooden bench by the door, where they waited patiently for ten minutes or so, at which point it became clear that the nephew who was to be the recipient of the elderly couple's postcard actually lived in Northam, a difference of three thousand miles or so. As the whole discussion began anew, Hartley threw in his hat and went to use the telephone.

He returned some minutes later in markedly better humour.

'What news on the Rialto?' the friar asked.

'I just spoke to one of my officers in Perth,' Hartley said, choosing not to engage with the mendicant's theatrical offering. 'No luck on the assurance agent as yet, but we have managed to locate a will.'

'Was it, by any chance, beside a way? I've heard the two are often in close proximity.'

Once again, the detective refused to dignify his companion's antics with a response. 'It may be something of a breakthrough. There was no trace of Fred's will and testament at Tolhurst, nor were we able to find anything in the care of any of the known officials associated with the family's affairs. The general consensus seems to have been that Fred simply never bothered to make one. It doesn't appear as though he was overly fond of lawyers.'

'I don't get the impression that he was particularly fond of anyone.'

Hartley had to concede that point. 'Regardless, he must have overcome his distaste to some small extent.

A solicitor in Claremont has come forward with a will made up in Fred's name — and quite a recent one.'

'What on Earth was Fred O'Donnell doing in Claremont?' The friar had been wandering around Western Australia long enough to recognise the name as that of a relatively well-to-do suburb between the Perth town centre and the sea.

'Dashed if I know,' said Hartley. 'It seems as though his movements were often a bit of a mystery. Took off up to the city fairly regularly, but never made a habit of telling his family when or why. They were probably just glad to be shot of him for a day or two. As for this particular trip — we'll have to wait and see, I suppose. My men are having a copy of the will sent down. I've asked them to include a statement from the solicitor, together with any records of communication with his client. With any luck, it'll shed some light on the state of Fred's affairs towards the end.'

'It's the state of his mind that interests me,' the friar said, appearing suddenly pensive. 'After spending decades with his affairs in total disarray, he seems to have experienced a sudden desire to set them straight. In order for him to arrange both a will and a personal policy . . . something must have changed, and not something trifling. It was sufficient to make him genuinely entertain the possibility of his own death. Perhaps this mysterious cloaked figure unnerved him more than he let on.'

'You could well be right,' said the detective. He paused to watch the elderly couple make their way to the door of the post office, giving them a polite nod as they left. The clerk excused herself, too, disappearing into the depths of the building for a few minutes. She returned smelling slightly of tobacco. The break must

110

have refreshed her, as she dealt with Hartley's enquiries most obligingly.

There was no official record of letters dispatched and received from the post office, but Kojonup's relatively small population and the clerk's almost prurient interest in the lives of others meant that she was able to deliver a broad summary of the O'Donnell family's recent postal correspondence. What the precis lacked in individual detail, it more than made up for in wild speculation and lurid conjecture. Following a relatively unconvincing show of resistance, the clerk also furnished the investigators with a small bundle of originating telegram forms, comprising every message sent by the residents of Tolhurst for the last six months.

Unsure whether to be grateful for the woman's information or alarmed at her willingness to dispense it, Hartley muttered a few words of thanks and withdrew. It was almost lunchtime, so he and the friar decided to repair to the Royal Hotel and go over their latest acquisitions in the comforting presence of sandwiches and a pot of tea.

According to the postal clerk's evidence, Fred O'Donnell had definitely sent mail at least once in the same week the assurance application had been submitted. This was not as edifying a fact as it might have been, however, as Les, Winnie and Edith had also made appearances at the post office. It was common, Hartley had learned, for members of farming households to send mail and telegrams on behalf of their relatives and neighbours, so as to reduce the need for multiple trips into town. This, together with the impossibility of knowing what was inside any of the outgoing envelopes — though Hartley personally wouldn't put it past the postal clerk to steam them open and skim the contents before resealing and sending them along — made it difficult to draw conclusions from letters alone.

The telegram forms were a different story altogether, providing a much more tangible record of the household's communication. Some prudent soul (probably Mary, the detective thought) had made the decision to purchase telegram forms in bulk, the ragged left edge of each message a reminder of where it had been torn from the book. There were around two dozen completed forms in a variety of hands, from Fred's now familiar lettering to the barely discernible calligraphic experiments in which Winnie indulged under the influence of whatever form of literature had most recently captured her fancy. The messages themselves were innocuous enough, for the most part. Some were of a mercantile nature, like the order from Hazel to Musgrove's in Lyric House, Perth, requesting a copy of the score for Rachmaninoff's *Piano Concerto No. 2 in C Minor*. Others were more personal, such as the note from George to one of his old mining companions in the Victorian goldfields, congratulating him on the birth of his first child. A few hinted at slightly less sentimental interactions, like the one enjoining an acquaintance to 'tell me absolutely everything about Tommy, you hideous tease, or I shall scream so loud you hear it in the Capital' and signed 'yours in Rural Boredom, Winnie.'

Of those that remained, one message in particular caught the attention of the investigators. It was written in blocky majuscule, each letter inexpertly formed in a way that reminded Hartley of a schoolchild's copybook. It read: 'THANKS FOR YOUR COUNSEL. HAVE

112

FOUND SUITABLE FACILITY NEAR ADELAIDE. DEPARTURE NEXT WEEK. NO NEED TO FOLLOW UP.' The telegram was addressed to a Doctor Thornally in South Perth and signed at the bottom by Les Thompson.

'Very curious,' said Hartley, passing the form to the friar. 'What do you make of it?'

The friar read the short missive several times, head tilted slightly. 'It certainly offers more in the way of questions than resolutions,' he said. Then, with a contemplative air: 'I don't suppose you speak Malay, detective?'

'Malay?' the officer blinked, taken aback by the sudden change of conversational pace. 'No. No, only the King's, I'm afraid. How is that relevant?'

'It isn't, really,' said the friar with a reassuring smile. 'Just a symptom of my mind's labyrinthine geography. Have you any idea who this Thornally fellow is?'

'Never heard of him. Must be a medical man.' He toyed with a teaspoon. 'The 'Doctor' in front of his name could suggest an academic position of some kind, I suppose, but Les Thompson doesn't particularly strike me as someone with university connections.'

The friar hummed his assent, still squinting at the telegram.

'What's this place near Adelaide, though? That's what I want to know,' Hartley went on. 'I haven't heard anyone else mention anything over the border. Whatever it was, he obviously didn't keep to his schedule.' He reached across to tap the date stamped at the bottom of the page. It had been sent on the third of July.

'Maybe the word 'departure' is in reference to someone else,' said the friar. 'Or something.'

'Could be.'

The pair sat awhile in thought, Hartley munching

on a sandwich and the friar cradling a now cool cup of tea. After a minute or two, the detective spoke again.

'I have an idea,' he said, 'though not a pleasant one, I'm afraid.'

'It could be said that entertaining pleasant possibilities is rather antithetical to your occupation,' the friar pointed out. Hartley was unnerved to feel the truth of this observation darken his mind, a cloud flitting across the sun. He shook himself free of the feeling.

'Les Thompson knew where he was going last night. The way he made straight for Edith's window made it clear he'd been there before. Now, what leads a young man to a woman's window in the small hours?' A loaded look followed. 'There's your motive for murder. Getting the husband out of the way. It could also explain this 'facility' business.' He dropped his voice, glancing cautiously around the near empty dining room. 'A hospital. Possibly one with a specialty in obstetrics, if you catch my meaning.'

The mendicant gave this his silent consideration. 'A pair of star-crossed lovers fleeing the farm to start a new family?' His voice was even, betraying neither encouragement nor scepticism.

'Well, it fits the facts, doesn't it? Strapping young lad, handsome woman. She realises a child is on the way, takes out a life assurance policy on her husband and does away with him.'

'. . . by locking herself in the room with him, shooting him in the chest and walking out through the wall?'

'I haven't worked it all out yet, clearly,' sniffed the detective, folding his arms, 'but it's a start, isn't it? If we can get Mrs O'Donnell's brother to admit he helped falsify the assurance application, we might be able to get something more out of her.'

114

15

Dr Parry smiled across the desk at his guests. He was a pleasant-faced man with dark eyes and a well-kept moustache. His sleeves were rolled up past his elbows, revealing strong, sun-reddened hands, and the polished mother-of-pearl buttons on his waistcoat did a passable job of drawing the eye away from the vague traces of various bodily fluids with which the fine fabric was flecked. Hartley chose to ignore these, just as he was ignoring the barbaric instruments of glass and curved steel lining the shelves of the physician's office.

'Sorry to have kept you waiting,' the doctor said. 'I was called to the Lawrence place to check on young Sally's cough, but there's always more to be done once you're out there. Boils to be lanced, the old man's ear impacted — I'm sure you get the idea.'

Hartley nodded, hoping the queasiness he felt was not too obviously reflected in his face. 'We won't take too much of your time, Doctor. It's about your brother-in-law, Fred O'Donnell.'

'I assumed as such,' the doctor said. 'His death was certainly a surprise.'

Not *a tragedy* or even *a blow*, noted Hartley. Merely *a surprise*. 'You didn't pay much heed to the threats he'd received, then?'

'I didn't actually hear anything about them until after he was shot.' The doctor's tone was almost apologetic. 'I don't make the effort to visit my sister and her family as often as perhaps I should.'

'Why is that?'

The doctor held Hartley's gaze. 'I suppose I have to be honest with you,' he said.

'That would certainly be appreciated, yes.'

'Well, then. I didn't often visit Tolhurst because I didn't much care for Fred. Couldn't stand him, in fact.'

'You were at his funeral,' the detective pointed out. He had, by this time, recognised Dr Parry as the man seated beside Edith O'Donnell at the service. The other woman must have been his wife.

'Of course. It was the proper thing to do, and I wanted to support Edith. Still, I hope you won't begrudge me the indecency of saying that Fred is far more tolerable in death than he was in life.'

'Why?' asked the mendicant. The other two men turned to look at him; it was the first time he had spoken since entering Dr Parry's office. 'Forgive the interruption,' he went on, 'but despite the fact that a sort of ambient hatred for Fred O'Donnell seems almost to be an essential part of the town's social fabric, I'm yet to hear anything in the way of specifics. What was it, exactly, that Fred did to make everyone despise him so?'

Dr Parry sighed, letting his forehead sink forward onto steepled fingers. 'That's no small question,' he said. 'How best to put it? Fred was . . . well, he was adept at being unpleasant. I don't know if it actually gave him any enjoyment — God only knows whether the old bastard was even capable of enjoying anything — but he pursued it as an artist pursues his calling. He honed it. You've heard of Jack?'

'Winnie's brother?'

'Fred and Edith's eldest child,' the doctor nodded,

116

'and their only son. When he was a young boy, around seven or eight, my wife and I gave him a book of fairy tales. Nothing peculiar; an illustrated Grimm collection. He was a keen reader, that child, and for whatever reason, he took a particular liking to the fairy book. Started carrying it with him everywhere he went. They'd find him looking for elves in the rose garden or trying to teach the cat to speak. All perfectly normal for a boy that age, you understand; a vigorous imagination, certainly, but the sort of thing that one grows out of.'

Dr Parry paused, staring at an indistinct spot on his desk. 'One day, though, Fred decided that enough was enough. Perhaps Jack was reading when he was supposed to be tending the vegetable patch. Maybe Fred simply thought the boy was getting too old for fairy stories. I can't say for sure. What I do know, though, is that Jack left the book on his bedside table, and in the morning it was gone. In its place was a cardboard box, tied round with a ribbon. Jack eagerly tore it open.' He shook his head. 'Inside was a pair of wings which Fred had pulled from a dragonfly and a single rifle shell. *That's all there is left of the fairy you found in the orchard yesterday*, he wrote. *Nasty things've been at the crops. Any other fairies you see, I'll get them too.* We didn't see Jack reading too often after that.'

'My word,' said Hartley.

'It wasn't just Jack, either. Fred found a way to get to everybody. He only ever referred to my family as 'those bloody papists', despite knowing full well that our grandfather converted around the time of the Crimean War. He refused to even acknowledge little Delia for the first three years of her life, for reasons known to God alone. He routinely pretended to be unable to understand George, due to his having a 'foreign' accent, which is ridiculous — not least because George was born on the banks of the Murrumbidgee, and it's actually Fred who came from overseas.'

'Where was he from?'

Dr Parry looked surprised. 'Ah, you never actually heard him speak, did you? He was from Birmingham originally. Came over here when he was still quite young, but never let his accent lapse.'

'If Fred really managed to make such great strides in the art of unpleasantness,' the friar wondered, 'what on Earth possessed your sister to marry him?'

The good doctor cast his eyes to the ceiling. 'That's the real mystery, isn't it?' he said, throwing up his hands. 'She was always stubborn. I think it must have been an act of protest against our parents. She clashed with them on every possible matter. Even used to go by 'Jane' for a period as a young woman, presumably to get a reaction from Mother, who had chosen 'Edith' in honour of an aunt. Our parents had a perfectly eligible lad lined up for her when she was sixteen, but she exchanged about four words with him before storming off. We didn't see her again for weeks, and when she finally came back, she did so on the arm of Fred O'Donnell.'

'You must have been disappointed,' said Hartley.

'Of course. We all were. Distraught, really.'

'You would have wanted to do something about it,' the detective pressed.

Dr Parry lifted an eyebrow. 'You've seen what my sister's like. What do you think I could've done? No, the best thing for it was to stay away. I made sure to visit the farm only when Fred was elsewhere and made it through weddings and Christmases by gritting my teeth and holding my tongue. For the most part, it worked. I hadn't spoken to Fred for two or three years before he came to visit me.'

'When was this?'

'About a month ago,' said the doctor. 'Actually, give me a moment and I'll be able to tell you exactly.' He reached for a mounted desk calendar and flipped through it. 'Here we are. The eighth of August. It was a Wednesday.'

Hartley and the friar exchanged glances.

'Why did he come to visit you?' asked the detective.

'He had a form he needed filled out. Part of a life assurance thing he'd sent away for.' The doctor's lips tightened. 'I was just getting ready to head out on a call. In he comes, the arrogant so-and-so that he is, and throws the form onto my desk. Tells me he'll be back for it later, turns on his heel and strides out again.'

'What did you do?'

Here, for the first time, Dr Parry hesitated. 'I filled it out,' he said. 'I'm not proud of it, but I thought it the course of action that would result in the least contact with Fred. I left the completed paperwork with my secretary and went off about my business. He came to collect it a couple of hours later.' The doctor spread his hands out upon his desk. 'That was the last I ever saw of him.'

'Can you confirm that this was the form?' Hartley asked, rifling through the sheaf of insurance papers to find his target. Parry squinted briefly at it.

'That's the one.'

'And that's your handwriting? And your signature at the bottom?'

'It is.'

'Will your secretary be able to verify the fact that

119

Mr O'Donnell returned to collect the completed form?'

'Certainly.' Dr Parry looked up, a touch of alarm in his eyes. 'Am I under suspicion of something, Detective? I've already spoken to the police — the local chaps.'

Hartley offered what he hoped was a soothing smile. 'I'm simply making sure I have all the details straight. The more people I can find to attest to Fred's movements, the better my report will look.'

The doctor seemed to accept this, for he relaxed a little. The friar then sat forward.

'May I?' he asked, gesturing to the piece of paper on the desk. Receiving permission in the form of a nod from both doctor and detective, he picked it up and began to read.

'Thirteen stone, five pounds,' the friar murmured. 'Rather a burly man, our Fred.'

'Indeed. That's an estimate, of course.'

'How's that?' asked Hartley.

'Well, Fred wouldn't stay for an examination — as I said, he just threw the paper down and left.'

'You didn't actually look him over, then?'

'I didn't need to.' Dr Parry smiled, either unaware of or untroubled by the fact that he was implicating himself in what would legally amount to fraud. 'When you've been a country doctor for as long as I have, you get a feel for these things. Whatever doesn't reach you through the rumour mill can usually be ascertained at a glance. Let's take you as an example, Detective.' He sat back, surveying Hartley through narrowed eyes. 'Six foot, I'd say, or a touch over. Pulse in the normal range. Age in the early to middle twenties. Weight would be — oh,' he clicked his tongue, 'roughly eleven stone, four pounds. Five, perhaps. How's that?'

Hartley was forced to admit that the doctor's figures very closely approximated those recorded on his personnel file in the headquarters of the Western Australian Police.

'Now as for you, Mr . . .' The doctor made a vague grasping motion, as if hoping to lay hands on a name for the friar. 'I must admit, you present something of a challenge. I'd put your height at five foot six and your weight around nine and a half stone. As close an estimate as that shapeless robe allows. Where age is concerned, however —' He shook his head. 'I think I may have to gracefully bow out, for fear of being so far wrong that I'd embarrass us both.'

The friar grinned, multiplying the lines on his face and further thwarting the doctor's ability to guess his vintage.

'You'll get nothing out of him,' said Hartley. 'Lord knows I've tried.' He let out a sigh and reached for his hat. 'Just one more question before we go, Doctor. Other than yourself and your secretary, how many people were aware that Fred had taken out a life assurance policy?'

'I've no idea.' The doctor shrugged. 'It's probable that Edith knows, and maybe Mary, but it wouldn't surprise me in the least if Fred went ahead and did it off his own bat, without telling a soul.'

Hartley paused, hat halfway to his head. 'You haven't spoken to your sister about it?'

'As I mentioned earlier, it's not often that we have the chance to see each other. When the occasion does present itself, we try to avoid discussing my brother-in-law. A conversation is rarely improved by the addition of any reference to Fred O'Donnell.'

'It's strange,' said Hartley, as they left Dr Parry's office and stepped out into the late afternoon sun. 'The more I hear these hideous anecdotes about Fred, the more I find myself wishing I'd met him. It's as if I missed a night at the theatre and everyone who was in the audience keeps laughing about how the leading man's beard caught fire. I don't mind missing the performance so much as being excluded from the camaraderie.'

'I understand perfectly,' the friar said. 'If the whiskers were to burn for sixty years, though, I can't help but feel that some of the humour might well be lost to the flames.'

The two men turned off Spring Street, passing the eponymous water source as they headed back towards the hotel. They kept to the shadows of the gums lining the stream. Though summer was still a way off, the sky was cloudless and the day warm. A flock of twenty-eights chattered unseen in the trees and fat, aimless flies muddled to and fro.

'I suppose there's a chance that Parry prepared his secretary,' said Hartley. 'Told her what to say, I mean, in order to make it seem as though Fred dropped the paper off, when really he conspired with his sister to write the whole thing up in secret.' There was a touch of hope in his voice, the sort that knows it is soon to be dashed.

The friar gave his head a gentle shake. 'A falsehood like that would be easily discredited. Again, you must remember that we're in a small town. People watch. People listen. Most of all, people talk. We'll find out soon enough whether Fred was seen entering Parry's office, but my instinct tells me that he was.'

'There goes the Edith theory, then,' the detective sighed. 'We'll have to start fresh.'

'Not necessarily. We have merely ascertained that it was Fred who took out the policy. Regardless of Edith's involvement in the decision-making process, she'd have a ready-made motive were she to learn of its existence.'

'Parry reckons he didn't tell her.'

'The doctor may be lying, though it's impossible to be certain one way or the other. Ultimately, the issue is academic. There are plenty of other avenues by which Edith might have come to know of the policy. Great Southern Mutual would surely have sent an acceptance notice of some kind, for instance, which would be easy enough to intercept.'

'You're right!' Hartley snapped his fingers. 'We've got to question her again. Sooner or later, she'll let something slip.'

'Later seems more likely than sooner, unfortunately. Dr Parry called his sister stubborn, but I fear he may not have done her justice. She's shrewd, and she knows herself to be under suspicion.'

'Time to take the hammer to the weakest link, then,' said the detective, straightening his hat. 'Tomorrow, we'll go after Les Thompson.'

16

Even with the hotel's kitchen boy waking him at dawn, Hartley arrived at Tolhurst too late to catch the shearers. By the time the rest of the household sat down to breakfast, Les and George were already down at the shed, knee-deep in merino wool.

'They wanna make sure the bulk of the work's done before it gets too hot,' explained Winnie, who had evidently not yet donned her affectations for the day.

Hartley looked round the table with some impatience, waiting for the friar to finish his soft-boiled egg.

'Are you sure you won't take coffee, Detective?' There was genuine concern in Mary Bamonte's voice.

Hartley rubbed his reddened eyes, feeling self-conscious. He was not a friend to the early morning, and his still-somnolent attempts to shave had left him with at least two nasty-looking cuts. Reasoning that time was no longer of the essence — he had already missed the opportunity to take Les by surprise, after all — he relented, accepting a large enamel mug of strong black coffee and sipping the bitter liquid with a mixture of relief and self-recrimination.

'What's on the agenda today?' asked Edith, at what the detective felt to be an indecent volume.

'I shall be taking a statement from Mr Thompson,' he replied, fixing her with a bleary gaze.

If the matriarch experienced any alarm at this prospect, she gave not the slightest indication. 'Charles can show you down to the sheep yards, if you'd like,' she said.

The lad looked up from where he had been impatiently folding and refolding a napkin. Both he and his cousin had long since finished eating but were forbidden to leave the table until everyone else was done with breakfast.

'Never mind the shearing shed,' the boy said, eagerly. 'If you're after something really brilliant, I'll show you the well we dug in the back paddock. It's half full and we dropped a handful of tadpoles in there. Some of them are still alive.'

'*I* dropped the tadpoles in,' little Delia corrected. 'You were too scared.' She turned to the detective and spoke matter-of-factly. 'I made a sling out of my pinafore and carried them. One of them wriggled out of and fell on Charlie's foot and he screamed.'

'I never!'

'Thank you!' Hartley held both hands aloft to quiet the clamour. 'Thank you, but my companion and I are more than capable of finding our way to the sheep yards. I'm sure you both have very important things to be getting on with. In fact, we should really be getting on ourselves.'

It was a moment or two before the friar appeared to catch the thrust of Hartley's tone. 'Quite right,' he said. He promptly polished off the last of his toast, and before long they were on their way.

* ★ *

The day was still fresh as they made their way down the hill. Dew sparkled on the wheat and the sun was yet to show the sting it would acquire towards

125

the early afternoon. The sheep yards were sat about three-quarters of a mile from the house, reached by a gently curving track of packed earth shaded by salmon gums. Though Hartley and the friar had managed to dissuade the children from accompanying them, Kaiser had not been quite as receptive to their arguments and was now ambling around them in irregular circles, sniffing at every tree root, fencepost and wheel rut. The first part of the journey was conducted in amiable silence, the friar breathing deeply of the cool morning air and the detective still shepherding his brain gently towards full consciousness. After a few minutes, the pair crested a slight rise, and the sheep yards came into view.

The sheep formed a heaving woollen mass, held barely in check by a tangle of runs and pens. The animals were audible even from a distance, their bleats and yelps dissolving into a sort of low-level hum as they pushed past one another. One end of the maze emptied into the shearing shed, disgorging the sheep through a darkened doorway. The shed itself was close to fifteen feet high, a simple structure of tin and pine planks. One side of the building was completely open, though only a sliver of the interior was visible from the onlookers' current vantage point. Patrolling the outer edges of the sheep yards, administering strategic nips and barks as needed to keep the herd moving, were the two working dogs. Upon catching sight of her comrades, Kaiser broke into a run and disappeared down the slope towards them.

'Oi!' George yelled, emerging from the open side of the shed. 'Kaiser! What the hell d'you —' He saw the nearing investigators and stopped short. Turning on his heel, he ran back into the building.

126

'That was odd,' said Hartley. 'Perhaps he didn't recognise us.'

'I don't think I'm flattering myself when I say that you and I form a shared outline that is uniquely recognisable, even from a distance,' the friar replied.

The detective ran his hands across the shiny brass buttons of his uniform and straightened his hat, finding himself unable to disagree. 'I suppose we'll find out what's going on soon enough,' he muttered. They crossed the last hundred yards or so in silence. When they were only a few steps from the tin wall of the shed, both George and Les appeared from within to greet them.

'Hello there, fellas. Lovely day for it.' Les wiped away the sweat which clung to his forehead despite the coolness of the morning. He wore rough trousers and a close-fitting undershirt. As Hartley stepped forward to offer a handshake, the two shearers moved almost imperceptibly closer together. They now stood nearly shoulder to shoulder, making it difficult to see past them into the gloom of the shed.

'What brings you boys all the way down here?' George piped up, with forced joviality. 'Looking for a haircut? I'll go and grab the shears, if you want.'

'I'm actually quite keen to ask Mr Thompson a couple of questions,' said Hartley. 'And I wouldn't mind taking a look around the premises, either. Just as a matter of procedure,' he smiled officiously. 'I'm sure you understand.'

'Orright, Blue,' Les sniffed. 'I'm due for a break soon, anyway. I'll just go and turn the machines off.' He turned back towards the shed, then looked over his shoulder at George. 'Do you wanna show them round the yards first, George?'

George hurried forward to lead the visitors round to the pens. While the dogs ran back and forth, herding lost sheep out of corners and chasing stragglers, Hartley and the friar were treated to lengthy, detailed descriptions of the shearing, wool classing and baling processes.

'That platform over there's a recent addition, too,' George said, gesturing across the sheep yards. 'They can just bring a cart or a truck around and we can load the bales directly from there. My idea, that one.' There was pride in his voice. 'Old Fred was against it, but he didn't come down here at all in the final few months. Last time I saw him down here was with that bloke in the coat.'

Hartley, who had been beginning to droop in the sun, brightened at the change of subject. 'Do you think you'd be able point out the exact spot you saw them?'

'It was over this way.' He took a couple of dozen steps away from the yards. 'Would've been about here, I s'pose.'

The detective followed, casting a careful eye across the ground. It was all pebbles and dust and wild oats drying to straw, a habitat thoroughly inimical to both boot print and tyre mark. Even if there had been something, he reflected, the local officers probably would've found it. They'd been over the area time and time again.

'This is where we saw that fella in the cloak, isn't it?' said Les Thompson, appearing at his colleague's side. 'Want one?' he asked, lighting a battered cigarette. When no-one took him up on the offer, he shrugged and pocketed his matches once more.

'What can you tell us about that meeting, Mr Thompson?' Hartley asked.

'Not too much, really.' The shearer went on to describe the encounter in much the same terms as George had done: a sunset silhouette, inaudible, indistinct. 'Whatever the bloke in the coat was saying, Fred didn't look too happy about it.' He took a drag on his cigarette. 'Mind you, that's not saying much. Fred was a miserable bastard at the best of times.'

'Were you party to the entirety of the interaction?'

'We could see the whole thing from inside the shed, if that's what you mean. Don't think they knew we could see 'em, though. They weren't out there for long. Argued for a couple of minutes and then took off as it was getting dark, both heading in different directions.'

Hartley thought for a spell, tapping his pencil against the top of his notebook. 'Who did you tell about the encounter?'

'No-one. Not at first, anyway. Fred was sitting in his study when we headed up to the house for tea. He looked all right. Didn't really seem like he was too bothered or anything. I'm not paid to gossip, after all, so I kept my mouth shut.'

Hartley looked over to George. 'And you, Mr Bamonte? Surely you would've mentioned something to your wife?'

George gave his head a vigorous shake. 'I like a peaceful marriage, Detective. We've been together nine years now, Mary and me, and one of the first things I learned, very early on in the piece, was to keep her father out of it. Everybody hates Fred O'Donnell — hated, I s'pose,' he corrected himself, 'but it's different when he's your dad. Mary didn't like him, as I'm sure you know, but if someone else was whinge-ing about him, she'd feel like she had to jump in and have a go right back at them.' He shook his head again. 'Problem is, you can't say anything nice about Fred 'cause there's nothing nice to say. So what d'you do? You just never mention him at all.'

There was a certain pragmatic wisdom to this, the detective conceded. Hartley had never given a great deal of thought to marriage — though he had noticed his mother bringing the subject up more frequently of late — and he found himself wondering if such strange compromises were a hallmark of every coupling.

'When did the rest of the household become aware of the cloaked man's visit, then?' he asked. 'If I have my notes in the correct order, this would have been the first sighting.'

George nodded. 'Winnie and Hazel ran into him about a week later, out by the chooks, like they told you. They were all pretty shook up by it, especially Hazel. Well, I didn't want them to think they were going crazy — imagining things, like Fred was saying — so I went ahead and told them about what we saw.'

Hartley made an absent-minded noise of assent, head bent over his notebook. Suddenly, he stopped, struck by something that he had heard while still half asleep. He flipped back a few pages.

'Hold on a minute,' he said, looking from one shearer to the other. 'What were you doing down here?'

'What were we doing?' Les laughed. 'The shearers, you mean? In the shearing shed, with the shears and the sheep? I think I can leave that sort of cerebral work to you, Detective.'

Hartley flushed. 'What I mean to say is why were

you down here so late?' He jerked his thumb in the approximate direction of the house. 'Winifred told me this morning that you were up before dawn, with the aim of finishing the rough work before the afternoon got too hot. How was it, then, that you were still in the shed when the sun was setting?'

To the detective's surprise, Les lit up at this question. 'Ah!' He clapped his huge, sun-reddened hands together. 'There it is. Didya hear that, George? Bluey here finds it unreasonable that someone should work from sparrow's fart to sundown. A bloody good point, if you ask me! See, this is exactly why —' In response to a subtle but unmistakable gesture from George, Les pulled himself up short. He stood in loaded silence, massive chest heaving with agitation as the other man took over.

'It's just too much work for the two of us,' said George. 'That's the honest truth of it. Fred used to do a lot of the yakka, but he'd been slowing down the last couple of years. Getting on a bit, y'know. As I said, he hardly made it down to the shed at all in the last few months. Most of what he did do was on the business side of things: trips into town to talk with breeders or buyers or sorting stuff out with the bank. Kept the purse strings pulled pretty tight, too. Mary was always on at him to hire some extra hands, but he wouldn't budge. Cheap old bastard.'

Hartley found himself reflecting again on the remarkable power of the deceased man to provoke ire. The more he heard, the more amazed he was that Fred had managed to make it through the six decades he did before being shot. At this point, it wouldn't have surprised him to learn that the whole household had planned his death in concert. Finding a motive

131

was, in the normal course of events, one of the fundamental struggles of detection, but Hartley was now learning that a surplus of motive muddied the waters even further than a deficit. With a sigh, he dismissed George. When Les turned to follow his comrade back to the shed, however, the detective held him back.

'Just a minute, Mr Thompson,' he said. 'There are one or two other topics on which I'd like you to enlighten me. To begin with, there is the matter of the telegram you sent on the third of July.'

'I didn't send a telegram on the third of July.' Les spoke simply, neither deceit nor defiance obvious in his voice.

'You didn't send a telegram?' Hartley struggled to keep the triumph from tugging at the corner of his mouth as he produced the incriminating document. 'Not even this one?'

Les didn't give it so much as a glance. 'No.'

'Maybe you'd like to go ahead and take a look at it. Just to make assurance doubly sure.' Hartley quietly cursed himself as he noticed the friar's habit of theatrical quotation making its way into his own idiom. He shot his companion a sideways look, but the little man had wandered a few feet away and was examining something amongst the weeds and wildflowers. He returned his attention to Les, who had made no move to take the folded paper from his outstretched hand.

'This isn't your writing, then?' he pressed.

The shearer simply shook his head.

'How can you be so certain? You haven't even looked at it.'

'I'm sure.' Les folded his arms and looked back at the shed.

132

Hartley felt the heat of frustration rise to his face. Before he could give voice to something regrettable, however, a hand was laid upon his arm.

'If I might be permitted to make an observation,' the friar said, 'Mr Thompson strikes me as a man who has spent much of his life working.' He smiled compassionately at his subject. 'When one spends his childhood on the land, his priorities are dictated by the seasons. Ensuring that every paddock is fully sown, for example, might take precedence over scribbling in one's schoolbooks, and the odd academic examination here and there might give way to the advent of the harvest.'

Les did not respond, but there was something like gratitude in the look he directed at the friar. Hartley couldn't believe how oblivious he'd been, or how tactless. The man was unable to read. He attempted to cover his embarrassment with a cough.

'To be clear, then,' he said, in a gentler voice, 'you didn't write, dictate or otherwise cause a telegram to be sent to a Dr Thornally in July?'

'I did not,' said Les. 'I've never heard of a Thornally, doctor or otherwise, and the last time I sent a telegram was at Christmas. Winnie took it down for me.'

'Winifred? Why not Edith?'

Les cocked his head in what appeared to be genuine puzzlement. 'What's Edith got to do with it?'

'She struck me as the member of the family with whom you have the greatest rapport,' said Hartley. 'You do work very closely with Mr Bamonte, of course, but I've yet to see you call at his window in the dead of night.'

The shearer blanched. Hartley could see the tension pass through his massive body.

'You *were* watching,' he said, tightly. 'I thought I saw the curtain move, but I told myself it was just a trick of the moonlight.' He swore. 'Listen, I know this is bad — I mean to say, I know this looks bad — but it isn't. Not in the way you're thinking, anyway.

'And what am I thinking, pray tell?'

'You think this has something to do with Fred, with him getting shot the way he did.' Les stood with his legs half bent, as if preparing to leap to safety. 'It doesn't, I promise. I'm giving you my word, whatever it's worth.'

Hartley smiled sadly. There was no joy in this for him. He wasn't the type of police officer to relish the chase or gloat over a quarry backing themselves into a corner. He didn't build noble stories around his own strategy or replay interrogations like prize chess matches in his mind of an evening. It was simply his job to find the truth. He was driven by curiosity and a vague conviction that untangling a problem, any problem, contributed in some way to the betterment of the world at large.

'I'd find you a lot easier to believe if you simply told me the truth,' he said.

Les began to pace. 'I can't,' he said. 'It's not that I don't want to, it's just —' He sighed. 'It's not up to me. Not my place to say. Understand?'

'I think so,' said Hartley. 'It's a matter of chivalry, is it? A woman's honour, that sort of thing?'

'What?' the shearer stopped, furrowing his brow.

'You don't want to — well, you don't want kiss and tell, so to speak.'

Hartley was shocked to hear his suspect break into slow laughter.

'Me and Edith?' Les chuckled. 'That's what you

134

were thinking? A secret meeting in the middle of the night for a kiss and a bit of a cuddle? You're off your rocker. She's hard as nails, not to mention as old as me mum.'

'Mrs O'Donnell is still a handsome woman,' said Hartley, a little defensively, 'and an inheritance of several thousand pounds often has the effect of enhancing one's appearance.'

Les sobered. 'I thought they hadn't got hold of a will.'

'I was referring to Fred's life assurance policy.'

Either Les Thompson was a particularly practised actor, thought Hartley, or his surprise was genuine.

'He took out a policy? You mean to tell me that the old man actually gave a stuff about what happened after he was gone?' Les whistled. 'People'll surprise you sometimes. Even the dead ones.'

'Am I to believe that you had no idea, then?'

'You can believe what you want, but this is the first I'm hearing of it.'

'It won't be the last, I'm afraid. Keeping your silence might seem like the noble thing, but that doesn't necessarily make it right. It'll be better in the long run if you tell me what you know.'

The shearer gave a sad shrug. 'I told you. I can't.'

'I think 'won't' would be a more accurate word,' said Hartley, but there was no malice in it. 'I shall speak directly with Mrs O'Donnell, then. You can expect to see me tomorrow, and each day after that. Until the truth comes out, I'm afraid, you won't be rid of me.' He turned to the friar. 'Come on. Time for the grand tour.'

17

Their examination of the shearing shed was less illuminating than Hartley had hoped. It was a simple
building, large and gloomy, with a raised platform for
shearing and several stout wooden ramps for shuttling
livestock back and forth. Though pairs of traditional
hand shears could still be seen hanging from nails
along the rear wall, the presence of a large clipping
machine and a diesel generator helped to lend the
operation a more modern air. This apparatus hung
in many-jointed arms over the platform, creating an
eerie arachnid impression in the half light. Tightly
wrapped bales of wool were piled high on two sides of
the shed, reaching towards the roof. A pulley system
had been devised to hoist them, the ropes now hanging slack amongst the rafters. Blowflies buzzed this
way and that, picked out at intervals by sudden shafts
of sunlight slipping through the perforations in the tin
walls. Whether these holes were the work of nails, rust
or bullets was not immediately obvious. The scene
was overlain by a heavy scent, the mingling of dust,
dung and sweat, together with the thick, oily musk
of matted wool. Oddly, despite the growing heat, the
restless sheep and their attendant insects, Hartley
found something comforting in the dim closeness of
the air. Lifting a handkerchief discreetly to his nose,
he took his time in wandering about the structure's
inner perimeter, poking his head into the adjoining
rooms. He soon found these to house baling wire,

tools and the rough cot in which Les slept. After some minutes, he returned to the main shearing platform, where George and Les had already resumed work. The friar was standing beside the far ramp, hefting one of the unused clipping devices and turning it over in his hands.

'Seen enough?' Hartley asked.

'It's warm,' murmured the friar, in a distracted sort of way.

'It certainly is. I can see why they want to get started early. Must be hell in here when midday comes around.'

With a final warning to expect further questions in the coming days, the investigators took their leave of the shed. Kaiser loped up to them as they reached the bottom of the hill.

'You knew already, didn't you?' said Hartley, when they'd put a respectable distance between themselves and the shed. 'About Les not being able to read, I mean.'

'What's that?' The friar looked up. 'Oh. I wouldn't say I knew, as such, but I certainly had some fairly robust suspicions. The telegram form was all wrong.'

Hartley fished the document out of his pocket and squinted at it. He turned it over. He even held it up to the sun and peered through it, searching for secret messages of the sort he'd read about in the *Boy's Annual* during his formative years. They were half-way back to the house by the time he finally admitted defeat.

'Go on, then. I give up. What's wrong with it? Some sort of code, I suppose, in whatever language you were asking about yesterday. Maltese, was it?'

'Malay,' said the friar. 'Come to think of it, though,

137

there's a good chance that Maltese has similar properties.'

'And what might those properties be?'

'Phonetic spelling, largely.'

'Meaning what? That words are written the way they sound?'

'More or less. It's a quality that makes for a much smoother language acquisition experience, depriving the learner of the joys of silent letters, mangled French borrowings and all the *I before E* uncertainty offered by our own tongue.' The friar shook his head, smiling. 'I grew up largely in the Straits Settlements, you see. Singapore. I always looked forward to Malay lessons. I had them every Wednesday evening after school, despite my father's objections. He preferred me to study what he called 'real languages' — French, German, Italian. The languages of the Enlightenment. In the end, though, my mother convinced him. She led him on with imagined diplomatic posts and a lot of rousing stuff about spreading goodwill towards the empire, when really, I think she just wanted me to help her eavesdrop on the servants.'

Hartley shifted his weight from foot to foot. Though keen to uncover more of the recalcitrant friar's background, the mystery of the telegram form was causing him almost physical discomfort. His attempts to conceal this must not have been particularly successful, because the friar took one glance at him and hurried the narrative along.

'Malay is not a simple language to learn, as such, but the precision of its orthography was a palpable relief after English and all its exceptions. If a word were spoken aloud, a relative beginner would be able

138

to write it easily enough. This is not the case, unfortunately, with our own mongrel tongue.'

The detective looked at the telegraph form again. 'I think I see,' he said. 'The handwriting itself is shoddy. It looks as if the person writing it is inexperienced or is copying it poorly from a primer.' He looked up. 'But there are no spelling mistakes.'

'That is rather the line along which my thinking ran, yes. If Mr Thompson — or anyone else, for that matter, with a limited literary capacity — were to attempt such a message, one would expect the result to be marred by more than just inexpert lettering. Look at the words used: 'counsel', 'suitable' . . . even 'facility' sounds as though it should properly be written with an *s* in place of a *c*.'

'What does that tell us, then? It was written by someone else?'

'I believe so. Further, it indicates that the writer knew, or at least suspected, that Les was not a strong writer, and modified their handwriting accordingly. For whatever reason — possibly an unfamiliarity with any language other than the King's — they neglected to consider the implications of irregular spelling.'

'That could help us to narrow things down, then,' said Hartley. 'Edith sounds well-educated. There's a good chance she studied languages, which would seem to be a point in her favour. It should be easy enough to find out, either way. And George is presumably familiar with Italian to some extent. He'd know about Les's trouble with letters, too.' He rubbed his chin. 'Not the sort of evidence likely to hold much water with a jury, but it might lead us in the right direction.'

The friar nodded.

'The other question to consider,' the detective went

on, 'is why anyone would want to imitate Les Thompson. Was it because of the recipient — this Thornally fellow, I mean, the doctor — or was it simply to avoid scrutiny?'

'We do not face a paucity of questions,' agreed the friar. 'Like the heads of the Hydra, one is cut down, only for two to spring forth and take its place. Still others arrive with no antecedent. I raise my eyes and find myself wondering, for instance, why Miss O'Donnell might find it at all necessary to watch us from a tree.'

There was a curse from somewhere above. Hartley spun and looked up to see Winnie balanced precariously on one of the broad, white limbs of a eucalypt, some ten feet above his head. Her lace-fronted blouse was tucked into gabardine overalls, her hair tied back from her face with a length of sky-blue ribbon. It was an odd ensemble, the detective reflected, made all the more arresting by the fact that its wearer was now slithering down the trunk like a possum. Executing a dismount which would not have shamed a professional gymnast, the young woman landed, barefoot and panting, before her discoverers.

'Gentlemen,' she said, and straightened up. 'Fancy running into you here. A socially vibrant sector of the property, this one. Can't budge an inch without coming up against an old chum or two.'

Hartley and the friar crossed their arms as one, determined not to engage with Winnie's patter. The girl sighed.

'I'll concede that the position in which you find me is, at first glance, an unfavourable one. In the ideal course of proceedings, I would not have had to be so indiscreet, nor indeed so arboreal. If you'll extend me the benefit of the doubt, however, I have no doubt you'll benefit from my testimony.'

'Please, Miss O'Donnell,' said Hartley, whose head was beginning to spin again. 'Just tell me why you were spying on us.'

'I should like to preface my response by objecting to your choice of terminology,' Winnie sniffed. Catching the warning look in the detective's eyes, she dropped the facade. 'I wasn't watching you,' she said, her accent antipodean once more. 'I was watching the shed. I thought you two might scare them out into the open.'

'Who? George and Les?'

'They're up to something,' she nodded. 'Ever since Dad died, maybe even before. They don't like anyone else going down to the shed. Delia and Charlie used to take their tea down to them in a basket, but one of the men comes up to the house to grab it now.'

'What do you think's going on?'

'I don't know. Not exactly. I have my suspicions, though, which is why . . .' she broke off and gestured at the gum tree.

The next query came from the friar. 'Were you able to discern anything of note?' he asked.

Winnie shook her head. 'Not from this distance. There was movement around the side door, but I couldn't see who it was. Might have been sneaking something in.'

'Or out,' said Hartley, rubbing his chin. 'We'll have to examine the place more closely when we visit them again tomorrow.'

'They'll be expecting us tomorrow,' the friar pointed out. 'It might be more prudent to make our move now.'

'Now? Surely they'll be on high alert now. We've

just put the wind up 'em, so to speak.'

'So we have, which is precisely why they won't be expecting us again so soon. I think they'll take this chance to cover their tracks or plan for contingencies. We may well be able to catch them in the act, as the saying goes.'

'Yes!' Winnie clapped her hands. 'Oh, go on! Let's swoop now!'

'You won't be doing anything of the sort,' said Hartley. 'For all I know, you're wrapped up in whatever Les and George are working on. This could all be an elaborate ploy.'

'All the more reason to keep me well in sight, then,' the young woman retorted. 'Come along.'

With this, she skipped lightly past the two men and began to jog down the hill. Kaiser leapt up from the makeshift bed she had arranged in the undergrowth and trotted after her mistress.

'Wait!' Hartley charged after Winnie and caught her by the wrist. 'We've got to make a plan first. At the very least, we'll have to do something with the dog. We don't want her giving us away.'

'Finally learning from Conan Doyle, I see,' the friar grinned.

18

So it was that, against his initial better judgement, Detective Constable James Hartley found himself crawling facedown through a field of wheat. His role in the farce was to approach the shearing shed from the east, coming quietly upon the side door which Winnie had pointed out from the top of the hill. At the same time, Miss O'Donnell was creeping around to the structure's open western wall, it being assumed that her discovery, should it occur, would cause the inhabitants of the shed more annoyance than alarm. The mendicant had been assigned the rather less physical task of keeping Kaiser at a distance from the other dogs, facilitating the surreptitious approach of his comrades.

Hartley's share of the work, ridiculous though it made him feel, progressed easily enough at the outset. He made his way towards the shed in a wide arc so as to stay out of sight, keeping to the cover of fences and trees. It was only the last fifty yards or so that he had to crawl, popping his head up every now and then over the rows of wheat to check his bearings. Whenever he did this, he was also sure to throw a glance towards the hill where the friar was hidden. If either Hartley or Miss O'Donnell showed signs of being spotted, the friar was to release Kaiser. The dog would then — her role having been patiently explained to her by an endearingly earnest Winnie — bound down to the shed, signalling the remaining infiltrator to rush forward with all haste

in the hope of pre-empting any attempts at conceal-
ment on the part of the shearers.

Despite the ignominious method of locomotion
and the attendant risk of damage to his treasured uniform, Hartley was surprised to find himself enjoying
the caper. There was an element of adventure inherent
in crawling towards an enemy position, even if said
fortress was filled with a ton or two of matted wool
in lieu of artillery shells. He was also aware, though
he would never admit to it, of a certain buoyancy, a
lightness of spirit which correlated rather neatly with
the presence of Winifred O'Donnell. There was a sort
of pure joy in the young woman's cavalier approach
to reality which enabled Hartley to forget, however
briefly, that he was in the process of investigating a
brutal murder and had yet to meet with anything significant in the way of success. This dreamlike state
persisted for a fair stretch of time even after Winnie
had taken her leave, or on the odd occasion when she
was separated from him by — to take just any old
thing as an example — a field or two of wheat and an
enormous corrugated-iron shed.

The heightening sun warmed Hartley's back as
he crawled forward through the grain, and the lilt-
ing warble of a magpie floated on the spring air. The
detective looked up to see a single towering wandoo
near the south-east corner of the shed. The magpie
was perched on one of the branches closest to the
summit, head thrown back in full dedication to its art.
Soon, a second bird chimed in from the shed roof,
making the song a duet. Hartley sank deeper into the
warm, peaceful haze, barely noticing the pebbles and
stubbly straw that caught at his hands as he crawled
onwards. It was the warble of a third magpie, closer

now, that finally gave him pause. The bird's cry had been altogether less musical than those of its comrades, high and shrill. Hartley felt his blood cool. He knew the sound, and it wasn't a mating call. It was a warning. Early spring, the time of year that the Noongar people call *djilba*, was when the wildflowers started to emerge, and the world began to grow warm. The magpies were building nests, preparing for the arrival of their young. They were vigilant parents, careful to keep their neighbourhood free of threats. Watching a fourth bird appear on a nearby fence-post level with his head, Hartley found himself reasoning that he was the sort of animal that could, in the circumstances, be construed as something of a threat from a magpie's point of view. He glanced back over to the wandoo, where several of the birds had clustered in the upper branches. That must be where the nest is, thought Hartley. The magpies were silent now, every eye fixed on the human interloper. The largest of the creatures, approaching the dimensions of a modest housecat, leapt to the shed roof and began sharpening its beak, dragging it meaningfully along the tin guttering. Hartley felt panicked childhood memories rise from deep within, vivid recollections of skinned knees and dropped sandwiches as roosting magpies swooped outside the schoolhouse.

'Nothing to worry about,' he murmured, lifting his hands slowly. He wasn't sure if he was trying to reassure himself or the birds. 'No-one's looking for trouble here.'

The magpie on the shed roof wasted no time in proving Hartley wrong. On the first swoop, it came within a foot of the detective's face, the brutal clack of its freshly honed beak ringing out over the wheat.

Hartley swore, crouching closer to the ground as he scurried onwards. As the second swoop knocked his hat free, the need for stealth sank below speed on his list of personal and professional priorities. He abandoned both hat and caution, sprinting the last few yards to the shed's side door in a flurry of wings and curses. Wrenching the door open, he slid inside and dropped to the ground, panting. His collar was wet, a mixture of sweat and blood. In addition to the headgear and the element of surprise, Hartley had lost a not insignificant chunk of his left ear in the attack. He felt gingerly around the wound. Nothing that a bit of iodine wouldn't fix, he thought, forcing himself to gulp a few calming breaths. Unfortunately, his composure could not be so easily mended. He was sprawled on the dirt floor of the shed in the murky shadow of a wall of wool bales. His eyes adjusted slowly to the dim light, and the air felt even hotter and closer than it had half an hour earlier. Strange sounds came from the other side of the bales, muttered voices and a sort of stifled scuffling. Hartley had just managed to pull himself to his feet when George's face appeared around the corner.

'Christ, Detective, what've you gone and done to yourself?'

Hartley waved the questions aside, pushing his way around to the shearing platform. There was still a chance, however small, of catching Les in the act. The precise nature of the act, of course, remained somewhat obscure at present, but Hartley was confident that all would be made clear to him at the time of discovery. He stumbled around the corner and pulled himself up short. The shed was all but empty. Les stood in the middle of the platform, halfway through shearing a

146

sizeable ram. The beast was splayed on its back, held fast by one hind leg, and had been denuded of wool from roughly the midsection down. It looked up at the newcomer with a sort of mild curiosity, and Hartley was left with the absurd impression that he had interrupted the creature in the act of dressing for dinner. He fought the urge to apologise for his impropriety.

'Been in the wars, mate?' drawled Les, nodding towards Hartley's bloodied face.

The policeman didn't respond. He was scanning the shed for signs of subterfuge, jiggery-pokery or otherwise distasteful goings-on. There were none. Everything was exactly as it had appeared on his previous visit, save for the slowly growing figure of Winnie O'Donnell, who could be seen in the field outside, approaching the open west wall at a run. She reached the shed a moment later, panting and flanked by dogs. Catching the detective's eye, she indicated via a rueful shake of the head that nothing untoward had been observed on her side of the building.

'Winnie?' said George. 'What's going on?' He glanced at Hartley, then back at his sister-in-law. His face hardened. 'Oh,

I see. While Les and I are sweating our faces off in this big bloody oven, just the two of us doing all the actual work, you lot up at the house are kicking back and having a bit of fun. Thought it'd be a laugh to sneak down here and spy on us, didya?'

Winnie and Hartley began talking over one another, layering hasty, half-baked excuses while George folded his arms and cast his eyes heavenward, an overwrought facsimile of the loyal wounded.

'The shearer doth protest too much, methinks.' This came from the friar, who had slipped into the shed unnoticed. 'You'll have to excuse my alterations to the text,' he added, apparently speaking to one of the ewes waiting her turn at the clippers. 'I'm a purist, by nature, but one must work with what one is given.' He made for the platform. 'I don't suppose you'd mind turning that device off, Mr Thompson?'

Les shook his head, scarcely troubling to look up from the fleece he was clipping. 'George is right, mate,' he said. 'Some of us have real work to do.'

Winnie ran across to the sputtering petrol engine powering the clippers and, with a deft hand, put it to rest. A sudden silence settled over the shed. Les straightened, grunting, with every indication of being about to give voluble expression to his displeasure, but the friar held up a hand to forestall him.

'Let's wait until the assembly is complete. Would you care to join us, gentlemen?' he called, seeming to address the latter statement to the rafters. 'This discussion will be of some relevance to you.' His voice echoed amongst the high shadows, then died away to silence. A couple of thin bleats rang out from the penned flock, but the rest of the shed was still.

'Look,' said Les, stepping forward, 'I don't know what you think —'

The friar ignored him, calling out again. 'The man with me is Detective Constable Hartley of the Western Australian Police.' He let the words sit before continuing. 'He has travelled down from Perth to investigate a murder. This is decidedly not the sort of thing you want to be accused of hiding from.'

The detective in question stood to awkward attention, attempting to project an air of authority. This was made particularly difficult by the fact that he had not the slightest idea who the subject of the friar's

148

admonitions might be — nor, come to think of it, *where* they might be, which left him puffing his chest and pointing his chin at various indistinct corners of the building. Fortune did not smile upon Hartley, and he was engaged in thrusting what he hoped to be a grim, no-nonsense face somewhere towards the north-west when a sharp intake of breath from Winnie revealed that the locus of the action was behind him. He spun round in time to see two men emerge from behind a row of wool bales. They were lean, dark-skinned and clad in simple working attire. Despite having spent the last few minutes crouched in a corner, the taller of the two men managed a look of calm defiance as he strode forward. He stood beside the clipping engine and folded his arms. His companion joined him shortly after, a touch of wariness lightening his movements. For several long seconds, no-one spoke.

'Would you care to make the introductions, Mr Thompson?' prompted Hartley. It was clear that the shearer cared to do no such thing, but his grumbling was cut short by the taller of the two newcomers.

'My name is Simons,' he said, in a firm, clear baritone. 'Edward Simons. This is my brother, Michael. We work here.'

Winnie yelped, clapping her hands together like a schoolgirl. 'I knew it!'

Hartley's brow furrowed. He had not known it, and still didn't. In fact, if he was to be completely honest with himself, he was a little hazy on the topic of what, precisely, might be said to constitute 'it'. The friar's look of triumph, however, made it clear that Hartley was alone in his ignorance — a situation he felt it prudent to conceal, for the time being. 'I think we'd all better sit down and talk this through,' he said.

'Now then,' the detective said, once all those present had regrouped to the pair of rough wooden benches by the shed door. 'Perhaps you would start by telling me, Mr Simons, whether you and your brother commenced your duties here prior to or following the death of Mr O'Donnell.'

'Well, it's difficult to be certain,' the man said, 'without knowing who Mr O'Donnell was, or when he died.'

Hartley stared at him. If he was joking, there was nothing in his eyes to show it.

'Fred O'Donnell is — or rather, was — the owner of this property. He was your employer. I find it hard to believe that you were unaware of his existence, or more to the point, its recent end.'

'We were told to keep our heads down,' said Simons, simply. 'We're not paid to hear things, or to see them. We're paid to shear the sheep, pack the wool and stay out of sight. And as for employers,' he added, 'we get our pay from Les, here. He and George are the only ones we've ever dealt with.'

'That's Mr Thompson and Mr Bamonte, to you,' said Les, automatically. Hartley disregarded the complaint.

'It doesn't matter. It'll be Fred's name on the permit, and —' He stopped short. In a flash, the whole scheme made itself clear to him. 'Of course,' he said, turning to look at Les and George. 'That's why you have these poor sods hidden away down here. You're employing them without a permit. How long has this been going on?'

'Only a fortnight,' said George, miserably. 'Fred just wouldn't listen to us. He was too busy to help out with the sheep anymore — and, let's be honest, getting a bit too old — but he wouldn't hear of bringing in anyone from outside. Too tight, he was, and too proud. Wouldn't spare us a penny to hire a white bloke, and getting the native permit takes weeks, so we had to do things on the cheap and keep it all under wraps.'

'Fred didn't know about any of it, then?'

George shook his head.

'He would never have stood for something like this,' Winnie put in. 'Not as a result of any sort of moral feeling, you understand. For all his antagonism, he was a stickler and a bore when it came to regulations. As long as he was seen to be doing the right thing, it didn't seem to bother him that he never did anything good.'

'It's neither good nor right,' growled an unfamiliar voice, which turned out to belong to Michael Simons. 'The whole idea's crooked, through and through.' The assembly glanced round at the man in some surprise. Hartley had assumed him to be simply reticent, happy to have his brother take the helm, but it now appeared as though he'd been biting his tongue. 'A day's work is a day's work,' he went on. 'I should be paid the same as the next man, black or white.'

'Or woman,' added Winnie, to the deafening indifference of those around her.

'Hold on, there's a point.' Hartley regarded the Indigenous shearers. 'What possessed you to take the job? A lawful permit-holder would pay the full rate for an Aboriginal labourer — though, as you've pointed out,' he added, in response to Michael's flashing eyes, 'it may not be a fair one. A fellow was jailed in Meekatharra not long ago for working off the books, and the farmer who employed him fined fifty pounds. Why run the risk?'

The detective was surprised to see both kinsmen draw themselves up, sitting straighter.

'None of the big places'll hire us,' Edward said. 'They know we're with the Native Union, see. Our uncle marched to Perth with William Harris.'

These words afforded Hartley the rare opportunity to act as educator for the usually omniscient friar. The ersatz holy man seemed to absorb information from the landscape as he strolled through it, but his adventures in Western Australia had been largely restricted to small towns and rural byways. Now, for the first time in the course of the investigation, the detective's urban origins were cause for something other than mockery. He'd been in the city centre that March day, months ago — a regular officer on the beat, then, not yet a detective. He'd seen the deputation from the Native Union march down Hay Street, straight-backed and proud, on their way to speak with the Premier. The crowd parted, murmuring. At the head of the group was William Harris, coat buttoned across his broad chest. People whispered that he was a half-caste, that he'd been educated amongst the whites. He certainly spoke like it, holding forth on the indignities of the *Aborigines Act* with the flair of a King's Counsel while Premier Collier listened in fascination.

'The papers all reported on it,' said Hartley. 'They said he spoke with the Premier for hours, made a real impression. There's talk of real legislative reform — not just work rights, but closing down the mission at Mogumber, too.'

'It's remarkable how often a man may suddenly be found to merit empathy the once he learns to dress and speak like his oppressors,' said the friar.

Michael scoffed. 'It's all talk, and it'll never be more than talk. Not while the Protector has anything to do with it.' He spat the word out in a way that made the title's irony clear. A.O. Neville, the Chief Protector of Aborigines, was known to be far fonder of prisons than pastoral care. 'I'll watch my kids grow old sitting and waiting for the laws to change. That's why we're gonna start our own operation. As soon as we learn the ropes well enough and get a bit of money put away, we'll buy some sheep and set up our own place. You don't need a permit to work your own land.'

'Here, hold on,' said Les Thompson. 'You never said anything about that before. This isn't a trade school, y'know. You can't just have us train you up and then go off to set up the competition.'

'I'm not sure that you're able to manoeuvre your way to the moral high ground on this point, given the circumstances,' said the friar.

The shearer sniffed. 'If it wasn't for me, they wouldn't even have jobs. A low wage is better than no wage.' He smirked, retroactively recognising his own rhyme.

'But you weren't actually the one paying them, were you?' Hartley broke in. 'The money came from the O'Donnells. And if Fred really had no idea, you must have had access to the family coffers.'

There was a crackling silence. George gave a start, noticing that all eyes were on him. 'What, you think I tapped Mary for the cash?' He chuckled. 'You don't know my wife very well, Detective. I told her how snowed under we were down here, and d'you know what she said?' He placed his fists on his hips, cocked to one side as he assumed the character of his beloved. ''Good! Might give you a chance to work some of that gut off!'.'

Winnie stifled a laugh. 'I have to hand it to you,' she said. 'That's not a bad Mary.'

'Quite a performance,' Hartley agreed. 'If you do tire of the pastoral life, maybe Hazel could put in a good word with her old theatre crowd. There is another O'Donnell, though, who had access to the money. She manages the household budget, I believe, and quite effectively, too.' He turned to Les. 'That was your reason for visiting Edith on Sunday night, wasn't it, Mr Thompson?'

Les held the detective's gaze before lowering his eyes. 'It was my idea from the beginning. She had nothing to do with it.'

'Spare us the chivalry. What was the conversation about?'

'I was just going to get the cash for the week,' said Les. 'We've been meeting every week since I first came up with the idea, about a month ago. It was a bit of work, but I convinced her that it'd be the best thing to do in the long run. We need to get the shearing done, and plenty more besides. Harvest's coming up soon, too, and we can't afford to drag our feet getting that in.'

'It must've been hard to speak with her unnoticed. Why not get George to do it? She's his mother-in-law, after all.'

'I think you just answered you own question there,'

George laughed. 'Not married, are you Detective? You'll understand one day. No, Edith's never been particularly convinced of my capabilities. A big, handsome lad like this, on the other hand . . .' He fetched Les a square slap between broad shoulders. The shearer shook him off, muttering.

'It wasn't hard to meet in secret for the first few weeks,' he said. 'A farm's a busy place. Plenty of errands to run. Plenty of opportunities to slip away for a minute or two. It was only after old Fred copped it that I had to get creative. Police swarming all over the place. That's the only reason I went to see her at night. There was no funny business, I swear. Other than the business itself, I mean,' he added, stammering.

'You seem curiously emphatic on that point,' observed the friar.

'I just don't want you to get the wrong idea, that's all. I wasn't up to anything.'

'Aside from the fraud,' said Hartley.

'What? Oh.' Les looked chastened. 'That.'

'Yes — *that.*' The detective let out a heavy sigh. His head was whirring. 'Just to be clear, then: you wish me to understand that this whole arrangement was in place weeks before Fred was killed?' Nods and sounds of general assent from those assembled. He took out his notebook. 'On the afternoon of the murder itself, both you, Mr Bamonte, and you, Mr Thompson, stated that you were in the midst of shearing. Am I to understand that the two of you were similarly engaged?' This last remark was addressed to the Simons brothers.

'When was this?'

'Monday the tenth.'

155

The pair nodded as one. 'We were working here the whole day through,' said Edward. 'Didn't leave the shed from dawn till dusk.'

All four workers, it turned out, were willing to swear to this. Hartley sighed again. He had entered the shed with hopes of uncovering a hole in the shearers' alibi. It was now twice as strong.

'Alright. I'm going to head back to the house and speak with Mrs O'Donnell. I'll be wanting to follow this up again tomorrow.' He tucked away his notebook, beckoned to the friar and turned to take his leave.

'Hold on,' said Michael. 'What about us?'

Hartley hesitated. 'Well, we can't send you anywhere now. This is a criminal investigation. You'll have to stay on, at least until the killer is caught.' He turned to George and Les. 'I'd suggest you start the application for that permit as soon as possible. Now that Fred's gone, there should be no objection. I won't charge you for a breach of conditions this time,' he said. Then, seeing the relief spread across their faces, he went on. 'Provided, that is, that Michael and Edward are paid at the same rate as Les. Whether that means an increase in their rate or a reduction in his, I can't say. That'll be up to Edith. Regardless,' he shrugged. 'A low wage is better than no wage.'

He strolled out of the shed into the morning sun, leaving a sudden and heated negotiation in his wake.

20

In order to better monitor the nocturnal goings-on at Tolhurst, Hartley opted to leave his hotel room empty and spend another night in the study. With the friar in his hammock on the verandah and his own ear pressed against the door to the hallway, the detective felt that all major avenues for skulking and sneaking were under surveillance. When he retired to the study, not long after dinner, he did so with a feeling of great satisfaction, to which Mary's roast potatoes and his own sound decision-making were roughly equal contributors. At this point in the evening, his mood was at its zenith. As the night moved on, it was destined to exhibit, with several minor fluctuations, a decidedly downward trend.

Hartley prepared himself to sleep in the armchair, it being the closest item of furniture to the door, though how he'd managed to doze off in the thing just a few nights prior seemed unfathomable to him now. The distribution of stuffing within the bulging upholstery seemed to beggar all known principles of physics, managing somehow to be hard enough to bruise while giving way at the slightest touch. The chair had a broad, high back, but whether this had been designed with persecution in mind or had simply been allowed to fall into advanced disrepair was not immediately clear. Each attempt to shift position only seemed to bring Hartley's vertebrae into communion with a new set of creaking springs. To top it off, the chair's leather had been worn so smooth and frictionless that any attempt to recline resulted in a gradual forward drift, and the tantalising touch of unconsciousness was more than once dispelled by the start of a slow fall.

After an hour or two spent battling the armchair, Hartley transferred himself to the sofa. There was an immediate relief in being able to lie horizontally, and the detective could have sworn he heard a grateful creak or two from his spinal column. Unfortunately, though, the sofa was about a foot too short. The comfortable arrangement of torso and head left his legs with nowhere to go; he could curl them underneath him, but they soon cramped or went numb. He wondered how Fred — who had reportedly spent most of his nights in the study during his final months — had managed it. He squirmed again. The armrests were too high to hang his knees over and too hard to lean his back against while stretching his lower limbs out straight.

It was at roughly this point in the evening that Hartley's memories of the starched sheets and well-fluffed pillows at the Royal Hotel began to take on an almost amorous intensity. Shifting the furniture around as silently as possible, he freed the faded rug from under the side table and laid it out in the space behind the sofa. Next, he spread his coat out over the rug and fashioned a makeshift pillow by stuffing his socks into his shirtsleeves. Lowering his body onto this feeble bivouac, however, served only to spur his memories to wider passion. No longer did his thoughts restrict themselves to well-made beds; he found himself lusting after the meagre cots on which had slept as a police cadet, the semi-damp swag with which he had

158

once camped on a childhood trip up the coast.

Incredibly, after an indeterminate period spent squirming and shifting, Hartley found it — the one configuration in which none of the bony parts of his body were pressed against the unyielding jarrah. He froze, not daring to move a muscle. His legs were splayed out towards the windows in the northern wall, his arms crossed over his chest. All significant joints were, if not painless, then at the very least not actively worsening. He lay in this precarious perfection for a long time, breathing slowly. Eventually, even the pain of his magpie-ravaged ear dropped to a tolerable background level. It was impossible to say, in the timeless gloom of the small hours, how long that peace lasted, but the precise point of its end was all too easy to identify. Hartley was well and truly at the gates of sleep when the realisation hit him with caffeinating force that he was lying in exactly the spot where Fred O'Donnell had bled to death.

The detective leapt up, all thoughts of slumber banished, and began to pace around a room that felt suddenly too close, too tight. There was just enough light creeping through the windows to cast shapeless shadows that clustered and crept around the high corners of the room. His bare feet clung unpleasantly to the polished wood of the floor, as if the house itself was trying to catch at him. He found himself craving a cigarette, though he rarely smoked. Instead, he stumbled carelessly through the dark, catching a bare shin against the side table, making for the windows. He pushed aside the curtains, fumbled with the lock — these damned locks, still confounding him at every turn! — and pulled the window open. He gulped lungfuls of cool night air, bracing and clear.

A couple of spiders skittered away from the window frame, indignant at having their webs interfered with, but he paid them no heed, merely following one breath with the next until his knotted thoughts began to loosen. When his mind finally cleared, he noticed movement outside. An indistinct shape emerged from around the corner of the verandah.

'Ill met by moonlight, proud Detective,' whispered the friar, grinning. 'Couldn't sleep?'

Hartley shook his head. 'What are you doing up at this hour?'

'I couldn't help but hear you redecorating.' The friar looked past him through the window. 'You certainly have an eye for arrangement. Hold on, though.' A note of curiosity crept into his voice. 'Have you got a light in there?'

'Give me a minute.' Hartley fumbled in the gloom for his matches, lighting the hurricane lamp Mary had lent him. He hoisted it high and stepped back as the friar clambered into the room. The little man made his way over to the jerry-built nest upon which Hartley had vainly sought sleep, then back to the sofa.

'The rug was here, wasn't it?' he said, gesturing to a patch of bare floor that swam in the flickering lamplight. 'I didn't think to look under it earlier.'

'If you're looking for a trapdoor or the like, I'll save you the trouble,' said Hartley. 'The local officers have been over it again and again. One of the poor chaps drew the short straw and had to crawl beneath the house to check it from below, too. Flushed a dugite out — can still hear him yelp as the thing slithered over his fingers — but the boards were airtight. Nothing went in or out that way.'

'Quite right,' the friar murmured. 'I don't suppose

160

he noticed these scratches, though.'

Hartley squinted. 'What's that?' He handed the lamp over and dropped to his knees, following the friar's outstretched finger. It took him a few moments to see what the mendicant had managed to glimpse from outside the window: a few broad gashes in the polished hardwood, obvious only from a certain angle. 'Someone's been careless when moving the furniture. It can't have been me, though,' he added, hastily on the defensive. 'I just nudged the sofa out of the way over here. Besides, it looks as though someone's tried to fix it up a bit. I think they may even have sanded it back.'

'I daresay you're right. And over here —' The friar froze, looking towards the door. Hartley had heard it, too: the slip and pad of stockinged feet in the hall. Rising as silently as he could, he began to pick his way through the inconstant shadows. He must not have been quiet enough, though, for he'd only made it halfway to the door when the footsteps came to a sudden stop and tapped out a hasty retreat. Scrabbling for the handle, Hartley was just in time to watch darkness retake the passageway as the sliver of light seeping beneath Winnie's bedroom door was snuffed out.

'It doesn't appear as if anyone's sleeping tonight,' he observed, returning to join the friar. 'At this rate, I'll have the whole house in here before morning.'

'They'd better be quick about it.' The friar nodded at the windows, beyond which the wide sky had begun to silver. 'The sun isn't far away.'

Hartley yawned. 'Well, if I get moving soon, I may be able to beat the shearers to breakfast. If nothing else, it'll give me a chance to shake my indolent urban reputation.'

161

He lowered himself into the armchair as the friar spread out on the sofa. Within minutes, both men were snoring. They slept through breakfast, neither of them stirring until just after nine o'clock, when the postman arrived with Fred O'Donnell's will.

21

There were three copies of Fred's will. Only the most recent held any legal relevance, but Hartley had requested all available documentation, regardless of currency. The O'Donnell family and their associates had gathered in the dining room, curiosity trumping any irritation at being kept from their duties. The fact that Fred had made a will at all was a surprise to anyone who knew him — with the probable exception, Hartley supposed, of his murderer — and the not insignificant value of the deceased man's estate only added to the intrigue. So palpable was the atmosphere of expectation that the detective, not usually prone to a fear of speaking in public, found himself afflicted with an uncommonly dry throat. In attempting to remedy this ailment, he availed himself of several glasses of water, multiple helpings of lemon juice with honey and the better part of a pot of tea, with the result that he was forced to excuse himself and dash out to the lavatory before having even removed the will from its envelope. At length, Hartley made the difficult decision to excuse himself from the anxiety of a speaking role, allowing the friar to read the documents aloud. This had the added benefit of freeing the detective to sit back in his chair and concentrate, scanning the faces of those assembled for any telltale reactions.

The chair in question was in the corner, looking out from beside the door to the kitchen. Edith O'Donnell had, quite naturally, taken her place at the head of the table, a daughter at each hand. Behind Mary stood George, kneading his wife's shoulders, nodding in sympathy as she lamented the continuing absence of her eyeglasses. Les leant against the opposite wall with the Simons siblings, who looked on with rapt attention despite their relatively recent and rather tenuous connection to the deceased. On the other side of the table, Winnie and Hazel sat with their heads together, whispering. The two youngest members of the family periodically appeared and disappeared in the course of some arcane game which, by a coincidence of cosmic scale, seemed to require them to run across the verandah at intervals, passing again and again the one room they had been explicitly forbidden from entering.

The friar pushed back his chair and stood. 'We have all gathered this morning in order that the wishes of Fred O'Donnell may be heard and, if possible, carried out.'

'Get on with it,' snapped Mary. 'Let's hear this so-called will.' Others voiced their agreement. Much of the preliminary chatter had centred on Fred's hatred of legal practitioners, which appeared to have transcended his usual background level of misanthropy and, apparently, spread to other members of the family. With a wounded air, the friar glanced at the paper in his hands.

'I have a feeling, Mrs Bamonte, that your misgivings may not survive the revelations contained herein.' He paused to clear his throat. '*To my daughter Mary and her husband Gino, I leave the lands, structures and assets of the Tolhurst farmstead, the deeds to which are enclosed, with the wish that young Charles be inducted into the management and custodianship of the property*

164

upon reaching an appropriate age.'

Hartley sat forward, elbows on the table, watching the brief sparks of emotion flicker over the family's faces. Surprise, he thought, from Mary and George, but undeniable satisfaction, too. Edith was inscrutable, stony as ever, while Winnie's face betrayed only impatience.

'From my accounts with the Bank of Australasia, an allowance of five hundred pounds each will be made available to my grandchildren, Charles and Cordelia, to be administered by their respective parents. The remainder of my assets, physical and financial, I wish to be distributed equally between my wife, Edith, and my daughter, Winifred.'

The faces of those referred to were more carefully controlled, now, with the exception of the two children, whose heads had popped into view again at the sound of their own names. Edith turned to shoo them away.

'Is there anything else?' asked Hazel, a poorly concealed catch in her voice. Hartley felt a tug of sympathy as he realised that she was the only member of the O'Donnell family not to have been named. He turned, as one with the rest of the room, to look at the friar. The little man glanced back at the paper.

'I'm sorry,' he said. 'The rest is copperplate, more or less. Just the standard legal formalities.' He handed the will to Hazel, inviting her to check for herself. Winnie laid an arm over her sister-in-law's shoulders, leaning in to whisper what Hartley had to assume were words of comfort.

'If that's the bulk of it,' said George, from across the table, 'then what's all this about?' He gestured to the sheaf of papers that still sat in front of the friar.

'I'm glad you asked,' the friar brightened. 'Perhaps

165

my associate would care to do the honours.'

Hartley was glad of the invitation, as he'd just been wrestling with the question of how best to usurp the speaker's role. The next revelation, he felt, would benefit from the authoritative backing of a uniform. With a quiet nod to the friar, he took up the papers and climbed to his feet.

'These,' he said, allowing his gaze to rest in turn upon each O'Donnell, 'are the others.'

'Others?' Mary looked up sharply. 'How d'you mean, others?'

'The testament you've just heard was only the most recent in a series of three documents that your father had prepared. It is, in fact, barely a month old.' He waited for the implications to sink in.

'He knew, then,' said Hazel. 'All the time that he was brushing off our concerns about the cloaked man, he knew to expect the worst.'

'And yet he continued to accuse us all of hysterical overreaction,' muttered Winnie, her voice sour. 'How very like him.'

Hartley returned himself to the collective attention by means of a curt little cough. 'It does seem as though Mr O'Donnell was apprehensive about the attempts on his life. The solicitor's correspondence bears that out.' He tapped the paper. 'An interesting development, certainly, but I'm more interested in the changes he saw fit to make in the face of his impending death.' He extracted a particular sheet of paper from amongst its compatriots. 'This is an earlier will, compiled in February 1923 and only rendered obsolete by the creation of its successor, whose contents you have just heard.'

'What'd he change?' asked George, with possibly

166

too keen an interest.

'As regards you and your wife, Mr Bamonte, not much has changed. Under the terms of the earlier will, you and Mary would still have inherited the farm.' He subjected the couple to a searching stare before continuing. 'The division of the other assets, though, is a different matter. It's clear that Mr O'Donnell still hoped to allocate his estate evenly to both his wife and younger daughter, but no specific monetary allowance is mentioned for the grandchildren. Instead,' he looked up slowly from the document in his hands, 'a considerable sum is to be set aside each year for use by another person. The name given here is Elizabeth O'Donnell.'

Hartley wasn't sure exactly what sort of reaction he'd been hoping for, but his audience left him spoilt for choice. Their faces ran the emotional gamut, from Les Thompson's straightforward shock to Edith's thin-lipped fury, with confusion of every calibre in between. Winnie, though, was the only one who seemed willing or able to put her surprise into words.

'Aunt Elizabeth?' she cried. 'But she's been dead for decades!'

The detective reached for his notebook. 'You knew her, then?'

'Only in the abstract. Elizabeth was my father's sister. They came out together on the steamer to Sydney after their parents passed away. She died shortly after, leaving him alone in the world — or so he told us. Clearly, there's more to the story.' So saying, she turned to train a look on her mother. Hartley and the rest of the room followed suit.

'I'm afraid I'm unable to tell you much of any interest,' Edith said. 'I, too, was under the impression that dear Beth — as Fred called her — had passed away. He rarely spoke of her. He avoided the topic as rigidly as he did anything else that had a danger of invoking sentiment or emotion.'

'Now, that's not quite fair, Mummy,' interjected Winnie. 'Anger is an emotion. So is scorn.'

Edith ignored her. 'When one is married for long enough, though, one becomes intimately acquainted with the moods of one's partner. Even a partner as po-faced and irascible as Fred will exhibit changes in temperament, if one knows what to look for.' She paused, possibly uncomfortable sharing such intimate intelligence. Seeing that all eyes were still trained squarely upon her, she continued. 'It was not uncommon, for instance, to find Fred contemplating his sister's portrait when faced with a difficult decision or some particularly taxing piece of work.'

'Of course!' Winnie leapt up. 'The portrait!' She vanished from the room and returned bearing the frame that had sat upon the mantel in Fred's study. Hartley accepted the picture, sharing a covert look of culpability with the friar, and set it on the table. It seemed inconceivable now, in a room illuminated by daylight, that they had ever assumed the subject of the sketch to be young Delia. While the likeness was still unmistakable — uncanny, even — the paper upon which it had been sketched was yellowing, the edges beginning to crack. Dating the image to before the turn of the century did not require an art historian.

'She looks an awful lot like our Cordelia, doesn't she?' said Edith.

'I suppose there is a resemblance,' Hartley dissembled.

'That picture would've been done a year or two after Fred and Beth were sent out to Australia. The exact date should be on the back.'

The detective turned the frame over. 'The twenty-ninth of May, eighteen eighty-one,' he said, reddening. 'Were you also under the impression that Elizabeth had passed away at around this time?'

Edith appeared thoughtful. 'Fred never gave a specific year. He just said that they'd grown up together, being shuffled around between orphanages and distant relatives. At some point, one of their mother's cousins offered to take Beth — she lived here in Australia and had other girls, apparently. Fred was in his teens by then, old enough to work, so he was sent elsewhere.' Edith paused again. 'Come to think of it, he only ever really referred to her as 'gone'. I assumed that she'd passed away, but it seems as though I may have been mistaken.'

'Or misled,' said the friar. 'It's possible that Fred preferred to think of his sister as beyond reach or redemption. A schism between siblings can often bring out the worst in us. The closer to one's heart a person is, the more damage they are capable of dealing.'

'But he provided for her in his will,' Mary pointed out. 'There must have been some feeling of responsibility there, if not love.'

Hartley nodded. 'That's true enough. All we can say with any sort of certainty is that Fred thought Elizabeth to be alive five years ago, when he created the second version of his will. Something changed prior to the drafting of his latest will, however. It's possible, then, that she had been alive all along, only predeceasing her brother by a year or two.'

'She may still be alive,' said Winnie, sounding thrilled at the possibility. 'My father was a capricious old goat. He could simply have decided that his baby sister was finally old enough to look after herself.'

'Fred was the older sibling, then?'

'Yes, by a few years,' said Edith. 'Fred was eight when his mother died giving birth to Beth. Neither had a particularly happy childhood, even before being transported. The family lived in Birmingham, cramped all together in one room of a back-to-back house. Fred's father was a rag-and-bone man, if I remember correctly. Poor as dirt, and none too hardy. He managed only a couple of years after his wife's death before succumbing to some disease or other and leaving the children to be bundled off to the colonies.'

There was a contemplative silence.

'Fred must have been proud of this place,' said Hartley. 'After such rough beginnings, to have a large estate, a home and a family — it must have seemed almost inconceivable.'

'He was grateful,' Edith nodded. 'In his own way.'

'Loath though he was to let us know it,' muttered Winnie.

Hartley hastened to pre-empt another escalation. 'Given what we've discussed today, I think the wisest course of action is for my associate and I to seek out news of Elizabeth O'Donnell. That alteration to the will wasn't done lightly. Fred travelled all the way to Perth to see it done. There's every chance that Beth holds the key to understanding her brother's murder.'

Edith raised a dark eyebrow. 'I thought you knew who was responsible.' Hartley turned, deftly deflecting the barbed remark towards the friar.

'I did,' breezed the friar, 'and still do. The time for that particular revelation, if you recall, is still two days distant.' He waved a hand, as if to bat away a pesky insect. 'Supporting allegations with proof, though, is rather a central tenet of the justice system, as I understand it. Bothersome, but necessary. The 'who' is nothing without the 'how' and 'when'. Personally, though, I must admit to a particular predilection for the 'why'.'

'If we leave now,' said Hartley, 'we'll make it to Perth by nightfall.'

'Hold on.' As one, the group looked up. It was Les Thompson who had spoken. 'What about the other will? You said there were three.'

'What's it got to do with you?' asked Mary. 'Would've been done long before you came on the scene.'

The shearer shrugged, looking as though he regretted drawing attention to himself. 'I dunno. Got me interested now. Can't expect me to stand around and listen to all this stuff all day without wanting to know the whole story. There were three wills, and we've only heard about two of 'em.'

With even the Simons siblings nodding their agreement, Hartley had to concede this point. He reached for the remaining document.

'It looks as though Fred took his cues from primogeniture on this one,' he said, shooting a sympathetic glance in Hazel's direction. 'It's from before the war. *To my son, Jack, I leave the lands, structures and assets of the Tolhurst farmstead, with the understanding that it be kept in the O'Donnell family for his sons and future generations.*' He coughed. 'The finances are split equally between Edith, Mary and Winnie. The allowance for Elizabeth remains.'

There were whispers from all corners of the room.

'At the very least,' Hartley went on, 'it tells us that the impulse to provide for his sister was not a fleeting one. She remained a part of Fred's life for much longer than he chose to let on.' He looked to the friar. 'The sooner we track her down, the better.'

22

It was almost five o'clock by the time they reached Perth. Hartley squinted into the sinking sun as he manoeuvred his vehicle on to the Causeway bridge. Below, the Swan River spread itself out in one of its milder moods, knee-deep and spotted with mud-flats around the low shore of Heirisson Island. It had been a long drive, much of it on 'unimproved' roads of pressed dirt, and the detective's hands were weary on the wheel. A shower would have gone a great way towards lifting his spirits — a fresh uniform would have been even better — but the day's work was not yet done.

'We'd better head straight over,' he said. 'With any luck, the office'll still be open.'

Having returned to terra firma, the car now carried them down streets lined with edifices of every conceivable size and description.

'No time for a spot of sightseeing?' asked the friar, bobbing his head to better see through the window.

'Absolutely not.' Fatigue hardened Hartley's voice. 'There's a chance we could get to the bottom of the whole thing tonight. I want it finished with, as soon as possible.'

'Some things are better not to rush. *Roma uno die aedificata* non est — and nor, I'm sure, was Perth.'

Hartley winced. He'd worked hard to bury the memories of his school-day Latin lectures and having them disinterred did nothing to lighten his mood.

'Tell it to the man who pledged to have this case con-
cluded by Friday,' he growled.

'A deadline which remains eminently achievable,'
the friar said. 'Have faith in your abilities.'

'Easy enough for you to say. You've made a career
out of faith.' Hartley accelerated to pass a clanging
tram in brick-red livery. He sighed. 'Look. We're
crossing Barrack Street now. If you make a right turn
here, it's only a couple of hundred yards to CID headquarters. The men within those walls are watching my
every move, but not with faith. Not with pride or hope
or anything else you might hear of in a hymn. They're
laughing at me. Always have done, since long before
I was made a detective.' A sharp twinge in the lower
back alerted him to the fact that he'd been hunching
lower in his seat, as if to avoid being spotted by one
of his professional rivals. 'That's how I came to be
assigned to this case in the first place. My commander
thought the whole business was a hoax. A farce of a
case for a farce of an officer.'

Hartley tightened his grip on the wheel. He could
feel the friar's cool eyes on him.

'I know one or two would-be wits who've worked
for years to cultivate such a reputation,' the little
man said. 'How did you manage to become so widely
regarded as a droll?'

'Why don't they take me seriously, you mean?'
Hartley shrugged. 'They say I'm too young, or too
earnest. They say I was only promoted because of my
father's status with the unions.' He paused to nego-
tiate an intersection. 'I suppose that, at an essential
level, they just don't think I have the capacity to bring
a murderer to justice.'

'Well?' the friar prompted. His look was intent,

174

expectant.

'Well, what?'

'Are they wrong?'

'How do you mean?'

'Are you fundamentally incapable of bringing a murderer to justice?'

Hartley flushed hot. 'Of course not,' he said shortly.

With a self-satisfied smile, the friar sat back. 'There's your faith, then. Not so hard to find after all.'

The detective opened his mouth, floundered and shut it again, lost for a reply. He drove the next mile or so in silence, finally bringing the vehicle to a shuddering halt outside a sandstone-fronted, two-storey building on the western stretch of Hay Street. Despite his professed haste, Hartley let a few precious moments pass before climbing out of the vehicle. The click of the cooling engine filled the silence as he looked over at the friar.

'Thank you,' he said.

★ ★ ★

Hartley couldn't say quite what he'd been expecting from Fred O'Donnell's solicitor — a Dickensian dourness, perhaps, a paucity of spirit, a smallness of character. The very antithesis, as it transpired, of Richard Gabrels.

'Call me Richie,' the man bellowed, ushering his guests in with a hearty pink hand clapped to the back of each. 'I absolutely insist upon it! Take a seat. Anywhere will do. You'll have something to drink, I hope? Business hours are behind us, after all. Whisky? Gin? Port? I have a decent sherry or two . . .'

The naming of liquors proceeded for some minutes,

175

Gabrels gesticulating at the huge variety of bottles (many of them nearing depletion) with which his sideboard was forested. After a token show of resistance, Hartley allowed a large tumbler of whisky and soda to be pressed upon him. The mendicant's request for a cup of black tea did not proceed quite as smoothly, Gabrels apparently having had some traumatic run-ins with the Order of Rechabites in the past, but once it was made clear that the friar was not operating as an agent of any known temperance movement, a kettle was found and filled. Soon enough, all three men were settled upon large, comfortable chairs, chosen beverages in hand and the noise of the city muffled away behind well-covered walls. Hartley let the thoughts ebb from his mind, lost in a welcome, companionable silence. Richard Gabrels was an expansive man, well over six feet in height and nearly half that across. He was furnished as richly as his room, a silk waistcoat stretched tight over his broad chest and comfortable belly and a pair of pince-nez balanced on a large, reddened nose.

'A toast! To poor old Freddie.' The solicitor's booming voice brought Hartley back to the matter at hand. He was struck once more by the unlikely pairing of the austere O'Donnell and the *bon vivant* currently draining his second glass of neat spirits.

'Did you know Mr O'Donnell well?' asked Hartley.

'As well as anyone, I imagine.' Gabrels topped up his tumbler. 'Which is to say, unfortunately, not that well at all. Never was much for speaking about himself.'

'You must've known him a good while, though. You prepared the earliest version of the will more than a decade prior to Fred's death.'

'Good lord, has it really been that long?' The solicitor shook his head. 'Swift fly the years, and all that, especially when one is enjoying oneself, which I usually endeavour to do. As a consequence, much of my life is rather a blur.' He laughed. 'Do you know, I honestly can't remember when I first met dear Freddie. The old boy always hated to be called that,' he admitted, as an aside, 'but there's precious little he can do about it now! I used to see him a couple of times a year, I'd say. A week or so before Christmas, then again around May.'

'Why May?'

For the first time, the lawyer seemed disinclined to speak. He reached for a cigar, rolling it thoughtfully between thumb and forefinger as silent seconds drifted by. Hartley was on the verge of pressing his query when he felt the friar's hand on his arm.

'Why would any pair of red-blooded modern gentlemen schedule a meeting in May?' posed the friar, rhetorically. 'Surely, only one reasonable answer springs to mind: to venerate Saint Rita of Cascia, patroness of impossible causes and marriage difficulties. Her feast day is the twenty-second, as I recall.'

Gabrels stared at the mendicant. His look of incomprehension slipped into a slow smile. 'Not bad!' he chuckled, resetting his pince-nez. 'I must admit, I wasn't expecting humour from a teetotaller. More fool me.'

The friar acknowledged this capitulation with a modest nod. 'Humour is but one of the services I am able to provide. I have also — with the assistance of my learned friend the Detective Constable, here — been swotting up on my induction, with promising results. I feel quite confident in postulating, for instance, that

177

Elizabeth O'Donnell was born in May.'

Perhaps, had Richie Gabrels trained as a barrister, blustering and preening each day before magistrates and the good people of the jury, he would have developed the careful, controlled expression of the practised liar. As the bulk of his legal work involved the drafting of documents, however — with any attendant deception carried out on a more bureaucratic level — it was the work of but a moment to read the shock writ large upon his face.

'How did you know that?'

Hartley, too, was eager to understand how the friar had arrived at his conclusion, though he had no desire to make his ignorance known to either of those present.

'It's really rather simple,' the friar said, sitting forward in his chair. 'Firstly, there is the matter of Fred O'Donnell's character. He has been described to us on several occasions as a man who sees *the done thing* — the expected course of action, if you will — as more important than any fleeting matters of personal feeling. Next,' he went on, after receiving a nod of comprehension from each of his attendees, 'there is the timing of his summer visits to Perth: just prior to Christmas. Any business he had to undertake with banks or other professionals would be better scheduled at almost any other time of year, as offices are liable to be closed or ill-attended over the festive period. After all, what is expected of a man at Christmas?' He didn't wait for an answer. 'To spend time with family and to give to the wretched. Fred, I believe, was attempting to satisfy both of these expectations at once. The only member of his family not resident at Tolhurst was his sister, Beth, so it follows that she was the one he was visiting in Perth. You have indicated, Mr Gabrels, that Fred also made annual trips to the city in May. On what other occasion is one expected to make some gesture of affection towards a relative?'

This time, he seemed willing to wait for a response. It was Gabrels who obliged.

'On one's birthday.' He shook his head, unable to conceal a smile. 'Well done, old chap. I have to hand it to you — bloody good work.'

Hartley murmured in agreement, but his attention had snagged on a particular word of the friar's monologue.

'Why 'wretched'?' he asked. The others turned to look at him. 'You said that Fred met with his sister before Christmas to fulfil a familial obligation, but also to give to the wretched. What was wretched about Beth?'

'I was hoping that you could enlighten us on that point, Mr Gabrels,' said the friar. 'The rest of the O'Donnell family had arrived at the idea that good old Aunt Beth had departed this mortal coil or had somehow lost contact with the flock. Fred did nothing to disabuse them of this notion. I think we can assume, in fact, that he actively encouraged it. What, then, was his motivation for doing so?'

Richie Gabrels was the question's clear target. He sat back with a sigh, swirling the dregs at the bottom of his glass.

'I don't know,' he said. 'Not officially.'

'But you have an idea,' prompted Hartley.

The solicitor hesitated, clicking his tongue. 'Yes,' he said, finally. 'Preparing and updating the last will and testament was not the only thing for which Freddie engaged my services. Some legal formality would pop

179

up from time to time relating to the farm, of course, but the lion's share of the work was in creating and managing accounts for the care and maintenance of Elizabeth O'Donnell.'

'What sort of care?'

'Miss O'Donnell was — ah — accommodated at various institutions,' said Gabrels, with what would have been a delicate cough had he been the size of a normal man. The following pause showed every sign of being indefinite until Hartley truncated it with a firm look. 'Her initial residence,' the solicitor went on, begrudgingly, 'was the Fremantle Lunatic Asylum. She was later moved to the Claremont Hospital for the Insane, and finally the Wooroloo Sanatorium.'

'And now?'

Gabrels gave a sad smile. 'She remains resident at Wooroloo, though no longer above ground, I'm afraid. Freddie saw to her burial in the adjoining cemetery on the twenty-ninth of June. Tuberculosis.'

'I'm sorry to hear that,' said Hartley.

'To tell the truth, I never knew her,' the solicitor said. 'Freddie was awfully keen to keep his legal affairs distant from those they affected. Probably for the best, though. You might not know it to look at me, but I'm a bleeding heart. Tend to go straight to pieces in the presence of the sorely afflicted.'

'What was the precise nature of Beth's affliction?'

'I believe it was largely the TB that necessitated the move to the sanatorium. Prior to that, though,' he sighed. 'I couldn't honestly tell you. Freddie wasn't forthcoming on the details, and I didn't like to pry. Aside from the doctors — and probably Beth herself, though it's hard to know how lucid she was — I'd say Freddie was the only one to know the whole story.'

180

'You must have corresponded with someone at the hospital, though,' said Hartley, 'if only on fiscal matters.'

Gabrels conceded this point. After searching through a number of drawers, he located the relevant file, copying the particulars onto an index card. He wrote in long, careful strokes, finishing each word with an ostentatious flourish, then handed the card to Hartley, who examined the lettering before pocketing it. A thought struck him as he did so.

'I don't suppose the phrase *with this, a little of what was wrong is now put right* means anything to you?'

He watched the lawyer hawkishly, but no flicker of recognition crossed the broad face.

'I'm not one for platitudes, as a rule. There's a dreary air of optimism to it, which I feel would require another bottle to properly appreciate. Or, come to think of it, a cigar.' He reached for a box on the sideboard. 'These were actually a gift from old Freddie, years ago. He gave them up for a long while but was well and truly back into the habit of late. Making up for lost time, I suppose.'

Hartley dismissed the cheroots with a distracted gesture. 'When was it that you last saw Fred?'

'I was blessed with several visits this year,' said Gabrels, counting them off on large, ruddy fingers. 'He dropped by in May, as usual, after visiting Beth on her birthday. He was back at the end of June to oversee her burial and the attendant paperwork, then again in August to redraft his will.' He checked a leather-bound agenda. 'That was the last time I saw him. The thirteenth.'

'How was he?'

'Well, he didn't seem awfully happy, though that's

181

not saying much. Freddie was hardly prone to gales of laughter at the best of times, as I'm sure you've already ascertained.' Gabrels sighed. 'To be honest, though, I think his sister's death was a deeper blow than he let on. They were orphans, you know. Sailed out from old Blighty together, just the two of them. I imagine it must've been hard for him, seeing that final link to his past slip away.' The solicitor stared off into the middle distance, then shook himself. 'These are just my impressions, you understand,' he said, glancing around the room as if he expected the deceased to burst in and accuse him of slander. 'He didn't actually say anything to that effect — nothing specific, at any rate — but there was something in the way he held himself. Something off, at an architectural level.'

Hartley raised an eyebrow at this image but noted it down regardless. 'The rest of the O'Donnell family must not have been quite as perceptive,' he said. 'None of them mentioned any particular expression of sorrow or loss on Fred's part.'

'They wouldn't have known to look for it, though, would they? Freddie kept them all in the dark about Beth.'

'True enough, I suppose,' conceded Hartley. 'Did Fred ever tell you why he considered such an omission necessary?'

'Not explicitly, no. I would imagine it was simply shame — her affliction, you know. Now that I think of it, though, he did mention something. It would've been a good few years ago. Someone in the family had been asking questions about Beth, wondering what became of her. Mrs O'Donnell, if I recall correctly.'

'Which one?'

The solicitor cocked his head to the side, doglike.

'Which Mrs O'Donnell?' he asked, appearing genuinely puzzled. 'To my knowledge, Edith is the only Mrs O'Donnell. Mary would properly be Mrs Bamonte, now, and young Winifred is still a Miss, as I understand it — unless some lucky young fellow has swept in and effected some exceptionally swift courting.'

Hartley could feel the friar's eyes on him, and hoped the heat in his cheeks was not indicative of a visible flush. He cleared his throat. 'I was actually referring to Fred's daughter-in-law, Hazel. Jack's widow.'

'Ah!' Gabrels leant forward, eyes sparkling like a village gossip. 'I think you'll find her to be Miss Allen.'

The detective took a short while to digest this.

'She and Jack were never married, then?' he said.

'Not in the official sense, no. Apparently there was some sort of ceremony amongst the stage folk over east. A few handfuls of petals, a bottle of something dire and dancing till dawn, I imagine — all very enjoyable, but nothing in the way of paperwork.'

'Strange. I wonder why young Hazel felt the need to conceal it.'

'I doubt she thinks of it as a deception,' Gabrels said. 'Things are different out on the farm, you know — it's all that horrid rising with the sun and turning with the seasons that does it — and the O'Donnells have been practically alone down there for years. They've developed their own way of looking at the world. I always had the devil of a time explaining the letter of the law to Fred. He preferred to see it as something more in the nature of a recommendation or a gentle suggestion. A simpler life, in many ways.' He stretched, reaching again for the decanter. 'But not for me, I think. I've grown accustomed to the creature comforts of life in the metropolis.' He shook the last few drops into his glass. 'Speaking of which, I daresay it's almost time to make the great migration down to the pub. You'll both join me, I hope?'

Hartley pushed back his chair and stood.

'Very kind of you, but we have work to do yet. Wooroloo isn't much more than an hour away by motor, I believe — with any luck, we'll make it out to the sanatorium before dark.'

The friar made a small noise which, while neither definitively a cough nor a sniff, was nonetheless unmistakable in its indication of disappointment. Hartley turned and cocked an eyebrow.

'In my experience,' the little man ventured, 'facilities delivering constant care of the sort seen in a sanatorium are wont to have the bulk of the administrative work completed by day's end, thus allowing their senior staff to disappear from the venue and partake of the creature comforts so enthusiastically indicated by Mr Gabrels.'

'A schedule which does not apply to a detective,' Hartley pointed out. 'Nor a priest, a vagrant or any combination of the above.' Seeing the tiredness in the friar's face, he softened. 'I do take your point, though. It's likely there'll be no-one around this evening to answer our questions, and it's true we've already done a good deal today.'

'Why not bunk down at that new hotel in Kalamunda?' offered Gabrels, in an easy manner reflective of long years spent interfering in the affairs of others. 'Supposed to be quite good. Only been open a few months. You could be there in under an hour, put your feet up by the fire and enjoy a decent meal. Then you'll be nice and fresh come morning, and already halfway out to the sanatorium.'

'You make a convincing argument,' said Hartley.

The solicitor grinned. 'Something of a prerequisite in my line of work.'

Hartley looked to the friar, receiving an enthusiastic nod.

'I suppose that's settled, then,' he said. 'We head for the hills.'

23

The brand-new Kalamunda Hotel was located so near to the old Kalamunda Hotel as to share a wall. Whether this should be viewed as a testament to the suitability of the site for lodgings or a sad indictment of the local imagination was a topic of much debate on the journey east from Perth. As the hills drew closer, the conversation began to ebb. This was largely a function of engine noise — the Australian Six complaining as it struggled up the slopes of the Darling Scarp in second gear — but it would be hard to argue that the scenery played no part. The friar twisted in his seat to watch the land slip away below, the city and its nascent suburbs spread out across the coastal plain as sunset's last blush set the wide sky aflame. Streets and railways were picked out in pinpricks of distant light, the familiar orange warmth of gas lamps still standing strong amidst the incandescent ranks of electric interlopers. The roads into the hills were nearly empty at this hour, and Hartley allowed himself to snatch a few glances, too, sating himself with mirrorfuls of the vista and one or two hurried over-the-shoulder looks before the car crested the rise and slipped into the darkness of the jarrah forest. The unnerving feeling that the world had winked out of existence did not fully abate until the detective was warmly ensconced in an armchair by the fire in the dining room of the Kalamunda Hotel. Finally, with naught but gravy left on his plate and a froth-capped pint of stout at his side, Hartley found himself — well, if not quite at ease, then certainly somewhere close by.

'Comfortable, isn't it?' said the friar.

The remark was innocuous enough, and it can only have been coincidence that it came precisely as Hartley's shirtsleeve caught on a rough whorl in the wood of what had, up until then, appeared to be a perfectly smooth dining table. The detective swore, watching his beer leap over the rim of his glass to spatter his trousers.

'Quite,' he grimaced, dabbing at his thighs with a handkerchief. He looked furtively about the room to see if anyone else had witnessed the gaffe, but his few fellow guests were too preoccupied with their food to notice. The only pair of eyes on him belonged to the friar.

'The thought occurs,' said the holy man, 'that we don't actually have a good reason to be here.'

Hartley said nothing, still preoccupied with his spill.

'We're an hour closer to Wooroloo, that much is true, but we might just as easily have saved ourselves the trouble, gone to bed in the city and risen an hour earlier in the morning.'

'What are you driving at?' huffed the detective, who knew quite well what his companion was driving at but had no wish to make things easier for him.

'It seems as though you were looking for a pretence under which to flee Perth,' the friar said, softly. 'The city made you uncomfortable.'

'I made no secret of that. I told you about the antipathy of my colleagues in the Department. Crossing paths with one of them when I'm supposed to be on assignment in the wheatbelt would give rise to all sorts of awkward questions.'

'Gambling does not greatly figure amongst the numerous vices in which I have indulged over the years,' said the friar, 'but I'd wager the odds of encountering another officer of the law in your own home are small, if not vanishingly so.' His eyes were unwavering. 'You do live in Perth, do you not, Detective?'

'You know very well I do. In Nedlands, not far from the river.'

'With family?'

Hartley sighed. 'I know what you're insinuating, and I hope you won't take it as an insult to your faculties when I say that you've missed the mark on this one.'

'Oh?'

'You're imagining my father — a rough man, hardened by years on the picket line — berating his only son for his inability to solve even the most provincial crime.' Reading no disagreement on the friar's face, Hartley went on. 'That picture couldn't be further from truth. My father is a warm, loving fellow, big but softly spoken. He's never offered me anything but unconditional encouragement. In fact, if I were sitting across the table from him now, he'd be telling me that none of this is my fault. He'd say that this case is clearly impossible and that I've done all that could be expected of me, especially given the fact that it's my first.'

'And that isn't what you want to hear.'

Hartley followed the pointed gaze down to his glass and realised that he was gripping it with both hands. 'It's certainly not what I need to hear,' the detective said. 'I don't need to be comforted. I need to find a solution. I need to see this case finished and put behind me.' He placed the beer back on the table and folded his hands together.

'And what happens when you've solved it?'

'I don't know. Move on to the next one, I suppose.'

The friar smiled off into the middle distance, appearing to be lost in thought. Then he said: 'Do you know the first detective story I remember reading?'

Hartley sighed. 'Conan Doyle again, was it?' he guessed idly.

The friar shook his head. 'The tale I have in mind pre-empted the good Dr Doyle by — ' he feigned a calculation — 'oh, a couple of millennia, at the least. You may even have come across it yourself, heathen-ish though your upbringing was. You studied the scriptures at school, surely?'

'I did,' admitted Hartley, 'though I managed to avoid retaining much. We had a dreary old master. An erstwhile deacon, if I recall correctly. Used to tug at his earlobes whenever he got angry.'

'Church of England?' The friar received a nod. 'Ah. Then you were probably spared this story. My papist brethren retain it, but Protestants tend to number it amongst the Apocrypha, or the deuterocanonical works. While not attested in the original Hebrew or Aramaic, it has its origins in the Greek Septuagint.'

Hartley smiled blankly through the jargon, guess-ing — quite rightly, as it transpired — that none of these details would be particularly pertinent to the friar's ultimate point.

'The story regards Daniel, he of the lion's den and the writing upon the wall.'

Hartley indicated that he knew the biblical figure in question, albeit not with any particular intimacy.

'Daniel was a young Jewish man who had been

taken to Babylon as a prisoner of Nebuchadnezzar. By the time of this particular story, though, he was serving in the court of Cyrus the Persian, who —' The friar must have seen that he was in danger of losing his audience, as he skipped the rest of the pre-amble. 'Daniel and King Cyrus were arguing about Bel, an idol worshipped in the palace. The king was of the firm opinion that the idol was a living god, as evidenced by the way the libations and sacrificial lambs laid out before it each night had been con-sumed come morning. Daniel, being a loyal devotee of the God of Israel — our old friend Yahweh, or Jeho-vah — was determined to prove that the idol was a thing of earth and bronze, nothing more. He advised the king to let the priests of Bel leave their sacrifices and offerings in the altar room, as usual, then lock and seal the door after leaving for the night. If the seal was undisturbed the following day and the food and wine had disappeared, Daniel would concede the divinity of Bel. A simple enough wager, wouldn't you agree?'

While not altogether delighted to be back on the topic of locked rooms, Hartley made a noise of assent, motioning for the friar to continue.

'The next morning, the sealed room was opened, and the priests were triumphant. The food and wine had all disappeared, proving that their beloved Bel was indeed a living god, not to mention a voracious one. When they turned to King Cyrus, though, hop-ing to finally discredit the interloper Daniel — a lowly foreigner and a heretic, barely better than a slave — they read no joy on their sovereign's face. For, you see, the king knew something that the priests didn't.' The friar's eyes danced in the dim light of the dining room as he leant forward with a confidential air. 'The previous night, after dismissing the priests, Daniel had urged the king to open the sealed door again. The pair had gone down to the altar and spread a fine powder of ash all over the floor before finally locking the chamber for the evening. The next day, as the priests were gloating, Daniel descended the steps and pointed out the dozens and dozens of footprints in the ashes. Using a secret door beneath the altar, the holy men had crept back into the room after midnight, bringing their wives and children along, and devoured every morsel set before the idol of Bel.'

'A neat trick,' admitted Hartley. 'Both the secret entrance and the ashes.'

'That was my thought, upon first reading the tale. It wasn't the subterfuge that made the greatest impression on my young mind, though.'

'No?'

The friar shook his head.

'When the king found out that his priests had been cheating him, mocking him with a clay idol while feasting themselves silly each night, what course of action do you suppose he decided to pursue?'

Even the ungodly Hartley knew enough of the Old Testament to understand that clemency was an unlikely outcome.

'I imagine he put the priests to death,' he said.

'Not just the priests — of which there were seventy, incidentally. No, as their wives and children had also partaken in the deception, they were put to death, too. In the scripture, this is shown as a victory for Daniel and the god of Israel.'

Hartley grimaced.

'Therein lies the lesson,' said the friar. 'You, Detective, are understandably eager to see this business reach its conclusion, but you must remember that the case doesn't end with the dissolution of the mystery. It ends with the righteous wrath of the god you serve: the Crown's justice.'

'What do you mean by that?'

'Only what you already know but are unwilling to confront. We have already reached the understanding that the person responsible for Fred's death is, in all likelihood, a member of his household. One of the people you have lived amongst for nearly a fortnight, laughed and broken bread with.' The friar held his associate's gaze. 'When we unmask the killer, they will almost certainly be hanged.'

'If that's the way the judge rules,' said Hartley. 'That is the law.' The words were dry and hollow in his throat. He reached for his glass.

'But is it right? Is it *just*?' pressed the friar. 'Can you think of no circumstances under which a killing might be merited? You've heard stories of Fred's behaviour. Atrocious enough, surely, but remember that these are only the incidents that others are able to share. What other acts might he have committed? Sins without witness, or whose victims were too ashamed to speak them aloud.'

'Is that what you think happened? Someone was driven to end Fred O'Donnell's life after being subjected to something untenable?'

'Not necessarily, no. The point I'm trying to make, though, is that not everyone is able to act with clear thoughts and a cool head. There are situations in which the only apparent option is an unthinkable one, through circumstances beyond the control of mortal man.' The friar's customary smile, which had been absent for a time, made an abrupt and unsettling reappearance. 'If you don't agree with me now, just wait until morning. We're sharing a room tonight, and it's been a fair while since I've had a good night's sleep in a comfortable bed. I've been made to understand that my snoring is more than enough to justify thoughts of homicide.'

Hartley shook his head and stood, draining the dregs from his glass. 'In that case, I shall be needing a nightcap,' he said. 'No chance I can tempt you?'

Making only the slightest show of waiting for a reply — he knew well the tenets of the friar's abjurations — the detective made for the bar. As he did so, he noticed one of the other patrons watching him. The man was seated alone by the door at a table littered with empty glasses. He was toying with his hat, and his eyes followed Hartley with such fiercely feigned disinterest as to draw immediate attention. For his part, the detective kept his gaze controlled, passing the man without so much as a sideways glance. He found a spot a few feet down the bar and hailed the publican. Making a show of perusing the available whiskies, he slipped his credentials discreetly onto the wooden counter and hissed a hushed instruction before returning to his seat, tumbler in hand.

'I'm afraid they didn't have any of the Irish stuff. Only Scotch,' he said, loudly. Then, under his breath: 'We're being followed.'

'How very unfortunate,' the friar said, at more or less a normal volume.

'Are you —' Hartley hesitated. 'Are you playing along with the whisky thing,' he whispered, 'or is that in response to the bit about the man following us?'

193

'Both, I suppose. Efficiency is my watchword, after all. I think we're probably safe to dispense with the act, though. He's well out of earshot and starting in on his sixth pint.'

Hartley sat back with a sigh. 'You already noticed him, then?'

'About an hour ago, yes. I wouldn't call him a particularly subtle character. His face is familiar, too, but I'm having trouble placing it. Did you get a good look at him?'

'Good enough,' said the detective. 'He was the chap in the grey suit at Fred's funeral. Remember? The quiet one who hung about by the front door the whole time and vanished before the end of the service.'

Recognition flushed the friar's face. 'Of course!'

'Not only that . . .' Hartley stopped suddenly, holding up a finger. The barman looked to be on the move. 'Listen,' his voice dropped again. 'I've spoken to the proprietor. In a couple of minutes, he's going to make a show of ducking outside on some business or other, then turn around and bar the front door. I'll dash over and station myself before the passage to the courtyard, which leaves you with the kitchen door.'

'To what end, exactly?'

'Well, when our fellow realises he's been discovered, he'll almost certainly make a run for it.'

'Yes, I managed to intuit that much, believe it or not,' the friar smiled tightly. 'I simply find myself wondering what good it'll do to place me between him and the exit. I hope you don't think I'm being even remotely modest when I say that I have never excelled in the physical arena. I was forced to participate in exactly one rugby match at school, and that ended

194

with the other lads making me the ball.'

'He probably won't come at you,' said Hartley, craning his neck to follow the barman. 'If he does, you'll figure something out. Play to your strengths. Take his legs out from under him with a cutting remark or hit him with a devastating quote from the Bard. Compare him to a summer's day but make it one of the really awful ones. The muggy ones that have you sweating through your collar. That'll stop him in his tracks.'

The look on the friar's face told Hartley that a piercing rejoinder was at the ready, so the detective took more than a little pleasure in choosing that moment to leap up from his seat and cut the conversation short.

'Now!'

The main door of the dining room slammed shut and he dashed to his station, one eye on the man from Fred's funeral. The chap must have been no stranger to inebriation, as the half-dozen pints he had consumed seemed barely to slow him down. He whipped round to stare at the barred door, hesitating for only a heartbeat before dashing back towards the kitchen. This door was also barricaded; however, the friar having managed to slip through and jam a chair beneath the handle. Turning, the man met Hartley's eyes. The detective steeled himself for a bodily altercation, but his quarry suddenly peeled off and ran towards the stairs leading up to the guest rooms. Hartley stood rooted to the floor. A fraction of a second later, a realisation hit him with sudden, coursing heat, sending him hurtling towards the half-turn staircase at speeds he would not have thought himself capable of attaining. It was only upon seeing the man in motion that his gait had become familiar, and the detective now knew that Fred's funeral had not been their only encounter. Heart racing and knees high, he took the stairs two at a time, skidding slightly on the soft carpet. The man in front of him fairly ricocheted from the wall of the landing and leapt towards the second set of stairs, panting audibly. Hartley flew after him, closing the gap between them with each thundering step until, just as the man set foot on the first floor, the detective was able to reach out and catch his other heel. The shoe came off in his hand, sending the man sprawling across the hallway. The fellow did not give up even then, scrambling on hands and knees towards the door of the nearest bedroom and lunging for the handle. He was not fast enough. The detective lashed out with a kick, striking the man in the chin with such ferocity as to knock him onto his back. Before he knew it Hartley stood over the semi-conscious figure, one boot on each wrist. Leaning forwards, he felt bones and tendons shift beneath his heavy soles as the man stirred and let out an incoherent cry.

'I think he's had enough,' said a quiet voice.

Hartley looked up slowly, as if awakening. The friar stood at the top of the stairs, brows beetling slightly in an expression that mixed concern and something more. Fear? Shock?

The detective felt his fury dissipate, extinguished by cold shame. He stepped away from his victim, who had no means of escape beyond the rooms lining the short hallway.

'That may have been excessive,' he conceded, 'but I couldn't let him get away again.'

'Again?' the friar looked puzzled.

'I didn't make the connection until I was running after him. This is the man who was hiding in the rose garden at Tolhurst last Saturday night. The one I chased off through the paddock.' Hartley turned back to the man now cowering on the carpet. 'I think we may have our killer here.'

24

'I've never killed anyone and that's the truth. Even back in the war, I was only a driver. You only have to look at my face to know you can trust me.' The detainee's voice, already high and rather nasal, took on a wheedling quality that did absolutely nothing to improve Hartley's opinion of him. 'You do believe me, don't you?'

The detective fought the urge to reply. His goal was to ask questions, not answer them. The room he had appropriated might have been tailor-made for the purpose: a narrow bedchamber with only a single chair and a high, dark window. A lamp on the cramped side table cast unstable shadows across the red-gold wallpaper, picking out each thorn from amongst the damask roses and lending the whole picture a discomfiting depth. Hartley had positioned his prisoner on the edge of the low bed, leaving the friar to take the chair while he himself paced the dark space between them. He was far too agitated to sit.

'If you've done nothing wrong,' he said, making a special effort to keep his voice low and steady, 'why run?'

'I didn't say I'd done nothing wrong. We've all strayed from the righteous path at times.' The man gave a smile that appeared to aim for ingratiating but landed much closer to ghastly. 'We're none of us perfect, are we, Inspector?'

'*Detective*,' corrected Hartley. 'And as for you — am

I right in referring to you as Harold Robertson, or does conducting business under a false identity number amongst your detours from the path?'

'Robertson, yes. Call me Harry.'

'I shan't be doing that.' Ignoring the proffered hand, Hartley leafed through the papers he had confiscated from his charge's attaché case: a motor driving licence, several receipts, a slim notebook and a sheaf of sales records. Besides providing the detective with his name, the documentation identified Robertson as an agent of Great Southern Mutual Assurance, and an apparently indefatigable example of the breed. 'You must be a busy man, Mr Robertson,' said Hartley. Though he'd taken a few minutes outside the room to peruse the papers at length, he now made a show of examining each policy in turn. 'Pinjarra, Ravensthorpe, Kulin. There are dozens of clients here, scattered over a not insignificant portion of the state.'

Robertson shrugged, toying with the brim of his cheap-looking homburg. 'That's the job,' he said. 'Never shy away from a bit of hard work.'

'You provide a comprehensive service, that much is clear.' Hartley selected a file and withdrew it from amongst its fellows, holding it before the prisoner such that the name on the policy could be plainly seen. 'I do find myself wondering, though . . . is attending the client's funeral a standard part of the package, or was Fred O'Donnell a special case, somehow?'

Watching Robertson's smile fall by a good half an inch, Hartley had to fight to conceal his delight. He'd landed a hit. The insurance agent must not have recognised him from the funeral or had perhaps hoped that his own presence had gone undetected. Now that the fellow had been disabused of this notion,

Hartley could almost see him working to understand his shifting position, eyes darting about the room as he made connections and untangled implications. When he spoke again, a trace of defiant cruelty could be heard in his voice.

'He's a pretty canny one, isn't he, this copper?' This remark was directed towards the friar, who sat with eyes half closed in an attitude of meditation, both unmoving and completely silent. Robbed of a reaction, Robertson shrugged and returned his attention to the detective. 'I was just passing through, as it happened, and thought it would be only proper to pay my respects. I'd do the same for any of my policyholders, given the chance.'

Though taken slightly aback by the speed with which his opponent had recovered — a practised liar, by all appearances — Hartley had his next move at the ready.

'On your way where, exactly? From Katanning to Katanning?'

Another pause, the clockwork cogs of Robertson's mind all but audible as they spun for traction. 'You've been snooping through my receipts.' He pulled his lips back over prominent teeth, his voice midway between smarm and scorn. 'Not much gets past you, does it, Inspector?'

'*Detective*,' Hartley amended, again.

'Well, *Detective*, I'll have you know that Katanning is a pretty handy place from the point of view of a commercial traveller. You can zip up to Wagin or Dumbleyung in no time at all, and there's a well-maintained road through Tambellup that'll get you on the way down to Albany right quick. And it's only about three-quarters of an hour from Kojonup, which is why

I could not, in good conscience, receive the news of Mr O'Donnell's unfortunate demise without looking in on the family.'

'Yet none of the family members were made aware of your condolences. They'd never heard of your contract with Mr O'Donnell, either. In fact, I'd go so far as to wager that Fred himself never actually met you in person. His forms were all submitted through the post, a practice that seems to be common to the vast majority of your clients.' He nodded towards the attaché case. 'It strikes me as a highly unorthodox way of doing business, and leads me to wonder what, precisely, all that trekking across the country is in aid of.'

'Oh, it's all dinkum, I can assure you. The legal fellows at the office have looked everything over, made sure the contracts are watertight, even when entered into remotely. As for the travel — well, I've got to cry my wares somehow, haven't I? We've run advertisements in all the regional dailies for quite a few years now, and they'll net a good few of the more provincial types. Blokes like Fred O'Donnell. Still, I tend to have the best luck in face-to-face conversations down the pub. Ply a fella with a few pints, spin him a yarn and leave him with a copy of the application papers, and you're all but guaranteed to find them in your postbox again in the coming weeks.'

'Why not sign him up then and there?'

'Well, there are the medical certifications to consider, but there are ways around that. No, for the most part, it's a matter of trust,' Robertson smirked. 'If I nag a prospective client to fill the form out while I watch — put him on the spot, so to speak — he's like to think I'm only out to make an easy quid. If, on the

201

other hand, I bend his ear for a spell and then leave him with all the information he needs to make the best decision for himself and his beloved family, he'll give the prospect the careful deliberation it deserves, knowing me for the honest sort of gentleman I am.'

'Oh, I wouldn't say you leave him with all the information,' the detective objected, with a dangerous smile. 'I doubt this hypothetical client is aware, for example, that rather than receiving any monetary compensation, his grieving children are more likely to glance out of the dining-room window of a Saturday evening and find you squatting amongst the rosebushes, leering at them.'

Another hit, thought Hartley, watching the colour flee his adversary's liquor-mottled cheeks. Clearly, Robertson hadn't recognised him from the verandah, either, or had again been hoping that his own face would go unremembered. To the detective's utter dismay, however, Robertson seemed to rally from this blow even more quickly than from the first. In fact, the scoundrel soon appeared on the verge of laughter.

'I can see it's no good trying to pull the wool over your eyes, Inspector.' He made a show of suppressing his mirth. 'Yes, I visited the property at Tolhurst that night.'

This time, Hartley was too aggrieved to correct the fellow's form of address. 'I think the decent thing would be to show some measure of contrition,' he huffed.

'What's the use? You saw me. I don't think there's much to gain in my acting sheepish.'

'Out with it, then! What were you doing there? Let's have your side of the story, for all the good it'll do.'

Maybe you're right,' Robertson began to titter.

'Might as well be hanged for a sheep as for a lamb.' The final syllable barely escaped the detainee's thin lips before he doubled over, his entire frame wracked by shaking laughter. Hartley could do nothing but watch, bewildered. Then, with a prickling shame, the significance of his adversary's abundantly fleecy idiom crept over him. The salesman must have glanced back as he cleared the fence that night, one quick look to gauge his pursuer's distance in the darkness. There could be no other explanation. He'd seen Hartley try to arrest the sheep.

Bizarrely, the detective's first instinct, as the mortification took him and the sound of the blood beating in his ears rose to fever pitch, was to look over towards the friar. If the little man bore witness to his humiliation, however, he gave no sign. He still sat with eyes half closed, hands folded in his lap, face unreadable. Hartley growled, spun on his heel and strode towards the door. Just before reaching it, he stopped and spun again, fists tightening, aching to visit retribution on the cackling Robertson. If not for the implacable presence of the friar, he might then have lost control, set dangerously free by the knowledge that his actions would go unobserved. How, he wondered, could one feel so powerless when the fibre of every muscle twitched with such fierce, deadly force? It was only the memory of the friar's expression in the hallway — that flicker of apprehension, genuine fear from a man whose friendship he had come to treasure — that finally forced him to turn away and fill his lungs with a succession of deep, quelling breaths. When he faced Robertson once more, the anger had ebbed away, allowing a steely resolve to surface. Whatever else the salesman threw at him, Hartley would finish the interview. The solution to the whole cursed mystery was within reach, and he would not be kept from it by jibes or taunts.

'You seem to be a man who enjoys his freedom.' The detective's voice became dangerously quiet. 'I'm not sure you appreciate how close you are to losing it forever.'

'What are you going to do? Lock me up for trespassing?' Robertson cocked a smug eyebrow at the stack of documents sitting beside him. 'Check the contracts. Somewhere around the bottom of page three, I think it is. Our clients confer upon us the right to surveil their properties for purposes including — but not limited to! — verifying the presence of such valuable assets as are mentioned in the policy, establishing the ease with which any malevolent actors might gain access to the premises . . .' He counted off the clauses on his fingers, a tobacco-yellowed nail falling with each example. 'It's all prettied up in the legal jargon, obviously, but you get the picture. Go ahead and see for yourself. While you're at it, why not take a look through the rest of my receipts? You've already got the one from the Royal Exchange Hotel in Katanning. The thirteenth of September till the sixteenth, correct? Well, go on and you'll find that on the nights of the ninth, tenth and eleventh, I was at the Denver City Hotel in Coolgardie. That's the one,' he said, as Hartley removed a dun-coloured slip of paper from the pile. 'Y'see? The day Fred was shot, I was four hundred miles away, right on the edge of the bloody desert.'

The detective peered at the receipt, holding it up to the light. He shook his head and stepped closer to the lamp, squinting as though trying to make out the words. Then, calmly, he lifted the lamp's glass cover and touched the receipt to the flame. Letting the paper fall to the floor, Hartley watched it blacken and curl before grinding the remnants to dust beneath his heel.

'Now, I'm sure you're tempted to tell me,' he said, turning back to the nonplussed salesman, 'that the proprietor of the Denver City Hotel will gladly corroborate your story, and that may well be the case. But how long will it take him to send word, and what other impediments can I dream up in that time?' Hartley's voice, though so quiet as to be almost a whisper, was clear and even. 'Make no mistake, Mr Robertson. When you do finally leave this room, it will be in the company of two constables from the Kalamunda Police, who will take you directly to the local lockup. The cells, as you'll soon see, are precisely as spacious as they are well furnished, and they will be your home for as long as I deem appropriate. Whether you walk out tomorrow morning or find yourself looking forward to a single, stringy mutton chop several Christmases hence depends entirely on how helpful you prove to be during the remainder of our conversation. It's in your hands now. You can shiver away on a limestone bench while your solicitor searches out a doctor to testify for the third time that the woman who gave birth to you is, in fact, your mother, or you can tell me what I need to know. Quickly.'

Robertson sat back, looking stunned. He sucked his teeth and said nothing for several long, stiff seconds, during which Hartley, terrified that he had overplayed his hand, struggled to maintain his composure. At long last, the captive sighed, sinking a clear couple of inches into the hotel mattress as the fight left him. It was all Hartley could do not to howl in jubilation. His stratagem had paid off.

'Well, here it all is, then.' Robertson looked at the floor as he spoke, and Hartley fancied that he could hear the level of scorn in the fellow's voice decrease almost imperceptibly. 'It's my father-in-law that runs Great Southern Mutual. He's not a pleasant man, but straight as an arrow. Not too fond of me, really — never has been — but so long as I keep the clients coming in and all the paperwork appears to be above board, he tolerates me well enough. The bulk of the firm's clients are in the bigger towns, you see, or not too far out. They come in and talk their options over, that sort of thing. It was me who had the idea to travel around the little places, out past woop woop, but it took my brother-in-law to convince the old man there was something in it. Bobby, the legal man. The apple of his father's eye but didn't fall within a mile of the tree. Crooked as they come, is Bobby.' This last judgement was pronounced with obvious approval. 'He's the one who wrote the copperplate for the contracts, and he did a hell of a job, I tell you. It's just about the perfect racket because it follows the letter of the law completely. The policies we do up for the rural types can be taken out in a matter of days. All you need is the application form and the medical record, filled out by a physician. When we started offering Bobby's special service, the yahoos went for it in droves. The payouts are enormous, you see — much higher than the competition — but our conditions are much more stringent. We make no secret of that; the clients understand it as part of the gamble, or they should do, at any rate.'

'What sort of conditions?'

206

'Well, for example, the small print specifies that if a client is killed or injured in an accident which a man of sound mind and body could reasonably have been expected to pre-empt or avoid, the policy will not be honoured.' He seemed unable to hide a grin. 'The word 'reasonably' does a tremendous duty here. Now, when it comes to murder, assault or comparable injurious actions committed by another party, there's another element at play. Any damages or reparations ordered as part of a court ruling are taken into consideration against the value of the policy. In other words, if you, Detective, were in possession of a thousand-pound life assurance policy and this chap,' he nodded at the friar, 'managed to knock you down with his motor car and snuff you out, the magistrate might order him to pay eight hundred quid to your family as compensation for depriving them of your sparkling wit and general good temper. In this case,' he hurried on, before Hartley had time to issue a reprimand, 'Great Southern Mutual would only pay out two hundred pounds, considering His Majesty's government and the killer himself to have made a worthy contribution and paid part of the agreed sum.'

Hartley was surprised to find that his opinion of the salesman's character had yet greater depths to plumb. 'But that's outrageous!' he spluttered. 'Surely it's entirely against the spirit of the agreement.'

'Spirit doesn't enter into it,' shrugged Robertson. 'It's all about the letter of the law, and the clients read the whole thing thoroughly before signing. At any rate,' he laughed, 'they should do. Not the most literate chaps in the world, as a rule, nor are they particularly fond of appearing foolish by asking for clarification. No, for the most part, they just sign.

So you see the alluring arithmetic behind the whole scheme. Plenty of men signing up and sending in their premiums — with a comfortable commission for me, mind — balanced against the odd claim, which, though large, is almost always attenuated somewhat by Bobby's devilishly clever contract work.'

'How often do you end up actually paying the full claim amount, then?'

The salesman leant forward, donning a confidential air. 'In the near decade we've been offering contracts of this kind, Fred O'Donnell's is set to be only the fourth to satisfy all the criteria for a complete claim.' There was an awed sort of satisfaction underlying the words, though whether it represented pride in his own cruel ingenuity or a grudging admiration for the magic worked by Fred's killer was not wholly apparent. 'Now you see, don't you, why I had to rush down to Kojonup the very moment I heard of the murder? In the first place, I had to establish whether his beneficiaries knew of the policy's existence. If they don't issue the claim within twenty-eight days, the whole thing is null and I'm off the hook. Secondly, I had to establish whether Fred's killer was likely to be brought to justice. In that case, our finances would at least suffer a lighter blow. Now, if the murderer was to be named as one of the dead man's beneficiaries, so much the better. In that case, there's nothing to pay at all, it being both illegal and — I'm sure you agree — unethical to benefit from committing a capital crime.'

'Quite,' Hartley all but spat. 'It's only appropriate if you benefit from it.' His distaste was such that it was nearly a minute before he could continue the interview. 'You'd have me believe, then, that you never met

Fred in person, had nothing whatsoever to do with his death, and only began to dog the footsteps of the O'Donnell family in order to establish how hard-hit your employer's coffers would be?'

'Something like that, yes. It's not just the money, you understand. Such a grand sum would cause my father-in-law to take a closer interest in my activities, and I can't have that. Not only could it curtail my earnings quite significantly, but he'd be all but certain to mention it to my wife. She's awfully fond of her father, see, and treats his word as gospel. She'll take his side, she always does. And as for our children' — he shook his head with vigour — 'no, it doesn't bear thinking about. I won't have my domestic affairs meddled with just because some farmer decided to go and get himself killed in the most inopportune manner possible. It's just not on.'

Hartley opened his mouth to reprimand the fellow for his flippant assessment but soon thought better of it. The interview had foundered too long in wrath and recrimination, leaving him no closer to catching Fred's killer. Downing the dregs of his pride, he made his final appeal.

'If you've followed the O'Donnells for more than a week, you must have come away with some useful information. Help us now and I'll see that your jail time is trimmed accordingly. Start from the beginning. Spare no detail.'

* * *

It was long past midnight by the time Hartley and the friar were finally able to retire. After the airless den in which they had passed the preceding hours,

209

their room seemed exceptionally wide and welcoming, each bed piled with soft quilts and well-fluffed pillows. The detective was half tempted to collapse upon the mattress fully clothed. He'd forced Robertson to go back and forth over every piece of testimony till the wretched fellow began to slur his speech with fatigue. Hartley's own faculties hadn't fared much better and when, at last, he had finally entrusted his charge to the care of the Kalamunda constabulary, he could manage nothing more cogent than 'Hold this for me, won't you?' by way of instruction.

He sat at the end of his bed and bent to unlace his boots, head still spinning with names and dates. A full analysis of Robertson's testimony would have to wait until he could spread his notebooks out upon a suitably spacious desk with a suitably large pot of coffee, checking the new data against his own findings. In the meantime, Hartley contented himself with the notion that while the night's questioning had furnished him with little in the way of fresh facts, it had at least been able to shore up his own observations with additional evidence.

'Not a complete waste of time, then,' he said, 'but I really thought we had our killer for a minute.'

'Did you?' the friar yawned.

Hartley bristled at his companion's nonchalance. 'I did. And if you're about to tell me that you knew he wasn't our man from the beginning, you'd better have a damned good reason for not coming out with it hours ago.' He unbuttoned his jacket and shrugged it off, rather huffily. 'Would've been a good sight more useful than humming and staring at the ceiling all evening.'

The mendicant smiled. 'Had you required my help,

I would gladly have obliged. Not only is unsolicited assistance rarely heeded, in my experience, but it can also give the impression that the receiver is incapable of managing things alone. An impression which, in this particular case,' he added, 'would be completely unfounded. You acquitted yourself, for the most part, very admirably.'

For whatever reason — exhaustion, possibly — Hartley found himself moved by this commendation. 'That's kind of you to say. The slimy fellow nearly had me a couple of times there, especially when I realised he'd seen —' He pulled himself up short, realising that the friar should still be unaware of his collision with the ewe. 'Well, he'd seen a great deal more than I expected.'

'He's certainly an attentive one. It's only a shame that he wasn't watching the property prior to Fred's death. Who knows what we might have learned?'

'There's something to be uncovered from amongst his observances, I'm sure of it.' It was Hartley's turn to yawn. 'Unfortunately, I can't see myself being any further use tonight.' He pulled back the heavy, starched sheets and climbed beneath them, reaching out to snuff the light on his bedside table. 'Sleep well.'

'I shall certainly endeavour to do so.' Was it the flame of his own lamp casting uneven shadows, or did the friar's lips twitch at the corners with mischief? 'If I do have trouble drifting off, I suppose I can always count sheep.'

Despite the burning in Hartley's cheeks, darkness took the room.

25

The Wooroloo Sanatorium was about an hour's drive east of Kalamunda, set back some way from the road amid the dense scrub of the Darling Scarp. The investigators followed a modest track through sparsely planted gardens before the settlement came into full view, a series of long, low residential houses arranged like the rows of an amphitheatre around the hospital proper.

A few of the inmates were immediately visible, partaking of the sun and basic fieldwork which formed the bulk of their treatment. While he couldn't say there was anything obviously oppressive about the scene, Hartley was aware of a grim, quiet sort of stillness. It was a place, he felt, of fatal and timeless routine, a place where victims of consumption, typhoid or leprosy could plod unhurriedly towards either death or convalescence, depending on their luck.

As he and his companion left the car and approached the wide, gable-shaded stairs of the hospital's main entrance, a few percussive coughs rang out like hammer blows in the tranquil morning, received with studious indifference by all those in sight. Perhaps this was part of the treatment, too; the refusal to acknowledge mortality in the hope that it might return the favour.

'I can think of few places better suited to a protracted demise,' muttered the friar, rolling his shoulders as if to dislodge some clinging, creeping thing.

After explaining their presence to an orderly in the entrance hall, the men were led down a series of passages to the office of the registrar, each footstep far too loud in the clinical hush. The walls were painted a germless, hopeless white, stretching the light admitted by meagre windows to its fullest effect.

The registrar rose to greet them, crossing the room with a quiet, careful tread. He was so thoroughly the picture of a career clerk, so entirely monochrome from thinning crown to starched socks, that Hartley found himself struggling to come away with a single distinguishing characteristic. The mere time it took to glance at his notebook was enough to forget every facet of the man; the detective took his name down as 'Cherwell', but there was a good chance that even that had been contorted by its bearer's crippling unremarkableness.

'You are seeking the medical records of Miss Elizabeth O'Donnell,' said the man, in a voice without weight or colour. Hartley and the friar could only nod, unable to determine whether the sentence was intended as a question or a statement. The registrar turned to the row of filing cabinets which lined the room's rear wall, opened a drawer and began to flick through the contents, his every movement metronomic. He returned with a worn-looking folder.

'Miss O'Donnell was admitted to Wooroloo on the eighth of March, nineteen twenty-five, with tuberculosis and general lethargy. Her condition showed no change for several months but began to improve by Christmas. Her health fluctuated over the next two years, complicated by a rather severe case of influenza. Following a general decline around Easter of this year, she passed away in June.'

213

'And prior to that?' enquired Hartley. 'She was a resident at Claremont, wasn't she? How long was she there, and why?'

The detective's tone must have betrayed too much eagerness, too much humanity, because Cherwell — or had he said Cheswell? — raised one grey eyebrow before licking his fingertips and beginning to leaf through the document.

'Miss O'Donnell was admitted to the Fremantle Lunatic Asylum on the ninth of October, eighteen ninety-six. Aside from two unsuccessful escape attempts, no violent or disorderly conduct was recorded against her. Designated *quiet and chronic*, she was relocated to Claremont Hospital for the Insane thirteen years later, just prior to the Asylum's closure, on the orders of the State Lunacy Department. Her tenure at the hospital was marred, at first, by a number of self-directed appeals and attempts to flee, but by nineteen fifteen, this errant behaviour had finally ceased. Her record for the next ten years appears to have been exemplary and she was later accommodated in an offsite care cottage. This arrangement ended with the illness which necessitated her removal to Wooroloo.'

'But why was she remanded to the Asylum at all?' pressed Hartley. 'What was wrong with her?'

This time, the eyebrow was lifted to the accompaniment of a prim little sigh, but after a trying silence, Cheswell — Cheswood? — bent to the pages once more.

'The precipitating factor in Miss O'Donnell's confinement and subsequent treatment appears to have been a series of disruptions to the peace. Three separate incidents are listed, each resulting in charges of both public disorder and offensive conduct. During

214

her stay at the Asylum — and, subsequently, Clare-mont Hospital — she continued to exhibit a range of symptoms, from lewdness, licentiousness, hysteria and unfeminine conduct to hallucinations, convulsive fits, somnambulism and histrionics. Treatment con-sisted of a strict diet, diverse nerve tonics, hypnosis, mesmerism and the application of smelling salts and scented oils. The success of said treatments can be seen in the gradual improvement of her condition throughout the years.'

'Throughout the *decades*,' corrected the friar, sitting forward in his chair. 'You'll excuse my interruption, Mr Cherwood, but as a man of the cloth, I have spent some time meeting the spiritual needs of those unfortunates who find themselves removed from the greater brotherhood of human society. In my experi-ence, an asylum inmate is usually released following treatment. A stay of six months would approach the upper limit of normal procedure, and internment for a year or more is customarily reserved only for violent or recidivist elements, deemed to pose a real danger to those of us on the other side of the wall. Are we to understand that Elizabeth O'Donnell fell into the latter category?'

The looks directed at Hartley, though intimating an unmistakable degree of disapproval, were nothing compared to the naked disgust levelled at the friar. Churlwood held the glare steady for nearly half a min-ute before referring again to the documents before him.

'There is nothing to indicate aggression or danger in Miss O'Donnell's record. While there are always details that must be omitted — the irrelevant, the incomplete, the overly intimate — it is important to

215

understand that these files are not intended as cheap entertainments, no matter how salacious the public might find them. They are tools of science and medicine, and every piece of data pertinent to the patient's condition is contained herein. Anything beyond that has no place in the files.'

The tone in which this reprimand was delivered left Hartley with no doubt that Chellworth viewed the populating and filing of records as the hospital's highest purpose. The patients, nurses and physicians, with all their noisy comings and goings, served merely to keep the files fed. Hartley was not at all surprised, then, to see the clerk shudder when asked whether he had known Elizabeth O'Donnell personally.

'I am required to conduct an interview with each patient upon admittance — for the records — but had no further communication with Miss O'Donnell, other than whatever was demanded by etiquette when encountering her in the hall or passing her at work in the gardens.'

'Did you ever meet her brother?'

'I did not,' said Charlesworth. 'The time and date of every visitation is recorded in the guestbook, which is kept in the foyer. You can refer to it on your way out.' With resolute, noiseless movements, he closed the file and stood to return it to its rightful place in the cabinet.

'Is there nothing more you can tell us about Elizabeth?' asked the friar, climbing to his feet. 'Nothing that might help us understand the part she played in Fred's demise? No personal impressions?'

'I am concerned with neither impressions nor the personal,' the clerk said. 'You are more than welcome to make her acquaintance and form your own

216

impressions. She lies in the cemetery on the hillside, just over half a mile north-west of here. As we have lost only one other patient in recent months, hers is the penultimate plot.'

26

The friar showed every intention of striking out for the cemetery immediately. While there was surely much more to be learned at the hospital itself, Hartley found himself unsure of where to begin, his thoughts clouded by the clinical, vaguely oppressive quiet. Reasoning that a stroll up the hill might well help to clear his head, he finally agreed to the expedition.

The day was wearing on, the cheery light of early morning hardening into something bright and insistent. Flies circled Hartley's head, seeking the sweat that shone at the nape of his neck, darkening his collar. A couple of crows rose, raucous, from the topmost wire of a fence, a willie wagtail snapping and jabbing at their backs. The friar, his face set, strode through the fields at such a brisk pace that Hartley hurried to keep up, tugging his hat down to shield his freckled nose from the sun. As the rows of staked vegetables gave way to wild grass and low wattle, the little man slowed, seemingly lulled a touch by the torpor of the bush.

The companions walked in silence, for the most part, the slight gradient demanding just enough breath to discourage them from speech. The landscape was largely open, the occasional redgum or wandoo erupting from amongst swathes of sedge and heath dappled with wildflowers. At one point, they startled a basking bobtail, stopping long enough to let the reptile stomp grudgingly across the track and vanish into the undergrowth before resuming their journey.

The cemetery itself could not have been much larger than half an acre, a clearing of orange-brown dirt set off from the surrounding bush by a low wooden fence. Though one or two of the plots bore headstones, most were marked only with simple rounded stakes of cast iron. Elizabeth O'Donnell's resting place was at the far end of graveyard, still largely grass free and distinguished by the freshly mounded earth of its more recent neighbour.

While Hartley had been harbouring a vague hope that the grave would offer some edifying proof of Fred's presence — an enscribed stone, perhaps, or a significant trinket placed at his fallen sibling's feet — a quick survey was sufficient to put this theory to rest. He retreated to the shade of a young eucalypt, allowing his companion the freedom to go about his activities in peace. The precise nature of said activities was not, as yet, completely clear. The subdued mood that had dogged the mendicant since the interview in the clerk's office showed no signs of dissipating, and he stood now at the foot of Elizabeth's grave, head bowed. If he hadn't known for a fact that the friar and Miss O'Donnell were not even remotely acquainted, Hartley would have described his attitude as one of mourning. Maybe, he thought, the details of the deceased's treatment — which struck the detective as unfortunate, if not entirely novel — had reminded the friar of some poor wretch encountered in his erstwhile role as a soother of souls, or he had simply lapsed back into the habit of administering last rites for the departed.

Whatever the motivation behind his actions, to scrutinise them too closely felt unseemly. As Hartley was in no hurry to return to the morbid gardens of the sanatorium, he swept the twigs and gumnuts from beneath his feet and sat with his back against the tree trunk, letting his eyelids droop in the heavy heat. He may have sat thus for only a short span, or it might have been an hour later that he stirred to the sound of rustling footsteps. Looking up, he saw a woman come into view just beyond the cemetery gates. She moved with furtive purpose, clad in the stiff, angled uniform of a working nurse. If she was surprised to see two strange men beside the most recent inhumations, she gave no sign, merely hurrying towards them. As she drew closer, she tore the rigid cap from atop her greying tresses and shifted it from one hand to the other, crimping the ironed edges in her excitement.

'You've come about her? About Beth?' she said, without preamble.

'Well, more or less.' Hartley clambered upright, brushing dust from his trousers. 'We're gathering information on her brother.'

The nurse's face calcified. 'Fred O'Donnell,' she sneered, with all the vitriol that Hartley had more or less come to expect in association with the name.

'You knew him?'

'Oh, that's one way of putting it! I have never, in all my life, held a man in such low —' She stopped short. 'Did you say *knew*? Not *know*, but *knew*?'

'That's correct. He passed away the Monday before last.'

While he was by now accustomed to the utter lack of sorrow with which this news was usually greeted, the unbridled glee that flashed across the woman's features still managed to take the detective by surprise. It was a second or two before she appeared able

220

to feign some more suitable feeling.

'I'm sorry,' she said, not sounding it at all. 'You must think me perfectly beastly, but . . . oh, I don't know where to begin.'

'Shall we start with your name? I'm Detective Constable Hartley,' he said, ushering the newcomer into the shade, 'and this is — well, let's just call him a priest. Of a kind.'

'Reformed,' the friar hastened to add, joining them beside the tree. 'As an apostate, I no longer trade in judgement or absolution, but I can certainly offer an open ear.'

The nurse treated him to a quizzical look, seeming on the verge of further enquiry, but soon shook her head and elected to simply start out on her tale.

'My name is Evette. Evette Goulding. I rushed up here as soon as I heard that you'd been asking about Beth. Word travels quickly in a place like this, you see, and people knew that I — that we —' She shook her head again. 'I thought you might be relatives. Over all the years she spent in places like this — horrid, grey places! — the only one who ever came to visit was *him*.' Once again, that familiar tone pointed the final pronoun unerringly at Fred O'Donnell. 'Not often, mind; only twice a year, but it was enough to throw everything into disarray. She managed to make out quite well, for the most part. Once you've been in asylum for long enough, you either lose whatever remains of your wits or you learn to turn things to your advantage and make your own sort of way, and that's what Beth did. She wouldn't have wanted to go back to her old life — or so she told me, anyhow — but every time that awful brother of hers showed up, it only served to remind her of what he did, of how things were before it all went wrong.'

'How *did* it all go wrong?' Hartley interjected. 'That clerk furnished us with dates and diagnoses but wasn't too forthcoming on the personal details.'

'Who, Chelmswith? That's no surprise. He wouldn't know human interaction if it crept up and interacted with his —' She stopped herself. 'He probably doesn't even know the truth of it, to be fair. It's not the sort of thing they like to commit to records. Not the sort of thing the doctors and directors understand, nor do they want to.' Evette settled a searching look on Hartley, then the friar, seeming to appraise each of them before coming to an abrupt decision. 'Elizabeth O'Donnell didn't much care for men,' she said. 'She preferred women. In fact, she loved them. Always had, or so she told me, for as long as she could remember. Even as a girl . . . you know that she and Fred were shipped over very young?' The nurse interrupted herself. 'Their mother died in labour with Beth, and their father didn't last much longer. I think the children left Birmingham when Beth was three or four. Fred must have been a few years older. They had a distant uncle in the colonies, and that's how they ended up in a rickety house in Albany, down by King George Sound.

'She always said she was a clever child, and pretty, too, and I have no trouble believing her. She seemed to have a good run of it at first, helping her uncle round the house and taking classes at the local school. The family was poor, but Fred was soon of an age to work out on the fishing boats, and then on to nearby farms. Beth had an idea that she might like to be a schoolmistress, so she focussed on her studies for the most part. Her brother was fond of her — hard though it may be to imagine, having seen the man he would become — and began to put a few coins aside, with the view of sending her up to board in Perth when she reached a sufficient age. It was there, in the dormitories of the convent school, that she began to realise —' Evette appeared to stifle a smile. 'Well, let's just say she enjoyed the company. She managed to finish her studies and find a situation as a governess, but her career was now only of interest in so much as it provided the funds to fuel her social outings, which had become more and more frequent. She cut a dazzling figure, by all accounts. She was quite a dancer, and not bad on the piano, apparently, but poetry was her forte. She devoured every bit of verse she could get her hands on, and before long she was giving public readings — just a modest circle of like-minded friends congregating in sitting-rooms after the dance halls closed, but to hear Beth tell it, she may as well have been holding court amongst bluestockings in a Left Bank salon. And that's where she met *her*.'

Evette sighed, eyes fixed on the stake of unadorned iron as though it were the only thing preventing Elizabeth from sitting up and wishing her a good morning.

'I don't know the girl's name. Beth never told me. It doesn't matter now. I suppose it never really mattered. The only thing that matters is that she loved her. Before Beth loved me, she loved *her*.' She fidgeted a little. 'I don't know why, but I used to always try and tease out more of the story, to find more about the girl I had replaced. It's awful, looking back on it now. Precious hours, minutes, seconds — time I should have spent merely glad to be in the company of someone who cared for me as much as I did her. Not that I didn't enjoy our time, you understand,' she hastened to assure Hartley, as though the detective might be taking this all down to be relayed to Elizabeth at some later stage, 'but now I know that there are no moments left, I can't help but dwell on all those I wasted. On jealousy, on doubt, on the fear of being found out. And after all, if it hadn't been for *her*, I never would've met Beth. And they only spent a short time together, really. In secret, naturally — at first, anyway — but Beth always did love too fully, too expansively. She wanted to walk arm in arm along the foreshore at Matilda Bay. She wanted to sit in cafes and laugh out loud. She wanted everyone she knew to bear witness to her affections. And so, at length, she asked this girl to marry her. Well, not her, of course — not Elizabeth O'Donnell. Even dear, wild Beth knew better than that. No, she cut her hair all short, had a couple of suits made, a hat with a nice wide brim to hide her face and some rags to pad her waist out into a respectable paunch. She took a job at a pub, of all places, and when she felt her new identity to be sufficiently established, she issued her proposal to the girl. The foolish thing accepted. I wonder, from time to time, how different it all would've gone had she seen sense and laughed it off, but she went so far as to set a date and have her father announce the business in the *Daily News*.

'Unfortunately, the father didn't stop there. He must have been unnerved by the lack of information on his prospective son-in-law's family, I suppose, or simply found Beth's handshake below standard. Whatever the reason, he began to look into the whole matter a bit more closely, eventually managing to make contact somehow with Fred, who rushed up to Perth the instant he received the telegram. Fred

224

was appalled, as you might imagine, ordering Beth back to Albany at once. She refused, weathering her brother's harangues and threats of violence with the stoic strength of a woman in love. Seeing that he was powerless to shift her, Fred began to fear for the respectability of his family name which, by this time, he had begun to establish. He was married and had purchased a small property near Kojonup with a view to expanding it and establishing himself as a prime woolgrower. Worrying that the community would mock him if it were to become known that his only sibling was a female invert, he made the choice to inform Beth's would-be father-in-law about her true name and background.

'I don't know what he expected to happen next, or whether he'd given the matter any thought at all, but I'd like to imagine for Beth's sake that Fred had no idea how long the repercussions would be felt. It just so happened, you see, that the father of Beth's beloved was a very powerful man, a well-known parliamentarian and close personal friend of Governor Smith. Within forty-eight hours of learning the truth, he caused his daughter to be shipped back to Edinburgh — where, apparently, she was forcibly wed to a distant cousin twice her age — and had Beth remanded to Fremantle Asylum, impressing upon the Surgeon Superintendent that his newest patient posed significant danger to the moral safety of the colony, that scarce hope should be held for her recovery or rehabilitation, and that not a single word from the woman's mouth was to be believed. Fred was too cold or too spineless to do anything. Maybe he even thought his sister deserved what was coming to her; either way, that was it for Beth. She'd taken her last breath of freedom, and they locked her away for the next thirty years.'

Nothing in Jamie Hartley's rather insular experience had prepared him for the mere mention of sapphic attraction. Faced with the plain, profound grief of a woman who had lost her love to a world which considered it never to have existed, he found himself utterly adrift. As the cloudless silence spread out before him, he cast frantically about for something comforting — or even remotely appropriate — to say. He moved to appeal to the mendicant, but the little man had placed his head against Evette's, wordlessly sharing her sorrow. He looked over at Elizabeth O'Donnell's grave, feeling the weight of decades and dirt. Finally, when he could bear the quiet no more, he simply opened his mouth, hoping that the right sentiment would find its way out of it. It did not.

'Locked away for so long,' he heard his own voice say, as if from a distance. 'A bit like a princess in a fairy tale.'

The friar and the nurse turned slowly to look at him, expressions almost identical. It was a look that was familiar to him, though he hadn't been its subject for some years: the quizzical look of a patient parent who, upon hearing their child experiment with an unfamiliar piece of vocabulary, is attempting to divine the young thing's thought process and thus decide whether to offer correction or praise. Then, to Hartley's great surprise, Evette began to laugh.

'Yes! Oh, Beth would've loved that. I always used to tease her about how snobbish she could be. Yes, she was a princess, locked away in a high tower. I suppose that would make me her Prince Charming.' She giggled. 'I'd only just finished my training and begun to work at the new Claremont Hospital when she was transferred there. She was thirty-two, beautiful and haughty and hilarious, completely undimmed by her years at Fremantle. The first time I was assigned to her ward, she reached out and took the cap from my head. She told me that nurse's hats are folded like envelopes to keep one's thoughts inside, and then pretended to reach in and take the thoughts out, reading them one by one. 'Scandalous!' she said. 'Why, what a thing to think about your poor, helpless patient! You'll have me blushing!' Of, course, I was the one who turned red as a beetroot.' Recounting the interaction now, Evette's cheeks glowed with a hint of the old heat. 'I fell in love with her almost immediately. It wasn't hard to hide the fact from the doctors or the others. An asylum isn't really a place for people to get better, you see — it's a place to put people you hope to forget about. Soon enough, Beth and I were forgotten, and that meant that we were free. We were happy, too, believe it or not. We couldn't come and go at will, we couldn't exchange vows, but we had no end of time together: in the gardens, in the exercise rooms, in the empty wards after dark. At first, I lived in the nurse's quarters and managed things so that we seldom went a day without seeing each other. Later, drawing on several years of incident-free conduct, she applied to be accommodated in a cottage away from the main institution, with me as her live-in nurse. We were all but free, then, only having to maintain the facade of sister and patient when the doctors checked in. There were dark times too, of course — when they wanted to try some hideous new treatment, or when Fred visited and left her all wistful and gloomy. Or, worst of all, when she came down with TB and was sent all the way out here. It took me a few months to secure a position at Wooroloo. The administration was sceptical at first, as the only open role was a junior one, and it seemed odd for me to willingly reduce my circumstances, but I spun them a tale about wanting to be closer to family in the hills. Before long, Beth and I were together again. When her strength started to fail, I was there to hold her. When the breaths came harder and bloodier, she used what precious air remained in her lungs to show me her love, and when she died, she died happy. I wonder if her brother, with all his treacherous freedom, could say the same.'

The fragile defiance of these final words convinced Hartley that Evette was sincere in her ignorance of Fred's death, but he was obliged to take the opportunity to question her regardless. Far from being surprised or appalled at the enquiry, she seemed to have anticipated it.

'I don't blame you for thinking I might've had something to do with it — I had motive enough, after all — but old Chensworth does a thorough job with the records. You'll only have to suffer through half a minute with him to get confirmation that I haven't left the hospital grounds for months.'

'Why stay here?' asked Hartley. 'Why not go back to your position at Claremont, or look for something . . . cheerier?'

'I will, someday. Leaving isn't such a simple thing, though. For years, this has been my home. I'm not talking about Wooroloo, you understand, but about Beth. She was home to me for so long. I can't leave her alone here just yet. There's not even a headstone, no record, no-one to remember her.' Evette knelt, dusting her white pinafore with dirt as she pressed

228

one open hand onto the warm soil. Then, suddenly, she looked up. 'There are others, aren't there? Fred's family — children and grandchildren?' The detective nodded. 'Will you tell them about her? I don't want them thinking she was a pitiful, mad old woman. I want them to remember my flashing, vibrant Beth.'

Hartley began to stammer something, taken off guard, but the friar stepped in.

'Why not tell them yourself?' he said. 'We'll leave the address with you so that you can write it all in your own words. I shall prepare them for the news. Winnie, for one, would be thrilled to learn about an aunt whose contempt for convention rivals her own. Thank you, truly, for entrusting us with your story.'

Evette smiled and let out a long-held breath. She returned her attention to the grave, making no move to rise from her knees. The mendicant took Hartley's arm and began to lead him quietly away. Before they had gone more than a few yards, however, a thought seemed to strike him, and he turned back.

'Beth — what sobriquet did she employ when courting?'

The nurse gave a puzzled look.

'Her name,' the little man clarified. 'I assume she wouldn't have had much success in passing herself off as a gentleman if she asked for another young lady's hand under the name 'Elizabeth'.'

'Probably not, no.' Evette chuckled. 'I wondered about the name, too. She didn't want to tell me, at first, but I ended up finding her out. She'd kept one of her old calling cards, you see. She used it as a bookmark, and I found it one day when I was straightening up her room. I still remember the look on her face when I asked her later, all casual:

'Who on Earth is Benjamin O'Donnell?'.'The nurse laughed anew. 'Why, it wasn't too different from the look you're both wearing now.'

Hartley turned his wide eyes on the friar, who stared back at him.

'Ben,' they said as one.

27

Hartley hurried back down the path, swatting profit-lessly at the circling flies. Emboldened by the midday sun, the tiny devils droned about his head, loud enough to rival the swarming thoughts within. Chief amongst those thoughts was this: how did Beth — or Ben — factor into Fred's murder?

If she'd been dead for months, there could be no question of her having pulled the trigger (Hartley was sure of this now, beneath a wide sky of cloudless blue, even if he might have entertained doubts in the wee sleepless hours at Tolhurst). Fred had feared her, though, going as far as to warn his children to be vig-ilant, and Winnie, at least, had made the connection between the mysterious Ben and the cloaked figure whose visits presaged the elder O'Donnell's murder. There had to be an answer in all this, somewhere. If only Hartley could shake the flies, the doubt. If only the mendicant would divulge his suspicions.

Despite his much longer legs, the detective found it quite a challenge to keep pace with the little man, who strode resolutely ahead through the bush. The conversation with Evette, which Hartley had hoped would signal the end of his companion's strange, silent mood, now appeared to have been only an intermis-sion. The friar hadn't spoken a word since leaving the cemetery, though the story of Beth's final days had visibly affected him.

'How did you know?' panted Hartley. 'About Beth.

About her . . . affections.'

The friar ploughed onwards, giving no indication of having heard the question.

'In the clerk's office, even before we met Evette, you guessed something. You must have.'

No response. No sound at all other than the flies and the dirt underfoot.

'I heard everything that you did, spoke to the same people. Somehow, though, you spotted something that I couldn't. You always do.'

Perhaps it was the note of self-reproach that did it, or maybe the mendicant's patience had simply worn through. Whatever the reason, he slid to a sudden halt and turned. There was an unfamiliar light in the usually even eyes — anger? Exasperation? Within a moment, though, the friar had mastered himself, and when he spoke, it was with his customary equanimity.

'You're not in the habit of fox hunting, are you, Detective?' Appearing to need no answer beyond the expression on Hartley's face, he pressed on. 'If you were to pick it up, you would soon see the merit in reading the forest, learning to discern here and there the slight disturbances in the undergrowth, the scat, the soft paw prints left by even the craftiest of beasts. In time, you might achieve a level of mastery, your expeditions ending in success more often than not. You might ride out with a hunting party every day, placing uncharacteristically careless wagers and staking your career, your reputation, your every possession on the outcome. You could, after years of painstaking practice, become a marksman to rival Artemis and Orion. What you could not learn to do — not with all the time and training in the world — is to detect the presence of a fox with anything approaching the accuracy of a bank vole.'

'I'm not quite sure I follow,' said Hartley, who was, in truth, entirely sure that he didn't follow. 'Are you . . . are you the bank vole in this analogy?'

'A bank vole, a stoat. Some sort of wallaby, if you wish to add a bit of local flavour. The point, which remains the same, regardless of the particular mammal at play, is this: you have become adept at sniffing out secrets, as demanded by your profession. Others become similarly adept for different reasons — gathering enemy intelligence, writing mystery stories or simply trading in gossip. None of these people, however — not even you — will learn to deal in secrets so deftly as those whose survival depends on it. That is to say, individuals such as myself and the late, lamented Elizabeth O'Donnell.'

'You and Beth?' The detective struggled to draw a line connecting the two.

'Come now,' the friar smiled. 'Word travels like wildfire through this tinder-dry country. Even before making my acquaintance, you'd heard enough to know that I might be of some use in solving a seemingly impossible situation. You must have heard other things, too. Facets of my personal conduct that might strike the man on the street as less than savoury.'

'Oh.' The implication settled with a sudden weight. 'That. I suppose I assumed it was all born of professional jealousy. Most of the rumours reached me via fellow officers, after all, and I'm sure they felt pretty foolish at having their work usurped by a man with . . . well, with not so much as a name to his name.'

'Nevertheless, you were undeterred.'

'I never really had much in the way of professional pride to begin with.' Hartley chuckled uneasily, feeling

233

almost as if he were playing for time. He had a vague idea of the information the friar was about to disclose, but absolutely no understanding of the appropriate way in which to receive it. His own feelings on the subject — one to which he had simply never given much thought, prior to reaching the Wooroloo Sanatorium — were something of a mystery, even to himself. Before he could give further rein to introspection, though, the friar had begun to speak.

'There is truth to the rumours,' said the friar. 'Or to one of them, at any rate. Just as Miss O'Donnell loved a woman, I loved a man. To many people, this marks me out as something different, something other. I have been called a sodomite, a homosexual, a pederast; the latter is particularly galling, I feel, given that the only man I have ever loved was precisely three weeks my senior.' He flashed a fond smile, and Hartley could all but see the image of the friar's paramour flickering behind his eyes. 'In recent decades, as you may be aware, the learned men of Europe have attempted to re-examine such tendencies through the scientific lens. It is not unusual to hear Ellis's 'invert' or Herr Ulrichs's 'Uranian' in lecture halls, where other terms might be deemed pejorative or simply uncouth. Magnus Hirschfeld's institute in Berlin is of particular interest, attracting attention from several notable physicians and offering a dangerous glimpse of hope for those of us who have been so long misunderstood.' While the smile retained its hold on the little man's lips, the rest of his face subsided slightly. 'Dangerous, that is, because I am now standing before a policeman and admitting to what remains, under the King's law, a capital offence. Not the most strategic move, I'll admit, and yet I believe there are two sound reasons

234

for acting thus.' He held up his index finger. 'Firstly, I am optimistic — perhaps foolishly so — that the tide of history is changing, that by talking freely about such matters and encouraging their discussion in our streets and dining rooms, we might progress towards a future in which each of us is able to love however and whomever we please. I do not labour alone in this aspiration. Just this month, a review in the *Herald* of Miss Radclyffe Hall's latest novel noted — with, admittedly, the odd disparaging jibe — that it was the third release in this year alone to feature a female protagonist's affection for another woman without the author indulging in condemnation or lecherousness. While these topics have always attracted a certain level of curiosity, it seems as though the public mind is at last ready to leave behind the scandalous particulars of the Wilde–Queensberry trial, the volatile affairs of Rimbaud and Verlaine, the tawdry obscenity of *The Sins of the Cities of the Plain*. This move towards acceptance is due, in part, to the medical men I have already mentioned, but the strides made by salon-goers such as Mathilde de Morny and the storied Mme Natalie Clifford Barney should certainly not go unrecognised. The group often referred to as the 'Bloomsbury Set', so venerated by your young devotee Winifred, have doubtless played a part, too, their insouciant disregard for tradition rendered somehow less dangerous by Cambridge diction and landed ancestors. Maybe even I, ragged and foolish as I am, can contribute to this great, collective thaw by speaking openly and honestly. And maybe you, Detective, can help simply by listening. Which brings me,' the friar said, 'to the second reason I have chosen candour. That reason is you.'

235

Hartley had begun to drift on the torrent of largely unfamiliar names, but his attention was now fully fixed. 'Me? In what sense?'

'You have asked for my assistance. I am attempting to render it. You wanted to know who killed Fred O'Donnell — a question to which, with the intelligence recently gleaned from Sister Evette, I believe I now possess the answer — but this is only the first real case of your career, and you cannot always count on being able to pluck a nomadic, nameless assistant from the bushes behind some pub or other. We aren't as common as you might think, and few have my capacity for observation.'

'Hold on!' It had taken Hartley a while to navigate the labyrinthine syntax. 'Do you mean to say you have the solution now? Who murdered him, and how?'

'I do.'

'Then why didn't you say something sooner?' bellowed the detective.

'To divulge the answer alone would be merely to bestow upon you the proverbial piscine gift, when you would be better served, in the long term, by some dedicated angling tutelage.' The friar gave a chuckle. 'I certainly don't mean to suggest, mind you, that the intimate details of my life — or Miss O'Donnell's — should be unearthed only to serve your career. You have no doubt noticed that I lack any real enthusiasm for the actual work of policing; while drawn to conundrums, I tend to find that the attendant business of judgement and sentencing rarely ends up resembling justice. I am sharing my story, then, in the hope that it will not make you a better detective but a better human being.' So guileless was the mendicant's manner that Hartley found these

236

words neither presumptuous nor hectoring. 'While it may be easy enough, in this particular place, at this particular time, to see yourself reflected in the people you pass each day, there are countless more who think differently, live differently, love differently. Until you acknowledge them — the displaced, the disaffected, the inconvenient — you will continue to dwell in a mere sliver of a world. You can see the high street, the town hall, the front page of the Sunday paper, but these are only glimpses, carefully curated for the pleasure and benefit of men like yourself. The greater scene, in all its beautiful complexity, still waits to be uncovered. Opening your eyes to the words and the ways of others will illuminate matters that might otherwise remain obscure. Fred O'Donnell's murder is one example, though there will certainly be more. It is my hope that you may even progress, in time, from squinting through the darkness to helping cast the shadows aside. I speak here not just of the criminal sphere, but also the civic.'

'I think you might be overstating my influence,' said Hartley, 'or my ambition, at any rate. I've never been one for political intrigue.'

'You have more power than you appreciate. You are able to have your voice heard in elections, for example, a right that does not presently extend to all who walk this land. Then, too, you are young, educated, respected — if not by your immediate colleagues,' he added, pre-empting Hartley's protestation, 'then by your family, friends, those of the general public who hold the law in high esteem. From your lips, the words of the disenfranchised may be attended, rather than derided or simply ignored.'

'I don't know about all that, really.'

'I do.' The mendicant's voice was firm. 'I have worked alongside you for a week, placing my talents at your disposal and my reputation in your hands. I will, before long, lay the solution to the whole mystery before you, making the thing plain. I have asked for neither remuneration nor recognition, but I make this request of you now: use your voice on behalf of those who cannot do so. Long have they clamoured, the suffragettes, the native associations, the workers, the lovers and the poets. Do not let their cries fade, but echo them, strong and clear. Will you do this for me?'

Quite overcome, Hartley was able only to nod. 'Yes,' he said at last, the words rasping in his throat. 'Yes, I will.'

'Excellent!' The friar clapped his hands together once and straightened, his usual ebullience flooding back like sunshine through curtains suddenly flung wide. 'Well, we'd better get moving if we're to make it back to Kojonup before evening.' With that, he strode off down the hill, whistling aimlessly.

'Wait a minute!' yelped Hartley, rushing to catch up. 'What are you planning?'

'Why, the denouement. Surely even you, with your curious aversion to detective stories, are able to appreciate the impact of having an audience present when the killer is exposed.'

'You'd better damn well expose yourself to me first.' The detective's agitation was sufficient to blind him to the double entendre. 'I'm not going to sit off to the side gawping like a slapped toad while you quip from the limelight. No, you'll tell me everything as we drive down, starting from the beginning, or I'll kick you out of the car before we've left the hills.'

After a brief show of hesitation, the friar grinned. 'Very well. But there is one final witness to speak to, in the name of completeness.'

Hartley let out a groan. 'Doctor Thornally,' he said. 'I'd almost forgotten.'

'Indeed. The physician mentioned in the telegram allegedly despatched by Les Thompson. Not to worry, though. I believe the whole thing can be handled with only a single, simple question. You noticed, I'm sure, the telephone wires running from the roof of the san-atorium? With any luck, we can raise the doctor on that device and have the whole thing tied up before we set out.'

Much to the detective's surprise, events unfolded in precisely the manner the mendicant had outlined, and within half an hour the two men were in the car once more, heading back to Tolhurst for the final time.

28

'Is this entirely necessary?' asked Edith.

Casting an eye around the room, Hartley felt that the question was not altogether unwarranted. Every surviving member of the O'Donnell family was crammed into the north-east room, to which each still obstinately referred by a different name. Edith had taken one of the armchairs and her brother, Dr Parry, the other. Mary, George and Hazel were lined up on the chesterfield, while Winnie had elected to stand with one elbow propped jauntily against the mantel. Les Thompson and the Simons brothers, who had also been called to bear witness, occupied the other side of the room. Michael stood, while Les and Edward were seated on a windowsill apiece. The sashes had been opened to let the mild evening attenuate the oppressive air within, and the shearers were tasked with keeping an eye out for Charlie and Delia, whose before-bed game of hide-and-seek seemed to bring them into suspiciously frequent proximity with the windows. In the very centre of the room, Hartley and the friar stood shoulder to shoulder — or, given the height discrepancy, shoulder to crown — a double act with a hostile audience in the stalls.

The mendicant drew a magisterial breath. 'One week ago, almost to the hour, I promised that I would return with the name of Fred O'Donnell's killer. It may all be a touch dramatic,' he granted, aiming a smile in Edith's direction, 'but let us not forget that the entire affair began with a cloaked twilight visitor capable of appearing and disappearing at will. I doubt it would be possible to conclude such a thing without a bit of theatre.'

'You might humour us with an attempt,' said Winnie.

'Yeah, go on.' Les lifted his chin in the direction of the clock. 'I've got a pint waiting for me down the pub. Give us the name.'

Here, Hartley stepped in. 'Take it from someone who's just spent days piecing the whole thing together. Without going through the preamble, the suspect's name will only have everyone up in arms. Unless you'd like to be here clamouring over each other till long after last call, it'll be better simply to let us tell it in our own way.'

A low murmur ran around the perimeter before the detractors fell grudgingly silent.

'I suppose it makes sense to start with the man in the cloak. That was the point at which I took up the case, after all. It's important to remember that I was never actually assigned to investigate a death. I came to Kojonup to determine whether the mysterious figure represented a credible threat or was, as initially believed, some sort of elaborate hoax.'

'It's a pity you weren't correct in that assumption,' said Mary, her voice tinged with resentment. Hartley was reaching for a rejoinder when the friar came to his defence.

'Don't be too hard on the good detective. As it transpired, his first instinct was not far wide of the mark. True, the theory does suffer from Fred's being almost immediately murdered,' he acknowledged with a blithe wave, 'but as we continued the investigation it became impossible to ignore the evidence that the cloaked man was, in effect, a clever contrivance. Does it not seem rather tidy, for example, that the mysterious visitor — apparently possessed of the ability to pass through walls, amongst other such talents — should be caught so often in the act of confronting Fred? All told, every member of the household managed to stumble upon the mysterious *tête-à-tête* at least once, though only in the company of one or two others, never the full assembly. The further fact that the dogs always happened to be elsewhere can hardly be a coincidence. Had they been present, their failure to raise the alarm would make it plain that beneath all the caped pageantry lay the familiar scent of an O'Donnell.'

There was a fraught silence, each attendee looking about themselves as if for the first time. It was Edith who finally spoke, her voice cool.

'You'd have me believe that the one responsible for this deception — and the murder — was a member of my own family?'

'We are all but certain.'

'And you intend to have us sit here fearing the worst of all those we hold dear, while you play at dropping crumbs and drumming up suspense?'

'I did not mean to imply that the killer was in the room with us now.' The friar's lips twisted in a cryptic challenge. 'Merely that he — or she — bears the family name.'

The collective consciousness chewed this over before Winnie snapped her fingers.

'Aunt Elizabeth!' she cried. 'She's still alive, then? You found her?'

Seeing that the friar would likely wring this, too, for all the tension it was worth, Hartley moved to take the narrative mantle upon himself.

'She passed away a few months ago,' he said, gently. 'We were able to learn her story, though. There's much in it that will fascinate you, I wager, when this is all over. She did try to visit once, nearly two decades ago. Fred wouldn't let her near the property, but she managed to make fleeting contact with young Jack. Barely more than a wave and a whisper, really, as she waited for him outside the school. She was, at the time, in the guise of a gentleman named Ben.'

Winnie and Mary locked eyes, an electric look passing between them. Before they could press for further details, though, Dr Parry raised an objection.

'If dear Aunt Beth predeceased her brother, she can hardly have had a hand in his murder,' he pointed out. 'While it's true that the science of medicine progresses apace and a country physician is not always at the forefront of his field, I've yet to see a patient capable of firing a revolver once decomposition has set in.'

'She didn't pull the trigger, no. She did, however, provide the murderer — a man who hated Fred more than anyone else — with motive, prompting him to make his move. To understand why, you must first appreciate the nature of the relationship between Fred and Elizabeth.' In as concise a manner as he could muster, Hartley relayed his newfound understanding of the O'Donnell siblings' lives, from their origins in Warwickshire to Beth's confinement at Wooroloo. To this, he appended the vital intelligence gleaned from that final telephone conversation before leaving the sanatorium. 'In July, only a week or two after his sister had finally succumbed to the illness eating away at her lungs, Fred discovered a tiny spot of crimson on his own handkerchief. He was able, with the help of patent medicines, to keep the cough relatively discreet, but he could not stop the blood. Visiting a Perth doctor by the name of Thornally, he was given a dim prognosis: total recovery was unlikely, and any progress against the tuberculosis would be hard won. The odds could be improved by retiring completely to a dedicated convalescence centre but, ultimately, Fred chose a different course of action.'

Here, by prior arrangement, Hartley yielded the floor to the friar. The tale thus far had been founded upon solid witness testimony but was now set to veer into the realm of speculation. While the detective had gone over the key points time and again during the drive back down to Kojonup, satisfying himself as to the soundness of their reasoning, he knew that his partner's more stirring narrative style would help the story find its mark in the hearts and heads of those assembled.

'It is a point of consistency across all the accounts we have received, whether from family members or passing acquaintances, that Fred O'Donnell was not endowed with any great capacity for affection.' The friar paused to acknowledge the murmur of general assent before continuing. 'In this sparse, somewhat arid emotional setting, Fred's love for Beth is an unexpected bloom, a spider orchid on a salt plain. There are three signposts that mark it out, though they are not equally conspicuous. The first is, of course, the portrait.'

Here, he crossed to the mantel and lifted the object in question.

'It may not be particularly ornate — I'll admit to having mistaken it for young Cordelia at first glance, so restrained are the lines — but it is the only image, aside from the wedding photograph, displayed in the study. There are family pictures aplenty in the dining room, naturally, but not even Fred's deceased son is afforded a position equal to Beth on the mantel in Fred's sanctum. Uncovering the second sign,' the friar went on, replacing the frame with care, 'required us to look further afield. It was only upon speaking with the family solicitor — whose very existence was, as I understand, something of a shock to the better part of said family — that we came to know of it. I am speaking, here, not of an object, but a habit: the biannual visits paid by Fred to his sister under the inexact guise of conducting business in the capital.'

Several audible indicators of surprise greeted this revelation.

'It is not merely the effort expended in these journeys that speaks to Fred's dedication,' the friar hurried on, pre-empting interrogation, 'but their timing, occurring as they did in the days around Beth's birthday and again in the weeks leading up to Christmas. Tender, familial occasions. The secrecy surrounding the trips leads us to the third and final sign of great and unusual affection: Fred's desire to keep all knowledge of his sister from the rest of the family. One could probably attribute this to shame, no doubt, or some attempt at keeping up appearances, but even the slightest scrutiny leaves such an explanation wanting. Would it not be easier, for example, to allow Beth to have contact with the rest of the family, on the condition that she never spoke of her romantic inclinations or her brother's betrayal?

'Fred might have just as easily told his wife and children that Beth was not mentally intact, and nothing she said should be trusted. If all this was too risky, or simply too much effort, he could simply have told the rest of the family that she had passed away long ago, as many of them ended up assuming. He could even have hidden the portrait away prior to courting Edith and chosen never to speak of her, thereby banishing the troublesome sibling from the collective consciousness altogether. Any of these options, callous and cold though we might judge them, would at least have exhibited some consistency, some clear resolve more in keeping with the pragmatic, occasionally ruthless man that most people understood Fred O'Donnell to be. Instead,' the little man turned on his heel and began to pace, 'he did neither one thing nor the other. He kept Beth's portrait on full display but would divulge nothing of her fate. He continued to visit her, paying for her care, but did nothing to ease the ache of her unfree existence. Acting thus held her in something akin to limbo, neither part of his world nor entirely absent from it. Out of sight, but accessible — on Fred's terms, obviously — as needed.'

'But what was it he needed from her?' asked Mary.

'To remember, and to be remembered. Beth was the only one who had known Fred as a boy, the only one who could see the child within the man. That's not to imply that he didn't share an intimate understanding with other members of the family,' the friar hurried to append, sweeping the room with an apologetic glance, 'but to them he had always been an adult, a man made harder and colder by life and loss. His visits to Beth, it seems, were almost like a pilgrimage. Part prayer, part repentance, connecting him to a time when he had been capable of kindness and joy. Then came the illness, and he was forced to watch the keeper of his lost innocence fade away, the last light

246

of childhood flicker out. According to her nurse and companion, Beth died without ever allowing Fred the forgiveness he sought. She welcomed his visits, occasionally even looking forward to them, but would not ultimately let him put aside the memory of his betrayal.'

He let the room breathe before proceeding.

'So this, then, is where we find Fred O'Donnell in early July, just under two months ago. Bereft, guilt-ridden, diagnosed at the not insignificant age of sixty with the same wasting disease that had just taken his sister. Recovery, if it comes at all, will not be swift. It will require him to be exiled from his family, not to mention the land he has spent decades working, or risk spreading the sickness to his wife, his daughters, his grandchildren — even the one he has yet to meet. We can only speculate as to which road he would have taken had he not encountered Harold Robertson of Great Southern Mutual.'

At this, Hartley took over once more. He cleared his throat and produced a stout folder filled with papers.

'It is not clear where, precisely, Fred crossed paths with Mr Robertson,' said the detective. 'The fellow is an unprincipled spider, spinning his webs in pubs and hotels from Meekatharra to Mount Barker. His policies tempt the unwary and the half literate with the prospect of a handsome payout, while employing every possible twist and trick to avoid ceding a single shilling. Being more astute than the usual mark, Fred must have seen clear through the scheme. Anyone taking out a policy with Great Southern would have to die in such a way as to satisfy more than a dozen exacting criteria if his beneficiaries were to have any chance at all of claiming the promised bounty. To anyone else, a deterrent. To Fred — ill, miserable and wracked with guilt — an inspiration.' A few audible expressions of astonishment or disbelief greeted the final word, but Hartley did not stop to acknowledge them. 'A practical man to the end, he set about getting himself killed in a way that would thwart investigation. In death, he would do his duty.

'But how? It could not appear to be a suicide, nor an accident for which fault might be attributed to any living party. Each of these would be in clear contravention of several clauses woven through the contract. A hired killer ran the risk of being caught and forced to confess. If Fred's body were simply to disappear without a trace, the claim would be negated on the speculation that he had fled and was still alive in some distant jurisdiction. We have to assume that he considered dozens of possible schemes, if not hundreds, before landing on his final method. It had a fair chance of success, it could be carried out without putting anyone else in danger and, above all, it would almost certainly leave the family in a position to submit a viable claim. There was a drawback, though.' Hartley paused to savour the thrumming silence before dropping a stone through its surface. 'He would need to take an accomplice into his confidence.'

The household burst into exactly the sort of hushed, hissing mix of questions and accusations that the detective had anticipated. He ploughed over the noise, excitement propelling him into the present tense.

'Now, Fred wastes no time. He annexes this very study, even sleeping here as often as possible in order to avoid exposing Edith to his illness. He visits his brother-in-law, Dr Parry, demanding an expedited medical document — though, crucially, he does not allow himself to be examined — which he then sends off to Great Southern Mutual with the rest of the policy paperwork, asserting that he suffers from no significant ailment. He names his wife as the sole beneficiary, knowing that she will distribute the money prudently. He also dispatches a telegram to the Perth physician, Thornally, telling him that no follow-up treatment or further investigation is required, as he is heading to Adelaide for a rest cure. Luckily for Fred, some crafty instinct had impelled him to adopt a false name from the very first visit to Thornally. Your name, as it transpires,' he nodded in the direction of Les Thompson. 'The telegram is thus sent in your guise, complete with assumed handwriting, exposing you to unfortunate suspicion later in the investigation.'

Having issued this almost apology, Hartley hurried onwards.

'Fred then initiates his accomplice into the affair, cast in the role of the cloaked visitor. Together, they contrive to be seen in various clandestine arguments, allowing imaginations to run wild and setting the stage for the killing itself. The plan succeeds admirably. The cloaked visits — bolstered by Fred's gunshots, presumably aimed over empty fields — prompt the harried family to call for police intervention. After some cajoling, the local constabulary send to Perth for a detective. The CID are able to spare their least treasured recruit.' A pause, a self-deprecating smile. 'Finally, Fred has a date for the event itself: I have told him to expect me in Kojonup at four o'clock on Monday, the tenth of September. He ensures that all members of the household will be visibly elsewhere, assigning his daughter-in-law to meet me and show

249

me to the property.

'While alone in the house, he makes his preparations, knocking items from the mantel and arranging the furniture in such a way as to suggest a struggle. He also takes the ladder from the auto shed and props it against the outside wall, using it to reach the chimney and feed a length of rope into the flue. Careful to cover his tracks, he sets the feet of the ladder upon a piece of stout board, preventing them from creating indentations in the dirt, and replaces everything neatly in the shed after use. When Hazel and I pull into the driveway, he waves to us — from a considerable distance, mind — so there can be no question of his having been killed earlier. He then retreats to the room, locking the door from the inside, and lights two cigars, reinforcing the idea of him having met with his killer. Finally, he takes out a pistol. Reaching up into the fireplace, he retrieves the hanging end of the rope, making it fast around the handle of the gun. He fires into the wall twice, giving the impression of someone attempting to hit a moving target. He then takes his place behind the sofa, turns the weapon on himself and pulls the trigger, shooting himself through the heart. His accomplice, having been instructed to wait for the third shot, now knows that it is time to approach the house and reel in the rope from the outside, retrieving the pistol via the chimney. Meanwhile, I come up from the other direction,' Hartley gestured towards the windows, 'and peer in at a dead man inside a completely locked room. While I am distracted by the seeming impossibility of it all, the accomplice is able to dispose of the weapon. And there you have it.' He clapped his hands together with firm finality. 'Quite incredible, but it does make a certain sort of sense, once the old man's motives are fully understood.'

The tale had an incendiary effect. Reactions ranged from Edith's outright disbelief to Mary's howled anguish, each expressed with equal heat. One notable exception to the general trend was Edward Simons, who could be heard quietly asking his brother if he knew who half the people in narrative actually were. The prevailing sentiment, however — expressed to the accompaniment of a vibrant palette of oaths, lent a particular depth by the diversity of the crowd — was a ravening desire to learn the identity of the accomplice. Hartley stepped aside to let the friar have the floor. So obvious was the little man's desire to regain the collective attention that the detective doubted he'd be able to act otherwise.

'The accomplice,' said the mendicant, 'is amongst us even now.' He let the words hang, pacing a portentous circle. 'It was clear from the beginning that the cloaked man must be someone close to Fred. After all, he would have to trust them with not just his life, but also his death. Beyond that fact, the trail initially appears to grow cold. The information offered by eyewitnesses is scanty and must be taken with a certain scepticism. We have already established that at least one of the people claiming to have seen the cloaked visitor must have lied in order to obscure their own role in the masquerade. Neither the hat nor the cloak itself have yet been discovered, with the pistol remaining equally elusive. It is fair to assume that each item is somewhere close at hand, but this property is a large one, and a thorough search of each paddock might go on almost without end. It is possible that the incriminating apparel will remain hidden until all this business is long forgotten. Yes, the duties of the

251

co-conspirator have been carried out commendably.'

The friar twisted suddenly on his heel.

'Perhaps too well,' he said. 'We have heard count-less adjectives used to describe Fred O'Donnell. Most of them, it pains me to say, were to some degree defamatory, but a few hinted at redemption: indus-trious, assiduous, dependable. Some have called him principled, though not in a particularly positive sense. We have learned, through the testimony gathered in Perth, that he was even capable of being affectionate, in his own way. On the list of words that have never been levelled at Fred, however, one will find items such as imaginative, curious and creative.'

The mendicant smiled.

'It is here that the accomplice has made a crucial misstep. It would be very difficult indeed to argue that the scheme staged around Fred's suicide is in any way devoid of artistry or vision. On the contrary, it is a work of considerable ingenuity. We are forced to conclude, then, that the accomplice found the origi-nal scheme too stolid, too unadorned to offer any real chance of success. Having already agreed to take part, the collaborator has no reason not to enrich the strat-agem with some measure of the significant wit at their disposal. In doing so, they have left clear indicators as to their personality and abilities. We are looking for someone intelligent, possibly even calculating,' the friar noted, fixing his eyes upon Edith. 'It cannot have been easy to anticipate the outcomes of all the possible variables at play and land upon a final, suc-cessful course of action. The accomplice would also need to be swift and able-bodied,' he went on, turn-ing his attention to Les Thompson. 'Staging so many coy colloquies with Fred and managing to get away without being followed is no mean thing. A rapport with the hounds would be equally essential.' This time, it was to George and Mary that the friar addressed his words. 'As would an understanding of where best to closet the sprightly canines. Above all, though, it is clear that the person we seek is a storyteller *par excellence*.'

He had come to a final halt before Winifred, fixing her with an implacable gaze. 'From start to finish, the plot progresses in much the same manner as a detective story; it would not be at all out of place in the pages of *Mesdames* Sayers or Christie, and I have already noted similarities to certain elements of Arthur Conan Doyle's canon. If I recall correctly, all three names are featured upon your bookshelf.' Winnie was now the centre of the collective attention. For once, the garrulous young woman appeared to be lost for words. She stammered, seeming to cast about for something to say in her defence. It was her mother, though, who came to the rescue.

'Preposterous,' she spat. 'On top of everything else, Winnie was with me and the children on the afternoon that Fred was shot. You've gone through the alibis time and again. Don't try to tell me you've suddenly found reason to doubt them now.'

Hartley stepped in. 'Quite right, quite right,' he said, in as soothing a voice as he could manage. 'Each alibi has been fully investigated, and our confidence in them remains steadfast. In fact, you might say that they provide us with the final piece of the puzzle. We have already asserted, you will remember, that Fred and his confederate had a hand in coordinating the rest of the family's plans on the afternoon in question. While the level of imagination behind the whole escapade might

253

well suggest a book lover, I would argue that the ability to have each member of the household in the appropriate place at the appropriate time — whether on the day of the killing itself or the many choreographed sightings in the preceding weeks — points to another skillset entirely. Cribbing neat tricks from paperbacks is one thing, but tracking the movements and motivations of an unruly troupe is quite another. To put it plainly,' he said, 'this business was not so much scripted as stage-managed. And there is, if memory serves, one amongst us who has undertaken a side-of-stage apprenticeship in the theatre.'

Winnie seemed to be the first to make the connection, turning an astonished gaze towards the sofa. Several others followed her lead.

'It cannot be coincidence,' Hartley continued, 'that this woman is also the only one lacking an alibi. She was, after all, in the presence of a police officer at the moment of the killing. Why should she need one?'

Every eye in the room now rested upon the impassive figure of Hazel Allen.

'Why indeed?' she said.

29

'I can't say for certain why he chose me,' said Hazel, 'but I have my suspicions.'

She had not moved from her place at the end of the sofa; any extra inches of bare leather were the result of Mary's withdrawal. For the most part, the rest of the family appeared to reserve judgement, their craned necks speaking to nothing so much as rapacious curiosity.

'I mean, It's not the sort of thing you'd want to ask one of your children to do, is it?' she mused. 'And I suppose Edith and George probably had too much to gain by his death, making them obvious targets for suspicion in the aftermath. As for Les — well, who knows? Maybe Fred thought he'd enjoy it too much.' She chuckled. 'So yes, you could look at it that way. A simple process of elimination, with me the last one standing. Just plain bad luck. But I think there's more to it than that. Fred felt that I owed him something: a favour or a debt. The whole thing goes back to dear Jack, you see.' She sank back, letting the chesterfield take her weight. Her eyes moved beyond Hartley to fix upon things long gone. 'I had so little time with Jack, really. We met in nineteen seventeen, during a tour of *On Our Selection*. The war was at its height, and we managed nearly a year together — eleven sweet, stolen months — before the recruiters finally got him. Then, just like that, he was bundled off to Egypt to fire at people about whom he knew nothing, other

255

than that they had been told to fire at him. I couldn't believe my luck the following November when they shipped him back in one piece, give or take the few holes gouged out by guilt and grief. I did what I could to breathe the hope back into him, but this time we were granted fewer than six months before the Spanish influenza laid us out. It ravaged the whole troupe, keeping us off the boards for the better part of a year, and while I eventually made a full recovery, Jack's weakened lungs could never again send his voice further than the first few rows. Even then, indigent and infirm, he would probably have preferred to chance it in our rented Newtown hovel than head back to Kojonup and face his father.

'It was the baby — Delia — who finally tipped the scales, I think. She'd started to make herself known at this point, pushing at my waistband and playing havoc with my appetite. Jack knew that I'd never had a family, and he didn't want his child subject to the same deprivation. He trusted that her aunts and grandmother would shield her from the worst of Fred's wrath, as indeed they did.' Hazel regarded the women in the room with thoughtful fondness. 'As it turned out, Jack needn't have worried. Fred largely ignored his granddaughter, at least to begin with. Jack and I were the main objects of his anger, until Jack's breath slipped away in his sleep, and I was left to bear the full weight alone.

'Fred blamed me, you see. For everything. In his mind, it was my siren call that had lured Jack away in the first place, and I was somehow responsible for his illness, too. I'd stolen his only son and left him a helpless baby girl in exchange. A poor deal for an old man with a farm to run. For the first few years, he was constantly threatening to turn us both out, these extra mouths in need of feeding. He'd insinuate that Delia wasn't even Jack's child. *You know those bloody theatre people.*' She let her voice drop into a gruff approximation of the O'Donnell patriarch. '*Not half an ounce of moral fibre to share between the lot of them.* He changed his tune — ceased playing altogether, in fact — when her curls grew in and the resemblance to Beth became undeniable.'

Hazel crossed to the mantel and took the portrait in her hands.

'It was strange. I'd often catch him looking at her, lost in thought. I had no idea what he was thinking back then, but he made it all clear when he inducted me into his scheme. He laid it out, very matter-of-fact, not asking me to take part so much as informing me that the decision had already been made.'

'You might have refused,' said Mary.

'I certainly could have tried, but Fred was very convincing. There was a pathos to the plan, something touching in his concern for those left behind. It was more or less as you've already described, Detective — the grief, the desire to exercise control over his own egress from a harsh world. I suppose you could say it made sense to me. To be completely transparent, I should note that there was something in it for me, too. Fred agreed to change his will.'

'But you weren't in the will,' objected Winnie. 'There were three versions, and your name didn't show up in any of them.'

'It wasn't *my* name I wanted him to include. I have enough trouble sleeping at the best of times. Accepting money in return for helping to kill someone — even at his own bidding — is not something I can see being conducive to sounder slumber. And, as has already been pointed out, anyone in the will would be subject to closer scrutiny from the police. No, I agreed to cooperate with Fred only when he offered to include Delia in the will. It might seem like a small gesture, but it legitimised her. For the first time, here was the name of Cordelia O'Donnell in writing, with Fred's signature beneath it. She was finally recognised as his lawful grandchild. I know you'll all say that the rest of the family had accepted her without a thought,' Hazel said, lifting her hands, 'but I always felt my position to be a particularly vulnerable one, especially once it became known that Jack and I had never officially wed. At the risk of labouring the point, memories of the children's home are never far from my mind. Having Delia in the will helped to assure me that she would be looked after, come what may. And, yes, the caveat that her inheritance should be administered by a parent gave me some similar measure of protection.'

'An understandable impulse,' said the friar gently. 'It is not hard to imagine that a mother with few assurances would be motivated by the promise of a better future for her child. Having enlisted you, then, how did Fred proceed?'

'He wanted to do a dress rehearsal of sorts, to make sure that his plan would work. I hope you won't all think me too conceited when I say that prior to my contributions, it was not a particularly strong one. He'd dreamt up the rope trick — probably, as you say, with the help of Winnie's collection of crime novels — and taken out the insurance policy, but that was about it. My initial role was fairly simple. After arranging a time when the rest of the family would be demonstrably elsewhere, I was to wait outside the

258

house for Fred to pull the trigger. I would then pull the rope through the chimney, bury the pistol beneath the house and call for the police, who would come and find the room locked from within. I couldn't help feeling, though, that more was required. There were too many ways in which the thing might go wrong. The police might take too long to arrive, for example, and find the scene suspicious, or one of the shearers might come back up to the house, having forgotten his cigarettes, and catch me scuttling down from the roof.'

Hazel shook her head.

'No, it was all too risky. Seeing as I had already agreed to take part, helping to concoct a stronger scheme didn't feel too compromising, morality-wise — in for a penny, et cetera — so I came up with the concept of the cloaked man. The garment itself was Jack's old army greatcoat, just as the pistol had been his service revolver. The boots and hat were originally costume wear; years ago, during an east coast run of *Penzance*, the producer had swindled the cast out of our wages, so we all made off with bits and pieces from the green room. All these things had been sitting in a trunk beneath the bed for years, half forgotten. With a bit of mending and the right light — I found that just after sunset worked best — the effect was rather striking.'

'It was you, then, in the cloak?' Les whistled. 'Had me fooled, I can tell you.'

'Now, hold on,' said Winnie. 'What about the time that you and I saw him arguing with Dad? Who was wearing the costume then?'

'No-one.' Hazel appeared unable to conceal her pleasure at having confounded the others. 'I simply hung the hat and coat from the wire on the far side of the chicken coop and had Fred yell at it. He wasn't a bad actor, your father. Ironic, really, given his antipathy towards the stage. As we had the children with us that night, I felt confident that you would not move to investigate such a heated row at closer quarters.'

With visible effort, she forced the smile from her features.

'I wasn't trying to deceive you just for the fun of it, though. The ruse furnished us with an impossible killer, a supernatural figure who took the blame for Fred's death and drove the thought of suicide from the collective imagination. It also netted us a policeman — a detective from Perth, no less! — who could clear me of any involvement and prevent the insurance company from challenging our narrative.'

'Quite,' said Hartley, not altogether thrilled at being cast in the farce. 'You mentioned minimising risks, though — surely running through all the rigmarole with the rope became even more precarious with a police officer standing outside?'

What Hartley really wanted to know, though he would've sautéed and swallowed his own hat before admitting it, was how the pantomime had been pulled off under his nose.

'That was my thought, too. Fred accused me of trying to undermine him, but I finally convinced him to walk through the whole thing while I stood at the front windows, playing at being the policeman. He ran through the front door, pretending to search for the key, then took a left into Mary and George's bedroom. He lowered himself out of their window, pulled the rope through the chimney and bundled the pistol under the house. Then he climbed back in through the window, ran into the corridor with the key (which, of course, he'd had in his pocket the whole time) and admitted me into the study. It wasn't a bad performance, for a gentleman of his age,' Hazel said, with an approbation that seemed alien in connection with Fred O'Donnell. 'Unfortunately, the entire performance took nearly two minutes and made an awful lot of noise. He also managed, somehow, to knock Mary's spectacles off the dresser on the way through the room and to crush them into the carpet on the way back.'

'My eyeglasses!' roared Mary, with an emotion magnitudes beyond anything she had shown at her father's passing. 'What did you do with them?'

'I'm afraid they were far too ruined to try mending. We swept up the remnants and buried the evidence out by the dam.'

'Ah, but you missed a piece.' It was the friar who now spoke, eyes gleaming. 'A sliver of one of the lenses, which lay in the deep pile of the carpet until last Saturday morning, when it found its way into the sole of poor Mr Bamonte's foot before he'd managed to get his boots on.'

A groan of sudden comprehension spread around the room.

'I wondered why you looked so ashen when I pulled it out,' said Winnie. 'You tend not to be squeamish at the sight of blood.'

Hazel smiled. 'No, it was the prospect of having overlooked some silly thing that might later serve to incriminate me. Well,' she said, upon consideration, 'that and the fact that you had poor George's foot up on the fine china. It's a wonder that Mary didn't slaughter us all on the spot.'

'I'm still not averse to the idea,' muttered Mary.

261

'You'd better get me a new pair of spectacles, quick smart.'

'It is the least I can do, all things considered. Their sacrifice was not in vain, though. After crushing them to pieces, Fred was forced to concede that his pistol-through-the-chimney scheme was not workable on a strict schedule. He finally allowed me to propose my own method, which was implemented on the day of the performance with great efficacy.'

Then, at long last, Hazel launched into a detailed description of her role in the killing.

'It was, I flatter myself, rather beautiful in its simplicity. Having met the policeman in Kojonup and travelled back to the farm, I gave Fred a wave from the gate, signalling that all was ready. Once the agreed-upon third shot rang out, I accompanied Detective Hartley down the driveway. We saw Fred's body through the front window and entered the house, finding the door to the study locked. Being sure to let the detective try the handle for himself first, I made a show of attempting to work the lock open with my hairpin, which knocked the key Fred had left *in situ* to the study floor. I pretended to venture into the house in search of another key, knowing that Hartley would go and try the windows. As soon as I heard his footsteps out on the front verandah, I crept back and used the spare key — which, again, had been in my pocket the whole time — to open the study door. Fred's rearrangement of the furniture and bundled curtains meant that the door was largely invisible from the windows, but I still wasn't keen to take any chances. I turned the handle but didn't push the door an inch until I heard the signal.'

Hartley slapped the heel of his hand against his

forehead. 'Those bloody trinkets!' he cried. 'The coin and all the rest of it.'

'Precisely. Once I heard them clatter to the ground, I knew that your attention would be elsewhere, if only for an instant. I opened the door just far enough to reach through and snatch the pistol before closing it up and locking it once more. Both the hinges and the lock had been well-oiled in advance, and Fred readjusted the screws so that everything was in perfect alignment.' She crossed the room and worked the handle several times. 'Listen — completely silent. As far as the pistol,' she said, seeming to read the detective's next question in the knit of his brow, 'we drew inspiration from Fred's original rope-and-chimney idea to ensure it wouldn't be seen. We took one of his ties' — this time, it was Edith's chance to emit a noise of comprehension — 'and knotted it around the handle of the gun. Before firing, Fred pushed the tie pin through the other end and fixed it to the back of the sofa; along the seam here, so as not to mar the leather. So, when the pistol finally fell from his fingers, it hung behind the seat, well out of sight. It was the work of half a moment for me to slip out the pin when I retrieved the pistol. Using a tie in place of rope — much more compact — meant that I was able to stuff the whole lot in my purse to be disposed of later. I knew I was unlikely to be searched, as I'd been at the detective's side when the shots were fired.'

'And all the while, I was squinting at that damn note,' said Hartley. He rubbed his temples, thinking not just of the day of the shooting, but all the subsequent hours spent puzzling over coins and shotgun cartridges. 'Do you mean to say that there was nothing more to it than that?'

'Well, I had to make it as misleading as possible.' Hazel's voice took on an apologetic tone. 'The more time you spent counting the teeth on a clockwork cog, the greater our chances of getting away with it all. The coin was part of Jack's collection. During the war, the soldiers swapped small change with each other for souvenirs. He traded with men who'd been stationed all over Europe and Asia, leaving me with a tobacco tin full of centimes, lira and rials. I chose one more or less at random. I then found that shotgun cartridge in the home paddock and pressed it flat, and the flywheel was taken from the clock over there.' She gestured towards the mantel. 'Fred had already let it run down. I folded them all inside the note because I thought you might be quick enough to catch one object, but the chances of catching all three seemed slim. I wanted to make sure I'd be able to hear something clatter to the ground.'

'What about the inscription?' Hartley was almost afraid to ask. 'We assumed it was a quotation, but even my well-read associate struggled to place it.' Out of the corner of his eye, he saw the friar lift his chin in a sort of challenge.

'It is a quotation, but not from anything you'd recognise.' Hazel rummaged about in the sleeves of her blouse and withdrew a small envelope. 'I copied it over from this. I've kept the original on my person for a fortnight now. It seemed the safest option. I promised not to reveal its existence for a period of at least five years, unless all were to be uncovered. Now that the everything else has been revealed...'

The detective took the envelope and removed a piece of notepaper, folded double.

I have tried to do what I thought best. The end is not far off, and I'd sooner meet it on my terms than make any more of a fuss. I have already outlived a sister and a son, and I see no great point in taking any more time. I doubt there'll be many tears shed over my passing, no matter what form it takes. I can't claim to have been much good as a father, a husband or a brother, but with any luck, my final actions will ease the burden on those left behind. She'll explain it all, I'm sure.

Perhaps with this, a little of what was wrong is now put right.
Fred

30

The eager gleam of a cigarette, distant but steady, marked out her location in the darkness. As Hartley made his way through the rose garden, the light blossomed and dimmed once more. He heard the heavy relief in her exhale, saw the smoke blush against the ember.

'Have one?' asked Hazel. 'I don't often partake. Edith is against the habit.'

'So am I, as a rule. Still,' said the detective, reaching for the proffered case, 'this is not a night on which the usual rules seem to apply.'

'They'll be applied to me, I assume.' It was a question, though she must have been too proud to phrase it as such.

'That depends.'

'On what?'

'On your family.' Hartley drew the smoke deep into his chest, realising how shallow his breath had been for the last few hours. 'They've been through a lot, as have you. It seems a shame to let Fred's sacrifice — if we may call it that — add to the suffering, especially when he aimed to alleviate it. I asked you to leave the room so that they could speak in private and so decide how best to proceed.'

He glanced back at the house. The same windows through which he had first seen Fred's body now framed the silhouettes of his descendants, deep in discussion. Around the corner, Les and the Simons brothers sat on the verandah with the friar, Kaiser snoring on the boards beside them. From the few snatches of dialogue carried over by the cooling breeze, their conversation appeared to consist largely of speculation around what decision, if any, the O'Donnell family would reach.

Hazel smoked in silence awhile. 'What if they decide to take no action?' she said, at last.

'Then none shall be taken. Life will go on, I imagine, much as it did before.'

'But that can't be legal. It's fraud, isn't it?'

'Amongst other things. You could face any number of charges. I imagine a decent barrister would be able to argue that you planned the whole charade yourself and forced feeble old Fred into it, somehow. Then there is the fraudulent element, as you say. Theft is theft, even when the victim is an altogether unscrupulous insurance operator. You lied to the police countless times, which should rightly result in another raft of charges. Then again,' he said, tapping a slow shower of ash out onto the soil, 'who's to say what a jury would think? They could easily agree that you had very little choice in the matter. That you acted as best you could, with the interests of the family at heart.'

'Why not let a jury decide, then? Why leave it to the O'Donnells?'

'If I take you into custody — make public everything I've learned here — then what happens to you next is on my conscience. You might be convicted, jailed, even hanged. I believe that would be neither right nor fair, regardless of the law.'

'Then surely *you* could make the choice not to take the matter any further. What the family wants is irrelevant.'

'I suppose I could,' Hartley sighed, 'but if I'm completely honest, I just don't have the gall. I don't know how to make the right choice. It's all that waltzing around with him.' Despite the darkness, he jerked his head towards the verandah, where the friar was even now expounding on some obscure element of the case. 'I find it hard to be sure of anything much anymore. As a detective, I'm expected to operate on facts, not emotions. The law is objective, impartial. Except, of course, that it isn't. Not one bit. Laws are made by men, and men are made of love and hate and fear and pride. These things writhe around inside us, and we can't lay them down, least of all when deciding what is right and wrong.'

He drew on the cigarette once more.

'I'm not cut out for this sort of work. Perhaps no-one is. I was determined to prove myself to my superiors, show them that I had the makings of a sergeant. It's clear to me now that I don't. I never did. Sending a man to the gallows, or a woman, for that matter . . . it would utterly destroy me.'

'You don't have the conviction to pursue a conviction,' said Hazel, with gentle humour. Hartley gave a quiet chuckle.

'I suppose not.'

'What will you do, then? Take up another profession?'

'I imagine I'll have to. There are a couple of friends upon whose hospitality I can prevail for the time being, but sooner or later I'll have to find another way to earn a living.'

'You might stay here a while,' said Winnie, from the shadows. Hartley spun round. He hadn't heard the

268

footsteps. 'With dear pater gone, we're down a pair of hands, and the harvest is almost upon us. Here, be a darling and let me have one of those.' She took a cigarette from Hazel.

'I'd be much more of a hindrance than a help, I'm afraid,' said Hartley. Then, before he could stop them, the words rushed out. 'I've actually been plucking up the courage to ask you if you wanted to accompany me back up to the city. I think it'd suit you. There are cafes and dance halls, and all sorts of modern thinkers around — especially now that we have the university — and I thought . . . well, to be honest, I had the impression . . .'

'That I liked the look of you? Now, how on Earth did you come by that idea?' Winnie tittered. 'You're handsome, and a good bit of fun, but I've just caught you confessing that your prospects are nearly non-existent. And to be honest,' she said, with a little less levity, 'I just couldn't leave the farm. As much as I love to mock this hamlet and its inhabitants, Tolhurst is my home. I can be myself here. More to the point, my family need me. I've a niece and a nephew to look after — with another on the way — and my mother insists on marching inexorably towards old age. That's without even mentioning my sister-in-law, of course.'

'You've decided not to turn me in, then?' Hazel's voice wavered with ill-disguised hope.

'Unanimously, my dear. There was never any other option. You're one of us. All we had to discuss in there was how long to keep you squirming.'

The two women embraced, laughing, then began to move towards the house.

'Do let me know if life in the capital begins to bore you,' called Winnie, over her shoulder. 'You'll have a bed here — for the time being, at any rate. I shan't wait for long!'

Hazel added her quick cry of thanks, and then they were laughing again, running to reunite with the rest of the family.

★ ★ ★

'My condolences.' The mendicant stepped down from the verandah to meet Hartley as he approached. 'It seems you are to return to the metropolis with neither suspect nor sweetheart in tow. Not a particularly pleasant trip to the country, all things considered.'

'Oh, I don't know.' Hartley shrugged. 'The scones were quite good, and I think I managed to make a friend.'

'I can only assume that you're referring to Kaiser,' said the friar, as the old dog nosed around for a scratch. 'All I really did, after all, was make you decide to pack in your profession. Not the sort of behaviour you'd want from a friend.'

'No, but probably the behaviour I need. If you really feel that bad about it, you can make it up to me by teaching me how to live on prayers and goodwill alone. You seem to make quite a decent go of it, and I think I may have a lean few years ahead of me.'

'I suspect you'll find roaring success in your new career path, whichever one it is you settle on. Between you and me,' the friar added, 'I've decided to make something of a change, too.'

'Don't tell me you're trading in your walnut-brown cassock for a russet version.'

The little man laughed. 'You're not far wrong. I do hope, before long, to dress in something altogether

270

more becoming. I've decided to make my way home.'

'To Singapore?' Hartley asked, in surprise.

'Further. To Hampshire. To the village which once sat at the heart of my parish.'

'Back to your old job, then?'

'No, but back to him,' said the friar. 'Hearing Beth O'Donnell's story made me look back on everything I've left behind. When I was first discovered, I felt that all was lost. I dropped it all and ran, tail between my legs. Beth didn't. She and Evette found a way to build a life together, even if it was a relatively sheltered and secretive one.' He took a resolute breath. 'If they did it, so can I. I'm older now. Not necessarily wiser, but perhaps that's for the best. Perhaps I've developed the sort of foolishness that gives rise to hope. Who knows? We may be able to live our lives in the sunshine, hand in hand, not slinking about in the shadows.'

'I wish you the very best of luck.'

'I shall certainly need it. All the luck in the world won't do me a drop of good, though, if I'm wandering about the Southern Hemisphere in sandals. I'm going to make my way back, reclaim my name and find the man I love. Then I'm going to treat myself to a decent bloody pair of shoes.'

Hartley laughed. 'I can start you off with a lift back up to Perth tomorrow morning,' he said. 'You'll be wanting to take a ship from Fremantle, I assume?'

'Thank you. I suppose that will be the best way to go about it. I no longer have a passport, but that's a problem to be tackled after a decent sleep and a cup of tea.'

'Well, I'm at the Royal Hotel for one more night. Will your newly loosened vows allow me to book you a room, or are you going to provoke the proprietors by stringing that ratty hammock across the balcony?'

'Now that you mention it, the breeze is rather lovely.'

Hartley laughed. 'You're not wrong. What do you think, Kaiser? A quick walk around the home paddock before we say our goodbyes?'

With the stars above them and the old dog at their heels, the two men strolled off into the evening.

Acknowledgements

To everyone who read *Death Leaves the Station* and expressed even a marginal interest in a sequel: look what you've done. I hope you'll take this as a lesson and be careful what you wish for in future. Thank you to Georgia Richter for accompanying me on this journey once again. Your manuscript returns are their own exclusive literary genre, to which I am privileged to be privy.

Thanks to the rest of the team at Fremantle Press for believing in me and not complaining when I respond to emails three weeks late.

I've always been quite a solitary writer, but I have come to greatly appreciate the support and encouragement of many wonderful Western Australian authors, both at industry events and online. I extend particular thanks to a Shirley, a Rebecca and rather a lot of Daves. Other invaluable support has come from the legends at The Literature Centre, countless libraries (especially Vic Park, Kalamunda and South Perth) and the various schools that have inexplicably allowed me to hurl words at malleable young minds. Thanks also to Roz, Simon and the rest of the Comms Crew for giving me the flexibility to pursue my side quests and listening patiently to 'fun' etymology facts.

To my family (in all its forms): thanks for shaping, inspiring and understanding me. Thank you, Sarah, for always, always being there. Thank you, Kris, for being a friend and a guide. Thank you, Mojy, for keeping poetry alive, Thank you, Ling and Adam, for being there when I resurface. Thank you, Riki, for reaching out, Anni for clicking on 'Buy now' (Jeff told me, obviously), and Kirsten for still demanding a name. Thank you, Sassy, for making every day brighter and keeping most nights pretty peaceful.

Finally, thank you to Lindsay for being my accomplice and allowing me the joy of being yours.